VISITORS

VISITORS

ROO STOVE

PuP

In memory of
Jae Scott
22 July 1970 – 9 August 2020
A good friend is hard to find, but harder to lose.

CHAPTER 1

By the Rivers of Babble On.

Ｍy fear is a time traveller. The same fear I had when I was four, can without warning turn up in the present. Carrying with it the same intensity and similar incapacities. Words are stolen, my bones become sapling-like, and I shake. Sometimes I even shit my pants. Shit is a horrible word, but its intensity is needed to portray the brutal and smelly taking of innocence. A four-year-old might poop in fear. And this one did.

Don't start the story talking about excrement. Disgusting. Yes, but truth can be, well, pretty ugly. I like pretty ugly worded together. It reminds me of my two-sided view of my own self. Most people aren't symmetrical, but my two sides are passively and aggressively opposed. Inside and out. Inside out.

My fear is a constant time traveller. It was there yesterday and is already waiting for me to arrive today and tomorrow, tripping over my own feet into next week. It waits. The patience of fear is extraordinary; it's kind maliciousness, sometimes incomprehensible. Fear's depth, fathoms deep, is unfathomable. It waits, to tighten its grip on my raw heart. To beat it faster. It waits for me to inhale and then it holds me tight in a strange air-filled suffocation. It waits.

Sometimes, when I sit all quiet on the outside, there's no quiet on the inside. I try hard to trace my fear back to its roots. If I find where it began, I can kill that time travelling shitty fear before it begins its wicked voyage. It's unfortunate, this belief, because it occupies my brain in a dangerous manner. It slides me into a childhood that I'd been relieved to grow away from. I haven't grown away, or up though. No girl interrupted here. Girl frozen. Girl stuck. Girl down. Medic! When girl wakes up, thaws, there'll be Hell to pay. How much? I've got $3.50. It won't be enough, will it? If I can't pay Hell the exit fee, the door might lock again. Locked in Hell. Throw away the key.

If it can't be you reader, it has to be me.

Often, it's likened to a cat playing with a dead mouse, looking back into your own history. People, no I don't know who these people are. People will say the past must be buried to move forward. But ask any archaeologist - to understand we must dig. Hand me my spade, or fucking shovel, please, I've things to learn. To have a good death I have to make good this life and cast off the debilitating fear that shadows me. Darkens me. Cue. Fade to black.

A lit candle drips its insides over its own shell and they both disappear. Light costs. Brilliance is not always wisdom; it can be optimism. We, the two or more crowded within me, will make it optimism. Light. Good light. Befriend me and help this archaeologist see the sepia-touched history and brighten the white and bring it new toward me without fucking fear. Or maybe, just fuck fear for a change.

Some might have faltered during paragraph two, stumbled on 'kind maliciousness,' perhaps questioning the linking of those two words. Even said, 'what?' out aloud on a bus as you read. I can't read on a bus; it makes me queasy. Queasy is a cheerful sounding word. Easy breezy queasy uneasy. Puke. Sorry. The kind maliciousness of fear. Stay on point.

When it is kind, fear can save you from death. It can assist a jump out of the way of a car not stopping as it should at a pedestrian crossing. Fear can urge you not to move forward over the yellow line at the train station and mind the gap. It can help you tell somebody they're too drunk to drive. It can make you brave.

And fear can turn nasty. The malignant side of fear, sometimes called anxiety, can tell you there's not enough air in this classroom and you're going to embarrass yourself by fainting in public. It can tell you your child is dying in a car-wreck while you're attempting to sleep. This side of fear can wake you screaming. A nightmare might sit for the rest of the day on your shoulder, tapping in one spot until the pain is unbearable. Torturous fear.

Sometimes it can be kind and malicious at the same time and your head explodes. Fear and loathing in transit, sometimes unintelligible, most often barbarous. Scrape your fear from the walls and try to hold it on the inside. Please don't taint the general public. Hold it inside, this nice foul emotion, this most-times incomprehensible eater of fun. Else people will gape at your ineptitude. They'll hold you responsible if this fear, your <u>hand-made</u> fear, gets away and infects innocent bystanders. Fear becomes your cottage industry, but other people profit. Stay inside. Stay inside your cottage. Don't leave the door ajar. Fear becomes you. Really becomes all of you.

So, I must dig.

I was born. Of this, there is no doubt. Or, is there? If I stop right here, at this thought, generations of my ancestors will crash into each other while in the queue for vicarious immortality and ask, 'What the fuck just happened? 'What do you mean she's not even sure she was born?' Existence is futile. Resistance gives you something to do.

No. I was born. There's a sigh and the querulous queue quietens. I'd like to point out I've alliterated with a q. That's no mean feat. That u almost always follows q is ancestral, too, like my queue. Blame the French, the Romans, the Etruscans and the Phoenicians. Q. Thank cue. Thank you. Cue. Cue music. The Electric Light Orchestra must have had an electrical conductor.

Put down those words, you don't know where they've been.

I was born. For my mother's sake, I emerged two months before the due date. Small and listless. Since then, I've made many a list. Groceries tops my list of lists, but I won't make a big to-do about them now.

Back then, in the middle-aged years of last Century they sent me off to a bigger hospital, away from my mother so that I could be truly, madly, deeply fucked-up by their do-gooder assistance. I know, I don't know who 'they' are, just people in charge of hospital decisions and whatnot. I'd like to meet them and say thanks in a way that I hope they realise is sarcasm. What knot?

I will die. Birth and death, to me are the same. Death may be kinder. There's a blessed return to the nothingness awaiting. Not that I want to go before the day fate chooses. It's funny that with all of my fears, death isn't one of them. As long as it's not a long painful searing voyage to the end. If I die screaming out my agonies on the side of the road after a car wreck, be assured, I won't be happy. I'll be cursing God, for sure, even though I'm not a believer. I might get locked back into Hell, again. Damn it. Damn me.

Terrorists killing in the name of religion took away my last vestige of belief in God. If they're not listening to a beneficent deity, what's the point? If a God is telling men and the occasional woman that their religion is better than any other, then I'd rather be a gentle human being on my own. Smite me. Smite us all and start over, your Supreme Beingness. This experiment has failed, unless it was to prove that humans are nasty, greedy, selfish, two legged animals. Smite me twice, because I'm feeling holier than thou right at this second.

Where was I? That's right; I was a bloody twisted wreck on the side of the road, screaming abuse at a deity I didn't believe in. Let's move away from there, step with care over my blood pooling on the ground like dropped dark shellac. I hate it when I see my death flash before me. Let's go down to the river and play. Water is soothing to the soul.

There's no non-believer's word for the piece inside of us that makes us unique. It seems a bit of a cheat to steal a religious word. When I'm rich, I'll patent an expression for Atheists and Agnostics to use in place of soul. Patent a word, coin a phrase.

To the river.

CHAPTER 2

Topography (/təˈpɒɡrəfi/ noun) of a voyage

Autobiographically speaking there's many years between now and back on that warm March afternoon when I entered the world in such a hurry. Geographically speaking there's 515.7 kilometres, or 301.91 miles as the tired old crow flies, from my starting point (birth) to right here ◈ right now. A lot can happen in that space. It is a space that's not the final frontier, but very close. The days between then and now then have added up and grown heavy over me. Each year that followed there was a more noticeable slouch of gloom in my demeanour and there were hours when I couldn't stand up at all, with the weight of all those days.

The melancholic is not addicted to melons, nor is melancholy a stomach ailment baby that melons might get, contrary to how the word sounds. The melancholic tends to have an easy-access file filled with horrific happenings that have blotted her landscape from earliest memory to now. Over there, you can see the good-times folder. ACCESS DE-NIED. Micro softly, softly, the blue screen of death. Reboot. I could kick myself. Twice. Re-boot.

Melancholics spend much of their time looking back to see if they can find the spot where it all went wrong.

Of times long past and glimpses of me, I wake to find I'm beside the sea. I look back to where I thought I'd be sitting, and there's a great wall of dark. Murk should not be unyielding; even so I have trouble seeing through it to the other side, to the map of where I've been. Until I catch sight of the small me perched on the front seat of a great creaking moving truck. It hauls the family's meagre possessions away from the red plains. Hours later, there's a chugging struggle up into the Blue Mountains and there, the truck deposits us into a heap of tiredness and old furniture.

This is not my memory at all. It's borrowed from my mother. There's no photograph or other social media proof that it happened at all. Except, I woke up in the mountains for a brief minute about a year later, a jealous green in colour, watching my brother go to school on his first-ever day there. Then I'm gone again apart from celluloid images flickering on a screen. Not me, but my ghost captured in old home movies. The ghost of Christmases past. The ghosts of Christmases pass. Forever March. Time marches. If you're quiet, you can hear its gentle footfall in time with your clock. Foomp, foomp, tick, tock.

The Blue Mountains raise you up. Their brutal beauty leaves you in awe of Mother Nature's maternal strength. The years she has spent carving into the landscape have taken their toll. How tired Mother Nature must be. How chronically fatigued it must have, without question left her, cutting great sharp edges using nothing but natural, renewable elements. Man would need fossil fuels and would ruin the Earth in his attempt to make it half as beautiful. But man has long since forgotten beauty and replaced the need for it, with money. Once the sun explodes, turning us to dust, beauty will be the biggest loss.

When next I awaken for a short while, we are living in a caravan in a boring city suburb which I grew to love and then to hate. I surfaced, slow due to my fuzz, into the real world. Most days, I was an automaton, but little things would thump my heart and wake me from my stupor. A spider in a paper bag. Holidays back on the plains. Holidays back atop the mountains. Whenever I was aware of my own existence, fear was with me. The stupor was a fine dissociative creation. It helped me survive, although sometimes I wished I was dead.

Hold yourself, prepare for the next sentence; look away, or go for a walk if you're feeling fragile.

Any fucking adult who has sex with a very young child, thinking his prey will be too young to remember by the time she's adult, is abhorrent and half right. The child's mind locks the memory away, 'forgets,' but the body never does. Prey, those who survive, are fucked up for life. It's not just rape. It's criminal damage. Malicious hurt. Permanent wounding. Unrepairable. The body memories attack the mind in a frenzied search for understanding. What happened? Why? The mind, in time breaks down with the effort of failed searches and turns on itself. More damage. Continual mutilation. What's left of the mind becomes a machine of perpetual emotion. Raw emotion. Bleeding. My childhood.

Sometimes, there is a great difference between a spoilt child and a spoiled child. Sometimes there is none. Spoiled or damaged, same thing. As a spoiled child, I know growing up put years between my body and the incestuous horror that flawed me. Floored me. My mind could not grip onto anything. I slipped and slid, tumbled, fell. Rose again. Not a battered phoenix. Just residue. Ash coloured. Unlovable.

School was a flatness underlined by teachers yelling, the shrieking dissonance that is a playground at lunchtime and the brilliant escape called 3:20 pm. Walking home was never done at speed. After the crossing guard had helped us across the school street, we were free to be killed or maimed by a car on any other road. Everybody walked back then. We didn't have great petrol guzzling four-wheel drives to choke school streets. Cars were a man's domain and they were never about when the school day ended. It was a man's world. Still is, I suppose. My great uncle owned a car. We lived in a caravan parked in his backyard. Uncle Cedric was never home before us, so at no time did we ride home, smug, in the car. He was a working stiff, until he became a non-working stiff, till he became stiff. Rigor mortified.

If you're lucky enough to have a childhood, relax, it doesn't last very long, in retrospect. When ankle deep in your infancy, phew, time has such elasticity, like youthful skin. Pain is time distended, a strange vacuity filled with sharp edges. I'm not sure if you're supposed to operate your life so that every decade is as affecting as the first. How exhausting that would be. Still, it puts a roll of consternation across my brow that an eighty-year-old man – or woman - can remain reactive to childhood trauma. The first ten years are so dangerous, so open to things, good and bad.

Do not fold, bend, mutilate, plus - wash carefully and don't iron young children, be vigilant during their inaugural decade.

The caravan year was perhaps my mother's happiest. Great Uncle Cedric or Uncle Said as we children called him, had secured my father a job at the engineering firm where Said worked in administration. If my blue-collar Dad wanted to get home at all he was reliant on a lift or he'd have to walk ten kilometres. This limited my Dad's alcohol consumption and he'd found a decent mentor in Uncle Said.

The move out of the caravan knocked me back again into my stupor. Much time passed before I woke up in the rental house. Although, it was two blocks away from Uncle Said's, I was in a new school and lost. As a five-year-old, I had a tenuous hold on my consciousness. I lost it, often.

Waking up is never easy, I know. Bloody nose. Vomit. Pain. Noise. Bloody noise. Spit and ugliness. That was school holidays for me back then.

Most of my adult life I've been homesick. I don't know for which home. My childhood places were never comfortable nests. It'd be awful to be returned to any of them. But some days, still, I find myself pacing about in the place I live, mumbling, 'I want to go home.' I imagine this makes me a failure as an adult, if I can't make my own house my home. If I dig, I might find what I'm hungering for is some sort of emotional maturity and stability. But mumbling, 'I want emotional constancy,' is a bit of a mouthful when you're pacing about. What I need is a place of safety and a sense that I can drop my guard. A place where no stress lives. It can be found sometimes in the bottom of a bottle, but you can't live there, for the sake of your liver and people close to you.

Places of no highs or lows, secure places, are home for me when I'm at the point where I need to pace about. 'I want to go home,' just blurts out of me, like the spoiled child I am. I don't understand why the words drop out of my subconscious so. It may take many more years of therapy to find my true home.

What if home comes from the inside? We spend so much money and effort fortifying a physical place, to find it feels like an extra wall holding in a big bundle of neuroses. Or is that just me?

Home may still be a physical place. I might know it when I find it. I might walk into a place one day and say, 'I'm home,' and sigh and be content for the first time since my initial gasp at air on arrival day. There's a short linguistical gap between being content and contention, but a world of difference in an emotional sense. I know what the sensation of being content looks like; I have a cat. I don't know what it feels like. The cat won't tell me. She's not going to interrupt a purr to try and explain the intricacies of being content. She'd say, 'just shut up, and be it, fuckwit.' She has a cussing problem. When the cat from next door comes in, you can almost hear her hiss, 'get the fuck out of my house'. She is at home in her place, and she knows it.

When next I awake, we are in a different house.

CHAPTER 3

Don't Think Your Children Can't Hear You Fighting

It's an asymmetrical kind of life. So lopsided sometimes, that I'm afraid of sliding off into the jagged obscure. We're a long time dead on either side of being aware. Life. Life on Earth's like an illness nothingness contracts. A feverish dream in the middle of dark nothing matters. You must make things happen or it's a waste of the strange accident that found you here in the first place. Imagine, billions of rocks in all of space and you landed – pulling all atoms together into a being – on this one rock, the third rock from the Sun. We are here as a mere dot on a timeline. Hate is such a waste of this time, but many fill their lives with it. Even me, to a lesser degree. A Bachelor of Arts is a lesser degree. I have one of those. B.A. Bugger All.

The person or beast I've hated with constant vitriol during my time here, is me. It came from within with such ease, I'd Initiated hating myself before I grew old enough to know this was what I was doing. But I would never think of turning inward hate outward, it seemed too powerful. Still does. Without concern for my own wellbeing, with a touch of masochism, I fell on a grenade for all. Like a child given their first allotment of pocket money, I spent my entire allocation of hate on myself and had nothing left over for anything or anybody who might warrant a good dose of hate. There's an art to being competent to turn any wrongness around so that you're able to blame yourself in full for it all. I am such an artist, sliding about in my asymmetrical life, wearing a brand of culpability. Mine's a designer brand, burnt deep into my hide.

We slid into our next weatherboard house in suburbia when I was seven, falling short of middle class by a shit load – given that the media seem to label middle class as the socio-economic group between the effluent and the affluent. My mother came from the middle classes. Now nouveau poor, she would pull us up from living in a rental to owning her own house with an in-ground swimming pool within a decade. Not without its price.

The front of this second house post-caravan, a rental too, I remember well. There was a veranda, with a wrought-iron balustrade that my brother and I quite often used as a surrogate tight-rope. Falling was unpleasant because rosebushes grew beneath. In this house, I became more aware of what? Than I'd ever been before. I remember the loo was in the backyard and the cistern hovered way above my head, to encourage a decent gravity-enhanced flush through the pipes.

In this house, I discovered razor blades. My father used an old-fashioned safety razor. With a twist of the handle, jaws opened to reveal the waiting blade. It called for blood in that little bathroom, painted as it was, in a coat of slapdash yellow. I gave the blood. A sad succumbing to fate. It felt inevitable. Pointless to procrastinate. Cut now, pay later. A room for the wounded. There too, in this room of fledgling self-damage, was a shower curtain that would wrap itself about you like a sticky child not wanting to be left with a babysitter. It was disconcerting and had a vague sliminess to it. Like life.

My brother and I were latchkey kids. Dad now drove a VW bug and we seldom saw him. Mum worked and was tired and angered by circumstance. It was my fault. I was a fault line that lay between my mother and any happiness I thought, or felt. Thinking wasn't my thing when I was seven. Too busy banging into walls. Too busy taking falls.

As soon as I realised I was unhappy on the inside I dressed in an idiotic smile on the outside. I wore that false stupid grin for so long, it became almost impossible to summons a smile that reflected spontaneity. There's been a long time since a smile has come to me, although I do have a well-built sense of humour. My smiles are just below the surface. Below the surface.

Razor blades.

Oh, bright litigious world, always looking for somebody to blame, I am your scapegoat. Beat me raw and I will whimper and wonder when death will find and steal me away. My father chose suicide – by the slowest method available to his Catholic sensibilities. He drank himself to death, a slow-release death. A church sanctioned expiry I guess, since it was a priest who gave my father his first taste of alcohol and perhaps worse. Ten-year-old altar boy looking for love, finding a ruined version. The altar boy, altered. It took forty-five years of concerted effort for my dad to die because he had the resilience of a coward and the heart of a lion. I could not save him, if you require somebody to censure.

My father was given the last rites many, many times, except the day he died alone in a bed-sit. He deserved a far more glorious exit on account of the years it had taken him to get to the turn-off. Alone. How sad. I take a drink now, in belated solidarity. Cheers, Dad. Safe travels. You've vanished now, not leaving a mark. Here is an X to say you were once alive, my dad. X.

In my dreams my father is no longer present. This is sad, too. I loved him in a way that defies classification. As a seven-year-old and up until late teen years, I lay in bed at night afraid that he might come home and also, very afraid that he mightn't. My father wasn't a violent man, but I think I could feel my mother's anger through the walls. In the dark, a discomforting expectancy held itself in, and me with it. Heavier than sleep. Without realising, I would hold my breath until my body fought back. The tension made me brittle enough to break.

Night after night after night.

As a child this repetition wore me stupid.

Night after night after night.

In the middle of heavy hours of darkness, I would wake in sudden anguish, afraid my father was already dead. My fault. Worried thoughts that saw him home safe, had fallen to sleep on the job. If dead, it was because I hadn't remained vigilant. In a panic, I would rush outside to check if the little beetle was in the driveway. If it was, the relief dumped on me, a mammoth undulation that rippled with such motion that it brought queasiness. Can you feel it?

If the car wasn't in the driveway my worries would begin again. Refreshed from their nap they took on renewed vigour; with graphic visual aids. Damn you, imagination. I saw the VW, my father at the steering wheel, mangled in a tree. I saw a pub brawl that left him bleeding to death. Sometimes, he just vanished and was never seen again. Unbeknownst to me, until well into supposed adulthood, this had happened to his first daughter. She sat across the ditch in New Zealand, wondering where her father had gone. Much of the time, when adults try to fix their lives, children must endure as collateral damage. Much of the time, when adults don't try to fix their lives, children must withstand secondary damage, become the fallout guys, caught in the mushrooming after-blast. It takes children a lifetime to recover from post-parental after-burn, and in the blur that is life passing, put a match to their own children's lives in the interim. Pain begets pain.

My Dad was a passive man, never a vicious drunk. Passiveness can still cause hurt. And hurtiveness[1] can still cause passive. By the time I'd reached the age of seven I'd abandoned standing up for myself, wounded to a place beyond caring. If indeed, I'd ever stood up. I reminded myself of a dog that winced every time a man raised his hand. My wincing and squirming were ninety-eight per cent interior, or must have been because nobody ever noticed. It was assumed my non-reactions were lack of emotion, combined with overall stupidity.

In truth, my lack of reaction was from too much feeling. Just once, I would have liked my father to stand up on my behalf, or anybody, but

...

Okay, that slipped into self-pity, as if I stepped onto a mossy rock and lost my footing. I need to tread with extra care. Pillage Spillage. I've dropped my memories and feelings all over the floor. Mop and bucket, Aisle 12.

I say *feelings*, but that's a misfire, a blank that flew out of the barrel straight through the silencer, and landed, pretending to be a real bullet. In my brain. We're waiting for the inquest, me and me.

Feelings are like colour. Black is all colours combined. My lack of reaction, or shutdown, was, and is all feelings combined. Frozen as a child, too cold for new feelings, I've yet to thaw. Because I'm afraid of the pain. Little pieces were amputated before the deadness spread. Collateral damage.

It would be nice to say to my Kiwi sister Anna, 'our father didn't leave you. He was led away by his passivity.' If I could be crass, I'd hint that he was led away by his dick. Anyway, he left one marriage and wasn't present in the next. Steered from place to place, he learned where the nearest pub was in case he sobered. My Dad wasn't a bad father, but he failed to be good.

It distresses me that I began to echo my father's behaviour. Passivity has been passed to me as if it's a genetic predisposition hiding in our DNA. Like him, I'm not against a drink or two. I fail abstention with ease. Unlike him, through what we might call learned evolution, I've attempted to succeed as a parent. Does that make my failure worse? My father had not given thought to his disaster as a parent, nor had he put much effort into child raising. He went on as he'd always gone on, without being conscious. This makes me sad for my Dad. If only we'd thought to wake him. With clemency, he can't be blamed for his sleep-walking. Alcohol and war quite often combine to protect the symptoms of PTSD [2].

My own war neurosis has lasted well past conflict's end, unless you count a Quixotic bent toward fighting windmills as an ongoing fight. I was plastered in Paris and never made it into the windmill that is *The Moulin Rouge*. Lost in France. But that's not this story.

Parents make mistakes. They often do. Not many own them. Children make mistakes all the time but are forgiven by virtue of youth and innocence. The parent who can own their mistakes and who can gift themselves forgiveness while they forgive their child, is rare. Parents seldom have time or make time to understand their mistakes and make amends until it's too late. I know, a simple 'sorry' takes seconds; it's the understanding part that takes years. Once an adult, healing old emotional wounds should be easy. It seldom is. Somehow a saboteur is implanted within the scars. When it sees you are almost healed it arranges an emotional plummet. To the depths. Drowning, not waving.

My father was not a stupid man, but he didn't recognise the extent that his drinking harmed those around him. He was an earthquake that couldn't see the resulting Tsunami because it was too far away. On the beach, unaware of the warning sirens my brother and I were often swamped. There were nights when we waited to be fed because my father was going to drive us to McDonalds' when he arrived home. On a few occasions my mother, so depressed and tired, felt the idea of pushing a meal together after a day at her own job quite unachievable. Child safety was not always the biggest issue. Matthew and I were flinched into the car by my mother's angry words (aimed at Dad but hitting us) and Matty would direct my father to the fast-food outlet. Being the elder, my brother would make the purchase then steer my drunken father home again. At times, Matty would physically steer from the passenger's seat.

It was also not uncommon for my Dad to piss himself on those post-pub journeys. One time he peed his pants the second he was out of the car in our driveway and I remember wondering if loving my father was compulsory or even necessary.

I did love him, but he made it tough. Tough love.

CHAPTER 4

Point 5

Peter Kitchener lived in a painted institutional-beige bed-sit owned by The Housing Department. Floor space was at a minimum. It was five steps to the bathroom and five steps on its reflective diagonal to the kitchen. Peter measured everything as a triangulation of lines that converged to a point at the end of his bed. If he felt lethargic he could vacuum the whole place while sitting at the end of that bed.

Peter had nothing else to do but neaten his home until the pubs opened. Life slid into habit not long after he'd moved in.

Clean self

Breakfast

Peel potatoes and do the prep for dinner later

Clean kitchen

Clean self again

Walk down the street

Make any necessary purchases

Go to pub.

Peter had just reached point five when he died, dropping like a rock to the bathroom floor, clutching a can of shaving foam. A clichéd drop yes, but there was no other way to describe it. He died standing up, and gravity did the rest with enthusiasm.

Death is not pretty. Anybody who has had to clean death off a tiled floor will know how hard it is to cleanse dried released body fluids from grouting.

Potatoes, peeled and ready on the hob, sat there for a full day before people became concerned that Peter was not on his usual stool at The Imperial Hotel. There's an Imperial in many biggish country towns in Australia. Locals often call these pubs The Impy because they're way too busy to round out words to their fullness, plus the pub name sounds cheery and mischievous stunted like that with a jaunty Y added.

Matthew Kitchener received the call about the death of his father. He in turn telephoned his sister on the coast and then his half-sister in New Zealand. Peter would have enjoyed how the triangulations of thought all converged at the point where he lay.

CHAPTER 5

Cease-fire on the Home Front

L ooking backward can give you quite a crick in the neck, and questions pop up like annoying internet spam. Why? An often-asked interior question, hurls out at the very second my retrospection twists over itself to become my ugly. Yes, my ugly. Now and again, I say or even yell, 'why?' out loud to the air. 'Phsht,' the air says. I take that to mean, 'Bugger off, I'm trying to keep the world alive. Hold your wishy-washy questioning to yourself.'

This is a loose translation, as the air has been about for a long time and speaks in an archaic tongue that I understand, just. Sometimes it resorts to blowing stuff around in my back yard because I appear to frustrate it to the point of anger.

Why is at the curious child's core. But, you know, sometimes we have to let the story go and look into the 'how?' How do I do the things I do? Makes a far better question. with a more logical answer than, 'why do I do the things I do?'

It seems easy enough, to ask 'how?' But when it comes to my mind's workings, how is as elusive as why. I've done experiments. How, how, how, Delilah?

If I look into the rear-view mirror again, I see that my mother kicked my father out of the house when I was still young. How? I don't remember at all. Perhaps I didn't even notice. The late-night checks of the driveway must have ceased. Did I sleep in peace? There's no corroboration, because I don't have access to this file. Turns out I was too young and too stupid to take anything in. I didn't realise my father was gone or living in the VW, a mere drunken stumble away from the local Bowling Club. Not even a five-minute walk from our now-vacant drive-way. The child-me remained oblivious. Oblivion is my home.

The separation could have been the end of it. That could have been the point where my father vanished out of my life like he had for Anna. That could have heralded a truce on the domestic front, signalled a cease-fire. But, no.

This is *how* it happened. My father living in his car, peeing in the gutter, showering at work and drinking his wages, had a massive heart attack. He was forty-five. Gough Whitlam, one of the more benevolent Australian Prime Ministers Australia, introduced Medicare to the public in 1975 but it was not a functioning entity until the mid-eighties. This meant that without a health fund, my father's hospitalisation had to be paid for by penniless him, or as his next of kin, by my mother. In my oblivion, I would not have seen her anger. Just felt it. Just. Unjust. Injury. The hip pocket nerve rips into a bloody gaping wound. Screaming.

The nurses may have thought my mother's tears sweet. Their bosses, the hospital administrators were not so sugary. They wouldn't release my poor (literally) and recuperating (momentarily) father unless his wife took him home and cared for him. It was the cheaper option for my Mum.

Hospitals held people to ransom in those days. They put their ultimatum under the heading, 'you have to be cruel to be kind.' Their selfish stupidity caused our family decades of pain and taught us all emotional immobility. The administrators, advocating for their one patient, made the lives of three familial bystanders wretched and doused in perpetual dis-ease. But, damn it, I loved my Dad which intensified my own dis-ease to the point of 'Argh!' There are no words.

As a consequence of my family's emotional stagnation and failure to thrive or progress, my father remained in our family home another ten years-ish after his first heart attack. The list of his ailments expanded with each annual Chemist Shop, complimentary next year's calendar.

One night Dad was coughing a bronchial gurgle on his drunken return from the pub. My mother, throwing empathy to the ground and stubbing it out like the end of a cigarette, yelled, 'If you're dying, could you please do it quietly?' Maybe, she didn't say please.

Love is. And then, it isn't.

During my long unenthusiastic life to the day my father died on his bathroom floor, I at no time witnessed my parents show an ounce of affection toward each other.

Affect – Touch, Move, Disturb, Mark, Distress, Upset, Shake. The order of the Thesaurus has the term increasing in intensity until it almost converts to physical violence.

Is that the natural order of *affect*ion? Is it the pattern of falling out of love?

These aren't answerable questions because: 1. You are reading just there, and I'm over here typing and scritching my dog on the top of his head. Scritch is a scratch without the blood. 2. There's both space and time between us. And, 3. Nobody would know the answer. I doubt my parents would know.

As an addendum, I am and was an unreliable witness. Most times my focus was inward, not outward. Or, I was unconscious. The closest I can recall regarding my mother showing consideration for my Dad was from the front passenger seat of the VW bug, she used to light a cigarette for him and pass it over. I feel, maybe in error, that her action was more about the art of self-preservation. For my Mum, there was an extreme dislike of being in a car and its awful proximity to possible sudden maiming or accidental death. She wanted my father's attention to remain glued to the road. My mother hated being in a car. Still does. All but assumes the crash position.

I began to assume the crash position outside of the car; perpetually braced for impact. Lying in bed at night, waiting for my father to tumble home. Soaking in the anger, my mother's anger, as it seeps through the gap under my bedroom door. My arms sometimes stretched up towards the ceiling in the dark, because it was dark inside my mind too, and I wanted somebody to pull me out—save me. Deep inside I am battered and bruised, a result of all the stumbling in the black, from bashing into hard or sharp parts of my fragmented self.

Often, I am dragged out of bed by my mother—my own bed, to be put in the double bed my parents still shared. It's not the rescue I crave. I will be used as ammunition when my father arrives home. A blame. I am a blame.

'Maddie's in here,' my mother calls, before my Dad ruptured through the front door, fighting to get his keys to release from the lock. He burbles beer-breath mutterings before falling into my room, into my bed—and I lie next to my Mum, feigning sleep and rigid with emotions that I don't understand. My mother sinks further into her inert surrender.

Later, she sleeps on the sofa most nights, rolling up her bedding each morning and shoving it into a cupboard. My bedclothes no longer smelt of ick. It's a dehumanising experience, is life. I loved my father, but from a very early age, I wanted my mother to be free. She's in a cage of a different kind now but is ⅝ happy. That's a better fraction than she managed with my Dad. Life is fractious on the whole. On the hole. In the hole of childhood.

There were days when I forgot to be unhappy: the last walk home at the end of the school year, those few weeks before the dreaded family holiday, exploring the neighbourhood with my brother when he wasn't treating me like excrement, the *Mr Whippy* ice cream van until I heard 'purse says no', lying on the back lawn looking up at the blue.

Those dreaded family holidays. We're not supposed to be apprehensive about vacations, but my anxiety knew no boundaries. There's a chance I could fill a book with my fears. *Madison Kitchener's Tour of Dreads*. Yes, I know - Madison. In defence of my moniker, I was given my mother's maiden name as my first and not named after an avenue in faraway USA. There's many female Madison's now, but back when

I went to school it was grounds for a teasing. Because life can't be hard enough.

Holidays - swimming pools, sunshine, Christmas Day, incest, long car rides and dread.

An old VW beetle, although cute is not an ideal car to take on a family holiday back to the red plains. I was born there and on occasion I thought I might expire there too. Done in by 'Matthew keeps looking at me' disease. That wasn't as painful as 'Matthew keeps pinching me' disease but far more annoying. Sealed in, without back windows that opened, without technological amusements, with a surplus pile of bags that didn't fit under the front hood plus the smell of fuel and cigarettes exacerbating an enduring touch of see-sickness (a form of motion sickness that you get in a car when there's nothing to see) for over seven hours, was nothing short of agony. I sometimes wished that 'Matthew's poking me' disease might be fatal. Matthew was never admonished when I dobbed him in. Instead, I was told to be quiet. My compliance took the form of sulking for two hundred kilometres.

Holidays away from home were the times we were 'family.' It hadn't taken long for our unit to break down. I blamed myself. A blame. I am a blame. The photographs of my brother, mother and father before I was born seemed family-ish. My arrival had, it seems, rendered the unit untenable. There are no photographs of the four of us looking at all clan-like.

Squished in the rear seat of the family car, another less-important reason to hate Hitler, we beetled toward the Never-Never without a song in our hearts. My dysfunctional memory does not recall meal breaks or even food. Mum, although frugal didn't let us go without nourishment or beverages. Gruel and water. Who knows? There were stops for petrol, perhaps time to pee but memory has jettisoned the information. To me it was a seven-hour incarceration, fun-free. Destination – Dreadville.

Red sand between my toes, outer space vacation and no recollection of adults being there at all. Cousins, many boisterous self-confident cousins, sped about while I remained the anxious little runt of the litter. The dog people want to take home from the shelter because it looks forlorn and then they find its permanent anxiety drives humans crazy. Times, I tagged along pretending to be a member of the gang. Times, I slipped off on my own and stared into the vast outer space oddity that is the Australian Outback.

Without concept of schedule, our return trip home felt as arbitrary as the date picked to start the holiday. I'd wake up and be tumbled into the V-dub for the drive. Not sure we were leaving until the outskirts of town passed beneath us and the realisation there was a pile of bags in the back seat with my brother and I, managed to infiltrate my awareness. I was not a young Einstein.

'Matthew's pinching me,' I'd say.

'Be quiet.'

Within weeks, I'd forget we'd been. Forget the sexual assault I couldn't and wouldn't ever speak about. I lie. I didn't forget. I buried it deep. Beyond excavating from others and beyond my own comprehension. In self-defence I became my *leftover* self; the fragments of a shattered being that didn't fit back together. I buried the memories of those holidays to a depth where I couldn't recall great chunks of time or what happened in them. This saved my life but served me up fresh and vulnerable for the next visit. Dissociation, fugue states are a blessing before they become a curse. Necessary. I never forgot to **not** speak the name of the offender. Never forgot. Even though I forgot the intimidation that made such a rule. As an adult, little bits would come back and floor me. Flaw me.

Never forget and forget. What a mess. I forgot where I'd left my only cardigan. Repression can be good for the soul, but losing stuff made my mother cross.

'You're so useless, Maddie. Where am I going to get the money to replace...?'

Zoning out, utilised and my mother would groan in exasperation and walk away. Traces of Einstein at it, somewhere in there. Oblivion is my home.

CHAPTER 6

Reoccupy the Crash
Position

If the preceding chapters treated my mother with undeserved harsh-ness, it was not acrimony, but the ripple or buckling effect of rear-viewing, using the eyes of my young, stupid and misunderstanding self. All mothers except the odd psychopath, try to do the best with what they have and with who they are at the time. My mother was not the psychopathic exception.

She struggled so.

The more knowledge, subsistence money and emotional stability a mother has, the better she might do as a parent. Except the narcissist, who places herself as the most important member of the family. There needs to be some altruism in parenting, it's the price you pay for having a child in the first place. That goes for fathers too. My mother had to be the sole breadwinner even though my Dad was working. He drank and gambled most of his wages on the day they went into his bank account and maxed out the joint credit card whenever mum wasn't looking. The absurdity was that knowledge, money and mental stability came well af-ter their children had left home.

My mother had begun her marriage to my father without any decent role models, nor did she have the mind-set that assists in a nurturing way to generate a stress-free personal growth spurt. (Spurt's a revolting word, eh?) Apart from Uncle Said, who my mother never confided in, there was no extended family nearby to assist in dealing with the carnage that comes from having two children a year apart in age. The bulk of our family was in New Zealand or way out on the dusty Australian red plains. Travel was an expensive, exhaustive time-consuming undertaking. There was an unspoken, unwritten rule too, that you didn't burden friends with problems. A rule I tend to abide by still – and more so when I'm moving about. To be frank, if Frank doesn't mind, I only have one friend. But one is a friendship that can be cherished and maintained. Not hundreds. How do people deal with sustaining more than a handful of friends? Even counting them on their fingers must be a trial. My daughter, Micah, has more social media friends than the population of a small country.

That's beside the point, or the ellipsis.

Drowning in her own river, my Mum was afraid to signal for help. In case it indicated weakness. She was supposed to be strong at work and at home. To roar. Floundering took the 'am' and the 'I' out of f-a-m-i-l-y. My Mum was out – absent unapproachable, scared, stressed, and more than a little bit angry at herself. 'Fly,' is all that's left when 'am' and 'i' are subtracted from the word. She was grounded. Wing-less. Stuck on a version of fly-paper of her own making.

'Help me!' echoes an old movie playing on a loop somewhere in my semi-subconscious layered in childhood. But I can't fly. I will always carry great apprehension if I'm to be sealed inside a metal projectile and flung at another country or state whilst I'm intense and occupied with imploring manmade engines to remain fighting gravity. I dream though of flying unassisted by mechanics.

I also dream of falling.

Forget flies, or life's sticky fly-paper. The credo, *you made your bed, now lie in it*, was the complete undoing of any opportunity for my Mum to find peace or happiness - ever. She needed to be vertical for any chance of an accidental stumble into contentment. Not lying unhappy but neat, in a bed she'd made. The antiquated adage ingrained itself right into Mum's poor young soul and has refused to be removed, like the perpetual stain that it is. The axiom is up there with *Stand by your man* as advice to keep women subjugated, if you ask me. You didn't? Sorry. I was presumptuous. Anyway, the fool who first threw such sayings at my mother, blemishing her soul forever, is long since dead. Or, perhaps still about somewhere, over one hundred years old and as bitter as bittery things are.

I believed both of the sayings for a long time, to my detriment. But we'll get to that later.

These days, I'm a believer in: *you made your bed, so go and lie down somewhere else, so's not to mess it up.* There's some OCD in me right where caring used to be. Or is it where not caring, or not knowing used to be? One day I would like to say, 'I'm absolutely foible-less,' but I fear the world is far too untidy for that to happen. Meanwhile, there's medicine. Ignorance may be bliss, but sometimes I can't go past prescription medications. (Use responsibly and in moderation). ◈ The small print. Life's not a game, you know. Okay, maybe it is.

Cheers, sweetie darling.

For the love of Jennifer Saunders, could somebody please get me back on topic?

Drinking has commenced before the sun pops over the yard-arm today. That first beer. For I need to take leave of my senses. An inner voice has become quite verbally abusive of late. A visitor. Nobody should have to put up with that kind of domestic viciousness. It's something to do with poking around in noir memories. Here's another adage I might try later; 'Write drunk, edit sober.' No, best not. I've a tendency to make things habitual.

Sometimes when looking back, anger rises. Even if I haven't honed in on anything in particular. Anger is there crouching and it attacks before making its motivation clear. An innocent bystander, I am injured by the sudden and brutal strike. Blurred lines, blurred times. The beer has taken the edge off for a while. Everything looks better in blurred vision, like me; the line across my face where a smile used to be.

Anger is such a wasted thing. It grows well out of proportion and potency. I sometimes confine myself into one room, so my anger won't shatter the entire house. Christmas break reminiscences bring out the worst in me.

*

When we resumed home life after our holiday, all crumpled and worn, my parents returned to work and Matthew and I were choofed off to Vacation Care. Where despite the name there was no vacation nor care. Where I'm certain, as a non-joiner I sat on a swing for four weeks. My memory is so very indistinct to the point that I'm not sure it's my recollection at all, but somebody else's that I've scavenged on the way. Anything salvaged from my depths is disfigured by the amount of time it's been in the deepness. What I recognise from a deductive point of view is this; I would not have been comfortable. Change is not as good as a holiday for me. There's a strong possibility that I would have peed myself because I'd not have known where the loos were and I know I wouldn't have asked. If I didn't pee myself, I would have become very uncomfortable by the afternoon and hurried home at top speed to reach the safety of a familiar or familial toilet.

Before we'd even touched double digits in age, Matt and I had keys to the front door of the house. It was the days before mobile phones were bonded to young people, melded into our youthful grasp by radiating unhealthy heat from the phone's internal organs. The house didn't have a landline either, because we were renters. Frugality and tiredness. My Mum's first big household purchase was a dishwasher rather than the rigmarole of a landline and dealing with a telephone company. There were no complaints from us, just the occasional argument as to whose job it was to empty the thing. The key to a quiet home is a fatigue-free mum. Some people get hangry, anger caused by hunger - my family is prone to tangry, anger caused by tiredness. Its genetic predisposition is carried through on the maternal line, no stops. An express anger that blasts out of me well before the realisation that I'm fatigued. Matt too.

The key to a happy home may not exist, but the front door key did. It hung around my neck and tried to kill me grabbing at things as I passed, attempting to garrotte me. I hung from a tree, managed to get myself somehow tangled in a bicycle's handlebars while in motion, and the act of opening the front door was fraught with danger if I didn't think to take the chain from around my neck before inserting the key. I was short and had to reach up on toe tips to make contact with the lock, so if the door flung open in a breeze I was dragged inside, unless I'd thought to take the necklace off first. I wasn't the brightest headlight on the highway so I entered the house choking on many occasions.

Matt was in charge of making sure we got on and off a bus to get to vacation care. As far as I know it was incident-free. Left to my own devices I would ride the bus in a fugue state until it terminated, ride another one back, back and forth, forth and back. I'd still be on a bus now, if Matt hadn't been there to give me a shove.

One afternoon, it was becoming quite late when Matt started to get a worry going. My mother was most days, home by five and it was close to 6.00 pm. As the dullard, I thought his fretting excessive, but unbeknownst to me there'd been a recent murder and the body of a woman had been found in the storm water canal system that ran like varicose veins throughout our suburb. So, our nine-year-old boy grabbed a torch and went out to scour the canals for his mother's body and his eight-year-old sister was left at home in case their father turned up, if the pub burnt down or something, so that he might be briefed on the situation that she didn't understand. She did know that she was left alone, and it was getting dark and there was no dinner and there was an overall wrongness.

Matt arrived back, unsure whether to be happy or sad that he hadn't found a mother-shaped corpse. He was not five minutes in the door before a car pulled up out front. It was nothing like a VW Bug. It was a fancy Holden with chrome that glowed. In the passenger's seat was my mother a little tipsy, being dropped home by her boss. They kissed goodbye. That's all I remember. My father would have arrived home much later and never learned of the drama. I'm not even sure if my mother knew that a miserable Matty had been searching the drains, very, very afraid of what he might find.

CHAPTER 7

John Fogerty, a Car Chase and an Explosion

My father never missed a day of work unless ordered to stand down by a doctor. It was one of the many reasons Dad never accepted he had a drinking problem. A drunk wouldn't be up at 5.00 am getting ready for work was his rationale. It's not beyond the sphere of possibility that he was never alcohol-free. The blissful ignorance Dad spent much of his life soaked in made him less susceptible to the crippling depression that attacked both the paternal and maternal branches of my family tree, like a mighty blight that began at its very roots. Most days found him keen for a laugh. Meanwhile my mother found out wine could be bought in a box. Dad drank out of habit. Mum, because life was a bit shit. My father became happier the more he drank. My mother became flammable.

After Dad recovered from his first heart attack, the effort required to separate from him again deflated my mother and she postponed the separation for well over a decade. Oneness; the quality of being one. It started about then, our family's ability to be four orbiting planets circling the house. Sometimes we aligned, most often not. Oneness; the inequality of being alone with others. Sometimes there was interaction, sometimes even laughter. Most times it felt like we had all inhaled and held our breath, to later exhale like pressure cookers over high heat - hissing and spitting—and hostile toward she-who-was-on-the-bottom-of-the-heap, the underling.

'Greetings from the bottom of the pile' – a postcard from young Maddie Kitchener.

I never knew what I was in trouble for, but I was always in it. My fugue states were broken by injustice or confusion, or both. Twice I found myself in the Principal's Office during the last days of corporal punishment, on the wrong end of the cane. My sins were not explained. The stick came swishing down. There seemed to be an assumption that I was conscious, and therefore I would know what I'd done. I wasn't. I didn't. If I'd discovered swear words in those young years I would have walked about in a state of astonishment, mumbling, WTF? Off with the fairies was used to explain my bumbling ways. In reality (or not often in reality) I was very close to being robotic with occasional bouts of rude awakening. My blurriness may well have been caused by exhaustion.

With my father back in the house my late-night vigilance was re-triggered and the older I grew the more complex my anxieties became. There were no words to explain them and nobody to reassure me if I'd been able to verbalise my worries. With constancy of fear, a poisonous anger began to fester. Bottling and gurgling up against Uncle too. Angry, Angry. ANGRY.

As the bum-end of the family totem pole, I had nobody beneath me to take out my anger. I turned it inward and lash out at my-self, her inside. I lay in my bed feeling internal wounds, listening to the sounds of resignation, a sighing acquiescence about the house. Over time, dysfunction becomes the accepted normal, and from the outside the family looked to be in working order.

Winter mornings often found my mother, dressing gown and slippers thrown on, pushing the stubborn VW down the street until my father managed to clutch-start the vehicle into a noise just a tad more powerful than a modern food processor. He chugged off to work with a little beep goodbye and there'd be an hour or so of quiet before the morning routine proper began. Sometimes the backing track included the rhythmic thud of the morning papers hitting front lawns and a cockatoo that lived a few streets away screeching 'Leslie! Leslie!' over and over, mimicking Leslie's mother's voice with wicked accuracy. Nostalgia. Neuralgia. Headaches and pain. Remembering won't put it back together again.

My bedroom at that house was at the front. It was the best bedroom I'd ever had or would ever have, right up to now. The windows opened onto the front veranda and it was an easy step out or in. One morning there was a squawk of the human kind and I slid over the window sill, out onto the veranda in the pre-dawn light, to see my parents chasing the VW down the road. My father had mishandled the part where he pushed from the driver's side door and jumped inside, swashbuckling style, to clutch-start the car as it rolled. They ran out of my peripheral vision but I soon heard the car start and chug off. Relief that it hadn't ended with a crash added humour but it was time to jump back through the window and into bed.

I knew by then that my mother wanted to be seen as an accomplished adult. Her veneer was to remain flawless no matter the day-to-day muck she had to wade through. If she'd known I'd witnessed her run down the street, chasing after a recalcitrant car, my mother would have turned her anger toward me. She did not want a witness to indignities, and not a witness with 'a stupid grin on your face'. I'd thought it comical and had not understood it to be yet another humiliation for my mother, brought about by a perpetual funding deficit. There was never quite enough money to throw at the problems brought to my Mum daily. My father was oblivious. To a point. He often lost all his money trying to gamble us onto Easy Street. If he'd just given the money to my mother, we might have made it.

My stupid grin was the sole weapon I had against my anger within. Anxiety sufferers know anger is very close to the surface. Caused by betrayal. Our experiences of trauma have caused our physiology to attack itself in ways that can lead to tears, the dripping kind. To tears, the ripping kind. To rips, the gaping sort.

Nobody wants to spend their life afraid. Nobody chooses the anxious life. It chooses them. An eight-year-old shouldn't be walking about in what I can now describe as a broken risk-management mindset. Back then I could jump off the roof of the house, hurdle my pushbike over a canal or climb the highest tree but when it came to protecting my psyche I was a coward. I let my emotional self be wounded time and time again. Harmful words felt like surgery without anaesthetic.

I never stood up for myself. I let my self-esteem go, unable to nurture my own ego, no ability to pat my own hand. On my face I placed a stupid grin and inside me, went by the name Door Mat. Door Matt. Door Mattie. Door Maddie. Poor Maddie. This allowed people to walk all over me while the stupid smile remained.

My brother, Matt was not a mat.

My little body had already been claimed by an incestuous relation of our inner family circle, one of the so-called trusted ones, not my precious Great Uncle Said but another, never-said. And my little mind had been claimed by anxiety. On both counts, what had been done could never be undone. I knew my life was over and I was killing time. And damn it, although I resisted there was always hope. I hate the hope that has maintained its place in my being, always keeping me going with false promises of better days. I did not want to keep going, at eight.

There was an old compact disk stuck in the CD player of the VW. One of my Dad's favourites, *Bad Moon Rising: The Best of Creedence Clearwater Revival*. It played on a loop in perpetuity. Whenever the player was switched on, like an omen *Bad Moon Rising* would be the first track played. Random. Not random. I cannot hear the song without thinking of that VW Bug, how my father once lived in that car and once almost died in it. How the car battery, whether new or fading/failing, never made it through a winter without my mother having to drag herself out into the street and help push the little car away. There was always hope. That little car always came back.

While I was waiting to die, I took up some habits that might assist its speedy arrival. At the age of eleven I began to smoke, but not very well. At twelve I began to decant some of my mother's boxed wine and take it to school. I knew I was playing with fire. I was testing an enjoyment of the forbidden. Aware through osmotic exposure of the dependence my parents had on alcohol, I toyed with the idea of letting addiction take me into its fold. It was my taunt to the universe, not an act of rebellion. 'Go on, take me.' Nobody tried harder than I as a teenager and beyond to adopt alcoholism as a lifestyle choice, but in a cruel twist I always became ill before I became drunk despite competing on volume. I could never enjoy the benefit of a happy buzz. My alcohol tolerance, perhaps because of my precocious start, climbed high. I could drink people under the table but never retreated under the table myself, never blotto.

Now, in my declining years, after two or three beers I begin to feel unwell. Drinking has morphed into refreshment rather than escape. Damn it.

I see a bad moon rising.

Cigarettes were more about having something to do with my hands and maybe to give the impression of being tough. A disguise. It was, in a family of many secrets, nice to have one of my very own; a secret stash. I would sneak off to the canals and lie back, look at the sky and make my own clouds. Nicotine made me feel a bit ill as well, but I was a survivor, a persevere-er-er.

One day down by the canal, my cigarette started to flare in an odd way and then it exploded. I jumped up, brushing smoulder off my blouse and let my emerging WTF? take over. My brother, Matthew had stumbled upon my secret stockpile of stolen ciggies. With precision, and what must have taken quite a bit of time he had pulled half of the tobacco out of five cigarettes, slid an illegally obtained tom-thumb firework cracker into each one and replaced as much tobacco as he could. I never smoked in complete comfort again. Always watching for sign of imminent explosion.

With wasted stubbornness I kept my self-destructive smoking habit up until a lung infection stole what little breath I had. By then aged eighteen it was obvious I wasn't a tough rebel type. Smoking hid nothing. Smoke screen failure. It's all done with mirrors. I quit cigarettes.

On occasion, decades since that child smoked, I miss the quiet contemplation that used to arrive with a cigarette and a view. Now I watch
a bad moon rising in the night sky with a cat by my side and a little hope
still in my heart. Damn it.

CHAPTER 8

Life Preservers

We moved one more time while my parents were still together, (*together* - not an accurate descriptor) into a house down the road from Great Uncle Said. The mortgage was an added worry to my mother's list, but it beat being at the mercy of landlords. My room this time was at the back of the house. It was a tight, claustrophobic suburb and the lack of green was disappointing. A storm water canal ran through, slicing the suburb in half but it was surrounded by housing, not wasteland. I liked wasteland. I missed the forlorn and feral dried-out scrub that had surrounded our old place. There was no middle of nowhere feel to our new suburb, one that I'd quite forgotten since our caravan years there behind Uncle Said's house. Middle of nowhere is a feel I enjoy; a 360-degree view without another person in sight.

As far as life was concerned, I was just phoning it in; even during my rebellious smoking phase. Suburban claustrophobia forced me to give up smoking by canals and now and again I smoked in the girls' loos at school. The atmosphere in there stank. My lacklustre mood may have saved my life. I couldn't muster up the energy to end myself. And there was always that stupid hope thing.

My brain didn't kick in until my mid-twenties. I began all my book learning way after I'd left high school which produced a most pitiful academic performance. Whether it was my lack of brain or a bunch of jaded teachers I don't know, but nobody lit any spark for me and high school was six of the most uninterrupted years of waste in my life to date. I've wasted years since but not that many in a row. As much as I like environ-mental wasteland, I don't like it laying across my space-time continuum. As a school-age teenager I was drowning the whole time, semi-conscious from a lack of tension-free air. The only period I did feel close to alive was after I'd had some of my mother's decanted boxed wine with my school lunch. The midday special, shine your light on me. Some days I didn't go to school at all. My grandmother must have died at least eight times in my last two years at the Girls' High but nobody bothered to question me about the high number of grandmothers in our family or their excessive mortality rate. In my real world I had one grandmother who resided alive in New Zealand. Nana lived well into her nineties and I credit my killing her off so often as a secret to her longevity, my per-sonal Dorian Gray effect.

Perhaps my weekly absences and often-repeated excuses should have been a signal to the school world that I was not faring very well. Much too subtle. I would have had to had to overdose in the playground to come close to seeing the school counsellor. Some girls did, and I think one classmate's brother walked down from the Boys' School to have his overdose in our grounds, with his sister holding his hand while they waited for the ambulance. So, my having eight dying grandmothers slipped well under the school authority's radar. Sometimes I stayed at school for the morning and went home after lunchtime roll call. My lack of attendance did not rouse any teacher's interest. At one end-of-year Christmas party the teacher asked if I was in her class. She'd thought I'd come in from a different lesson to enjoy the crisps and stuff she had laid on for her girls. I thought it was hilarious at the time.

Drowning at the same time, nobody's girl.

My consciousness registered hilarity but I soon realised not one per-son gave a shit whether I was at school or if I wasn't. It didn't improve my ever-diminishing self-esteem. Decreasing, deceasing. On one hand I felt invisible with an almost Ninja quality and that was cool. On the other I was invisible - which somehow equated to worthless. Throughout those six wasted, wasteland years of high school, if I now had ten dollars for every time I was asked, 'Are you okay?' I'd have zero dollars.

Close to Chaplinesque. Comic. Tragic. That is how a soul can split in two.

Humour became my weapon. My sense of the absurd quickened. I laughed when I should have cried. A clown was born. Not the face-painted kind, they're just creepy. I was the kind whose quips annoy teachers. *If Madison put as much effort into her school work as she does her smart comments, she'd be a genius.* Mrs Chase, music teacher - Year 10 report card. I took the comment as a compliment. Yet, I was drowning. Except at swimming carnivals.

My mother hates surprise expenditure, much like I do now. In high school when I said I'd made it as far as the Area Swimming Carnival (that's two above ordinary school swimming and one below state level competition) and that I needed a one-piece Speedo™ swimming costume, Mum stared at me. End of no-conversation. I may as well have asked for a million dollars and a small private plane.

'Swimmers take your marks.' There I was on the starting blocks next to girls in one-piece swimming costumes, caps emblazoned with swimming squad insignias plus flash-looking goggles, and me in the bikini I'd worn the past five years, quite frightened I'd lose my top when I dived in.

At least it was a sanctioned day off school. I defaulted on trying at that point. There was no way I wanted to reach the next level of competition. People seemed to be taking the whole activity as important, so I swam at a pace a sloth might envy, to the other end, enjoying a dip in the pool on a hot day with the added bonus of annoying the unsmiling marshals who sought to get the next race started as soon as possible.

My other accidental sporting aptitude was for cross-country running. Again, without training, I'd bumbled my way as far as the Area Carnival. I began keen enough but when I saw ahead that I was expected to race up a steep hill to the finish line, a rugged challenge after running for much longer than I enjoyed, I slowed to a dawdle. Sports weren't my thing. I had no survivor spirit when any situation wasn't life threatening. When the contestants from the race that had started after mine overtook me, I thought it humorous. Out of breath I also considered giving up smoking for good as I wheezed up the hill, not bothering to go over the finish line but veering off to sit on my bag on the side-lines.

Nothing seemed to be my thing. I was drowning. A drowning sloth.

*

The mood behind the closed front door in our new house was not light. My mother would grab her first glass of wine the moment she was inside after work. For amusement or some sort of revenge, Matthew would sprint out the back door, up the side path and around the front to ring the doorbell. My mother would jump and thrust her glass in a cupboard before going to answer the door. By the time she returned shrugging, Matthew would be sprawled on the floor watching TV as if he'd never left the room. A cupboard drinker, my Mum, which I assumed in relation to size, was smaller and therefore less devious than full-on wardrobe drinking.

Keeping up appearances was an understood priority etched into our family code. It must have been a bit King Canute for my Mum. trying to hold back that tide of constant disappointment. With my Dad rolling home from the pub each night and Matthew and I underachieving at school, my mother had very little to brag about to her friends and hospital admin colleagues.

'My daughter has been accepted into The University of Sydney,' a fellow-professional might say.

'Mine's learnt to whistle with two fingers in her mouth,' was the one accomplishment from my thirteen years of school worth a boast. I bet my house my mother never volunteered it though. I'd also learnt to write an entire note of absenteeism in my mother's handwriting. I suppose it's not a skill to be proud of, but it is noteworthy. Worthy notes.

Without psychiatric skills or qualifications, my brother and I had both realised that we were never going to be brilliant enough so trying would be exhausting and futile. And my father - he just liked beer. Quite the family unit. Including the cupboard drinker. Nobody in our family was changing. Nobody was growing. None of us were living.

Or was it just me? Never were there dreams or plans for my future. I didn't think I had one. A sense of doom followed me everywhere. Sometimes I didn't always notice its shadow; other days it was so dark I contemplated suicide just to get it over with, like ripping off a Band-Aid with speed. When you feel more dead than alive something has to happen to take you to one side or the other. That's when fate decided to kick me while I was down, in the dark.

But, before we head away from the light here's some preamble. In a self-protective way (the scrap of self I still had left) I didn't tell anybody that I was going to attempt my driving licence test. No public humiliation for me if I failed. But I passed, first go. There was me, walking out of the Department of Motor Registry gripping my Probationary Driver P-plates with my signature idiotic grin on my face, meaningful for once.

That day I arrived home earlier than my mother and when she walked in after work, I held the plates up, proud of myself.

'Look what I've got.'

'What car did you steal those from?'

My heart kind of sank as I explained that I'd passed my test and showed her my new licence. 'Then you might as well pick your father up from the pub tonight.'

My first solo drive in the family car was from our driveway to the local pub, four blocks away. Matthew had gained his licence the year before but had not been required to chauffeur my drunk father about. Matt had purchased an old car of his own so he didn't have to jump through hoops to use the family car to go for a drive. Some nights, instead of bringing my father home I'd have to detour to the Emergency Department of the local hospital. Sometimes my father had pneumonia, or he had to be stitched up after face planting on the curb. Sometimes he was just a horrible colour. Making this kind of health decision was not easy, a burden alone, scary and humiliation-by-parent at the hospital. Dad was always healthy enough to get to the bloody pub. I knew

I hated the whole business; sitting in that creepy under-lit carpark behind the street of shops, watching and waiting. It wasn't for the faint-hearted, but there I was anyway. Ordered-by-mother. Watching grown men stumble out into the night from the back door of the pub. Peeing as if the whole world was their toilet. Spewing, swearing, leering, sneering and spitting, and the occasional woman doing the same. It was unpleasant to an extreme I registered deep in my black place, no light, so no shadow.

We never talked, my father and I on these evening drives. I was so rigid with fear and loathing that I could not move my jaw. Never did I ever have the nerve to tell my mother or father to fuck off. I'm not doing this anymore.' I'd placed myself so low on their or any other ratings list that I didn't know how to think I deserved better.

Inside, I was dying one piece at a time. One peace at a time. My stupid, conflict-weary, bashed-about sense of hope was the one life preserver left.

WARNING: If you think the narrative has moved to the dark side, please DO NOT read the next chapter. I'll let you know when I turn the light back on. There'll be a candle in the window.

CHAPTER 9

Near Completion

When I get to Heaven, I will be more silent. I will not step forward and try to explain my life. I can't begin to validate my Earth time because so much of it has been wasted. Because I have been unable to remember most of it. And because only garbage gets thrown away, forgotten. Isn't this so? I know I've fucked up and if Heaven is anything close to what zealots proclaim the Divine will know that too. When I get to Heaven ...

I'm without religion, so perhaps I won't make it there at all. I believe there might be a Heaven because I've already been to Hell. I'm a believer in natural balance.

When I get to Heaven, I will be silent. Inside and out. Balanced. Debit and credit equalled.

*

I don't remember how it went wrong. Trying to create a balance sheet of myself is as though a camera has zoomed in from a great distance to catch me at my worst. Points before and points after have been lost. To make sense, I'll try to gather information like puzzle pieces. I'll start at the edges. It's difficult because they are all black.

Here's the sharpest edge. One late afternoon I walked off. Just walked off. In my head, I was going to hike to Melbourne, 857 kilometres or so. I carried nothing. From this distance, years later, I assume I was walking out on my life since it seemed untenable at the time. There was anger in my stomp. My adult brain had still not formed so there may have been a bit of tantrum in my action.

It grew dark. I kept walking. It grew late, I slowed. It grew later, I reduced to a stroll, the anger lost from my step. I'd walked, at a guess twenty kilometres. Like a clockwork animal I'd begun to wind down.

From the dark in front of me, a man emerged. He carried an over-sized canvas bag made larger in comparison with his small build. We passed and I kept walking south.

'Hey!' he called. 'Do you wanna beer?'

I stopped walking.

*

Can you believe it? That's all it took.

Papers have been written about individuals who have been molested as children having no skills to evaluate others, powerless to read body language or understand personal signals. A high number of survivors are later raped in adult life. You can add me to that statistic.

*

I did very much want a beer.

We sat in parkland. The man talked. Turned out that day he'd been sacked. Been working as a jockey or a strapper at Warwick Farm Race-course, not ten minutes away from where we sat. He was angry at being fired. The man was angry.

I did not feel threatened until the threat. He'd grabbed a stirrup from his bag. A stirrup. It looked solid, heavy.

'Do as I say or I'm going to smash your pretty face in with this.'

Cue fugue state. From beneath him I heard a garbage truck empty-ing rubbish bins on the perimeter of the park. I remained frozen.

'See me,' I pleaded. Invisible. You know how it is. I don't know if I said it out loud.

When he was done, I was pushed away. With belated flight response I jumped and ran in the direction of home. Laughter followed me, haunts me now, sounding villainous like a stupid cartoon character. I ran until I was sure there was no chase. Blisters had burst, seeping on my heels, soaking fluid into my socks. My running shoes were sandpaper rough at my heels, to the point of scarring me. But I kept walking. Retracing my steps as the sun was coming up. On the highway not five kilometres from home. my mother passed me in a colleague's car on their way to work.

Our eyes met. It's the first time I'd been seen in years.

No, I did not go to the Police. I had accepted the offer of a beer. I had been out walking alone through the night. I didn't know why I'd been where I'd been. Fate had brought me to my knees. So, I did not go to the Police. My shame was entrenched.

No, I did not go to a doctor. My shame threw me into the shower at home and I scraped myself clean with a scouring pad from the kitchen cupboard. I sat down on the tiled floor and stayed in that shower for five hours. Maybe six. My heels bled. My heart bled. I hurt so bad back then and since. I have not cried—yet.

Right now, I'm opening a beer at eleven in the morning and I don't know if that means I'm accepting an offer of a beer from myself without shame, as a sign of recovery, or if I'm drinking to take the edges away. The black edges.

It was a long time ago now, in another life, but it was a hideous landmark in my travels toward being. It closed me down further than I thought possible. It was as if I'd scoured the interior of my soul as well. Leaving me clean but bland. I died. Was clean, new but without life. I drifted.

When my mother arrived home from work, she burst into my room where I was shivering under the bedcovers although the weather was mild.

'How dare you,' she spat and it felt as painful as a physical slap yet she was across the room. 'If you're going to stay out all night, like a slut, don't you dare come home on the same road as I'm travelling. You looked disgusting. Brenda asked if that was you. It was humiliating.'

With that she left my room, slamming the door closed. The house shook with her anger. I died again.

My mother doesn't know the story of that night. I will never tell her. She will never know how her words ripped me again. How much I needed a mother.

I left my bed and went to have another shower, again trying to wash my shame away. There was deep pain within, where a scream was waiting, seeking oxygen. Instead, I washed again, put on clean pyjamas and went to help my mother prepare dinner.

'Are you going to wear those to pick up your father?'

*

My life had changed so much—and had not changed at all. Everything I had walked away from was still there. Now defeated, I lost the will to leave. That next day, the first back at home was a day of giving up. It was the day demons began to knock.

The time lapse between this rape-and-return event and the day I heard my first voice, I'm not sure, but it didn't feel like long. Not minutes, maybe days. You cannot eat that, it said.

Then began a fight for my life. You must die, to begin again. I thought I had, but no, I hadn't died deep enough. From the outside I was still the clown. I pursued laughter as if it was gold in a rainbow's light. I grew thin though, and weak and voices pursued me like I was the waiting gold, the prize, the destination. I was a few months away from a lifetime of psychiatric meds. If I had known what was coming I might have let the voices win. I needed to die. My sense of failure was so very near completion, complete, to complete, will complete, may complete, completed.

Without knowing, I was choosing life every time I walked into a doctor's office. Every time I swallowed a pill. Every time I swallowed some food.

You need to die it screamed, relentless. It multiplied into a dissonant choir at its own behest, me the unwilling listener. 'Death is your out.'

'True,' I would reply, 'but you know, no rush.'

CHAPTER 10

Candle in the Window

In a stomach-churning see-saw type of motion, I spent the next month both shrinking and growing. Undulating. Queasiness spewed over me, a constant ick doing little to assist my fight against the voices that were tormenting, ranting and easing me toward death by self-perpetrated famine. In a last-ditch attempt at survival, I went to the doctor's. Without telling my mother, on a sunny Wednesday I went, jittery as a mouse in the waiting room, ready to scuttle away.

'You're too skinny,' the doctor said, once I was lying vulnerable on the examination table, unable to escape. 'I can evaluate most of your skeleton and vital organs without the use of an x-ray machine.' He paused, brow ribbed with pretending rows of concern. Could you be pregnant?' he asked, kneading my abdomen and surrounds.

'No of course not. Yes.'

My confusing answer reflected back at me from the doctor's face. His left eyebrow rose in question, almost disappearing under his hairline.

'I... um... maybe. Maybe I should be tested for that, and STIs,' I said before leaning over and throwing up into the waste bin.

When I'd recovered we did a pee test to rule pregnancy in or out. The result arrived in no time. With gentle cinematic-like fade-in came the blue (+) sign at the end of the stick. I smiled, a very small smile at the visual indication that there was to be an addition to our family.

'We won't do bloodwork yet,' the doctor told me. 'I think we need to build you up a bit first before we start sucking vital fluids out of you. Also, you've got some thinking to do.'

I was handed a long list of supplements to buy at the chemist and a referral to the diagnostic people to have my blood tested for every disease known to man.

'Wait until next week before you make an appointment at the pathologist's so that some of the supplements can kick in. In the meantime, eat, or you will die. I want to see you again in a fortnight.'

Eat, or I will die.

*

It could be that I went into shock. I was carrying the child of a ... My brain shutdown for at least two days and the voices went away for a while too. Sweet respite. I ate like somebody rescued after being stranded for weeks. Gluttony occupied my mind and my belly. It seemed impossible to feel full, to be full. Within a week I'd put back on a kilo although I couldn't see where. Maybe my earlobes were bigger.

Eat or I will die. It was ever so tempting to go with dying. The doctor had told me to do some thinking and I knew he meant I had to decide about the foetus. I couldn't force myself to contemplate termination. Or motherhood. Perhaps I'd starved my brain to its near-death and it could no longer piece a thought together. I did eat. Was that a decision? That the survivor in me would be victorious? Was that me eating for two? Had I chosen?

I must have. Instinct in charge. Conscious mind awol. Eat. Have a baby.

I sat in the carpark waiting for my father to stumble out of the pub, slamming Macca's Drive-thru meals down my gullet. There was no taste and brief chewing. It was a lazy person's fuel. A habit formed in that I began buying extra fries because my father could smell the fat they were soaked in as he slid into the car, and every time, he insisted on eating some.

'Glorious,' he'd say.

The sound of him chewing just about made me puke but we kind of bonded over our awkward secret. There was a childish don't-tell-mum message in our indulgences. The whole time I was pushing decision making far out of my mind because in truth I felt I might be going out of it. My mind. Do you leave your mind or does your mind leave you? Is my mind out in the ether, abandoned, frantic, looking for me, its protective shell?

Trying to push lava back up into the volcano was futile.

*

'What are you going to do?' the doctor asked during my next visit.

'Do I have to make up my mind right now?'

'You have a small window left for a termination if you require one. But in two or so weeks that'll no longer be an option. Now, you'll be pleased to know your blood tests are fine, except you're anaemic which is no surprise, and your sugar is low. Keep taking the iron supplements.'

'No STIs?'

'No.'

'Just a baby?'

'Yes.' His frown returned. 'How about you come back in a week? I'll check your sugar and you can tell me if you're going ahead with this pregnancy. Or not.'

When it came down to it, my failure to arrange for an immediate abortion was my way of telling myself I was willing to continue with the pregnancy. Once I had this in my mind, the part I was clinging onto, I began to think like an expectant mother. My point of view jumped to the perspective of somebody who believed they had a future. It was simultaneously unfamiliar and phenomenal to plan ahead.

'I'm going to have this baby,' I told the doctor the next week, as he was pricking my finger to test my sugar level.

Thanks to his years of training I guessed, he didn't react as if I'd made a good or a bad decision.

'Fine. I'll have a referral to the hospital clinic made out. Does the father know?'

The spilling lava got away from me and I burnt red. 'I... No ... I ...' The pain of my shame was excruciating.

'Perhaps you should tell him. He might be very supportive.'

'I don't know who he was, is,' I admitted. Did I note some judgement? No, but these words blurted from my mouth anyway, 'I was raped.'

It was like Pompeii in the year 79AD in that office. I was desperate to get away from the burning, liquid fire but I didn't know how to save myself.

'And, you're absolutely sure you want to keep the baby?' the doctor asked.

I stumbled on, verging on incoherent, thought-to-word new and jumbled but there for me when my resolve had to be spoken. 'I ... Yes ... I don't connect the baby with the rape at all.'

'You should probably see a therapist. I'll write you a referral for that, too.'

'Yes. I should, probably, but I don't want to. I'm okay.'

Except for the voices and the shame.

'Spawn of Satan,' said a voice.

'Gift from God,' said another.

I left them to their argument. Religious nutters in my head.

*

In the short-term there was the matter of telling my parents. The need to reveal was gaining awful momentum in my thoughts and I was quite petrified about the outcome of the eventual exchange. This step I would postpone until the pregnancy was obvious and undeniable—and beyond termination. If I procrastinated long enough they might approach me first. That might cut down on my uncomfortable anticipation of hostilities.

On odd occasions, in my head I played out the scenario of telling my mother. The dummy-run enactments always ended with me waving a white flag. Sometimes in these try-outs she killed me; my mother put her hands around my neck and strangled me blue.

My neuroses began acting up, to the point of melodrama. I was becoming pre-stress disordered about something that hadn't happened.

'Calm down,' I said to myself. 'You're a grown-up now.' I was nineteen.

'Spawn of Satan,' the voice yelled again, and I wished I could decant some of my mother's boxed wine and take a giant slug.

Optimism was the key to a healthy pregnancy. I knew that. I had to think of nothing but the little life growing inside me. Someone who was going to love me unconditionally. Something, someone, I could love without being hurt. There would not be a price to pay. The words of poet Philip Larkin reverberated in my head, *They fuck you up, your Mum and Dad.* Now I would have my own chance at being a parent. Inadequate, terrible parenting might be something at which I would excel, given my role models. Or conceivably and hopefully, I would be a different parent than my parents, one with a flair for bringing a new being into the world and shaping them into an admirable human. (I'm sorry for 'conceivably,' but it sat there for the punning). Conditions were such that it was possible, almost probable that I would do a better job than my own parents managed. Worse case, I'd get to fuck somebody up for myself.

Optimism was the key.

'Spawn of Satan!'

Spawn of Satan. SOS. Go back, you're going the wrong way. An argument of voices erupted in my head most mornings while I was throwing up. It wasn't the best way to start a day but it was the only way I had. Optimism was the key ... 'Oh fuck off, you and your optimism.'

I quit my job. After leaving school I'd worked with diligence to move up from dish pig to short-order cook at the local steak restaurant. It was a job I hated but I didn't think I could do better. My Higher School Certificate was worthless; my choices were limited to unskilled or unskilled in the labour market. Employment was just another environment where I appeared conscientious but inept. My work ethic made up for lack of natural ability and I was very good at putting out flash fires.

As my bulge grew the assortment of smells in the steak place turned me a shade of pesto-sauce green and I made it through a shift by a small margin. Workers at places like these are quite transient so there was no shock when anybody left. No party. No good wishes. You were there one day and just not there the next. It was an easy job to turn my back on and I walked away with no regret.

The very next day, dragging my shame with me I walked into a *Centrelink* office and signed on for benefits. It seemed I would be doing a lot of walking. The way I was going, I would never be in a position to afford a car of my own. Walking. Walking was how this had all begun. No good came from walking. Now I'd walked out of a job and into poverty.

Money was needed as none of my clothes fitted over my growing bump. This roused me from the quiet suspension of reality that I'd been hiding within and took me to the brink of informing my parents about their first grandchild.

There was a morning with a rehearsal of what I might say to them. I deferred the real thing again though, because of the sudden disintegration of our family unit. Everybody had seen it coming but it was a harsh surprise and sad when it happened. Matt and I were so accustomed to the frigid emotional landscape of our so-called home (think sanctuary? —not), we didn't have a conversation about it ending or what that would mean for us. We were accustomed to discomfort.

Within a month we were all living in separate places and I still hadn't told anybody about the baby. The bump. My bump. My reason to live.

CHAPTER 11

Raison d'état

Most humans don't need a reason to live. They've found themselves here on Earth and ready to make the best of it. Others want a motive or else living is just pain upon pain and life becomes an endless endurance test and list of unfortunate events. I fell into this latter category. Not on purpose. Like most people who fall, I tumbled by accident. Nature and nurture had collided mid-air to wreak a strange havoc on my life and I was struggling on most days to find lightness. Puberty blues had morphed directly into adult clinical depression, without let up. It's not how I meant it to be. I don't know how I meant it to be, but I knew that wasn't it.

The little being in the making, nestling, incubating in my belly needed a better start than most to overcome the elements stacked against it: miserable genetics, an outstanding predisposition for complete wretchedness, and the slight madness I brought to the table. The contribution from the paternal side was even creepier.

'Kill the Spawn of Satan,' demanded a voice. But the voices weren't worrying me for the moment. This one didn't concern me until it repositioned its cruel suggestions to outright threats, reinforced with a statement of intent. 'I will kill the Spawn of Satan,' it proclaimed. 'From here, from within.'

The idea that something inside of me would or could kill something else inside of me seemed possible, however, improbable. Until I went to the loo and saw blood in my underwear. 'Spotting,' people say. 'Panic,' my brain said. I knew there would be much more blood in a miscarriage, but I didn't know if miscarriage started this way and built up to blood-soaked awfulness.

It took me two buses to reach the hospital. Now that our family had fallen divided, I didn't have easy access to a car. My father had re-taken to driving the old vehicle straight to the pub after work and staggering home to his nearby flat after closing time. He'd won custody of the car but no one fought over me or Matt.

'I'm killing the Spawn of Satan,' the voice sang at me all the way to the hospital.

'I won't let you,' I shouted, and the person in front of me on the bus turned around to gape.

'Do you mind?' I demanded. 'This is private.'

The person moved three seats further away, closer to the driver. From there he kept turning around to stare. getting on my nerves. He pressed the communication button and left the bus at the next stop, much to my relief. The person off the bus still stared up at me as the bus moved away. I poked out my tongue. It was fortunate the person on and off the bus had taken my thoughts out of dark places for a few minutes. The voices in my head had calmed down a little, easing off from their homicidal rantings. But by the time I reached Accident and Emergency at the hospital I'd worked my way back up to distraught.

After I'd explained what was going on I was told to take a seat. The triage nurse seemed unconcerned. I'd expected to be swept into a treatment area with every available person there to help.

'I'm going to kill the Spawn of Satan. Now,' it said.

'No,' I yelled, overwrought at being placed in the 'accident' category rather than 'emergency.' I lowered my voice a little when I realised other bleeding people were staring, 'It's my body,' I told the voice.

'Mine too,' it said.

'That's ridiculous! You're beaming your voice in from somewhere else.'

'No, I'm not. Watch this. I'm going to move the right leg.'

My right leg twitched. 'That's a coincidence,' I said.

'I'm going to move the left hand.'

My left hand jolted up into the air just as two nurses arrived and hustled me into a room away from the waiting area. The involuntary movement of limbs had frightened me and must have frightened the staff, too.

'I've given the nurses the power. They're going to kill the baby,' said the voice with believable assuredness. Things were getting serious. 'I'll make them do it right now.'

I lost my mind.

The voices roared and groaned and cried. They were too hurt to love and too dazed to hate but they terrified me just the same.

'Back off,' I yelled. 'I have a baby to defend.'

Then a wave, a tsunami of panic knocked me down and bloodied my knees and I thought I was ended. Through the dark arrived my enemy, on horseback, his face hidden by a rusting iron mask. One voice amongst the many, had taken over. 'The Spawn of Satan is mine.'

From nearby I heard equine movement and the clink of agitated bridle metal.

'Give us this day, our new king.'

My enemy rushed toward me, a sword with an evil point aimed at my belly. 'No!' I screamed.

'She's waking up,' sang the chorus.

After the rumble of the sea eased, I could find it in empty shells rattling in my headspace. No horse or rider remained, but the echo of the storm swished through me, ear to ear.

*

I had a room to myself. A woman opened the door, pushing toward me a rattling blood pressure machine on such undisciplined wheels she battled to move it in a straight line, and it banged itself to a halt near the head of my bed. Although not dressed like a nurse, she wore an ID label with a hospital's logo visible.

'I shouldn't be in a private room,' I said. 'I'm a public patient. They've put me in the wrong place. I can't afford this.'

'Everybody has a single room here,' she told me as the pressure arm-band gripped me hard.

'Oh.'

'Your blood pressure's a bit low. You should get up, have a shower, go and join the rest outside. Have something to eat. You missed breakfast. It's a beautiful day.'

'My baby is...?'

'Your baby's fine. You've just had a bit of spotting, nothing to be worried about. Everything's fine.'

'Fine,' I repeated. 'Everybody's fine.'

'Come on, let's get you up and about. It'll do you good.'

After I'd showered in the small en-suite bathroom (the nurse knocked twice to make sure I was okay and didn't rattle away with her blood pressure contraption until she'd heard the water stop), I dressed in my street clothes and stepped, or stumbled into the fluorescent-lit corridor, wondering which way to turn. A TV or radio was prattling at volume and I headed toward its noise, expecting to find new mums and newer babies scattered about the common area, like arranged deco-rations. I was almost ashamed about the amount of time it took me to comprehend that I was not in a maternity ward. I was in a psychiatric unit.

'There's been a mistake,' I called out when the realisation struck me hard.

Nobody took any notice of me. There were no nurses about, just an assortment of mad folk looking like they'd come from auditions for Psy-chiatric Patient Number One on a TV drama series.

'This is wrong,' I murmured.

There was movement behind a glassed-in office and I saw the nursing staff bustling about on the other side of the transparent partition. They might as well have been in an aquarium. We stared at each other through the thick glass until I moved up to the counter. There was a small window, like at the bank.

'There's been a mistake,' I called again, moving my face closer to the gap where you'd take withdrawn money at a bank. 'I came to the hospital because I was bleeding. I'm not insane.'

There came a harsh murmur of voices from behind my back, but I paid them no mind while I tried to get any nurse to acknowledge my existence.

'Hello?'

I saw the nurse who had taken my blood pressure earlier. She acted now as if I wasn't there.

'Hey! Tell them I'm not a psycho. I don't belong here.'

'Madison,' said a man coming up to the window. 'We went through this yesterday. Just relax.'

'What? I only came in today. I've never been here before,' my temper was tattered and unravelling, revealing brand-new anger. I knocked on the glass. 'This is crazy!'

'Should we get her something?' the nurse at the window asked his colleagues and I felt invisible again. 'Go to the medication window,' I was advised.

'The what?'

'Go to the medication window.'

In the direction he was pointing was a window in an otherwise bland, cement, institutional-coloured wall. It had a grey roller shutter. As I stared, the shutter rose and a nurse appeared in its place and beckoned me over to the small countertop. I shook my head. This was stupid.

'I'm not taking drugs. I'm pregnant.'

'I'll have whatever's going,' called a voice from a lounge chair near the television.

'Come on, Maddie, we've been through this.'

'I'll calm down, honestly,' I assured the nurse, startled out of a tantrum by the diminutive use of my name, but not persuaded by this strange familiarity to take the offered medication. 'I don't need your pills.'

'Is it Loraz? I'll have 'em,' somebody, maybe the same body, yelled.

I walked away, walked out of the building via the one exit available to me. A thick metal and glass door which opened wide to a high-walled, inescapable bricked-in courtyard that smelled of the real world. If it wasn't for the sky, blue and brilliant above, I would have suffocated on the spot.

It was hard to get my bearings. Was I still at the local hospital? Was I in my right mind? My left mind? 'This is stupid,' I muttered to myself as I moved toward an unoccupied wooden bench beneath a thick-trunked tree at the obvious centre of the symmetrical yard. There were a few sleeping bodies strewn over the lawn, enjoying the sun but upsetting the symmetry. 'Stop talking to yourself, idiot,' I ordered myself. 'No wonder they think you're nuts.'

'The Spawn of Satan will die.'

'You shut up, and all. It's your fault I'm in here in the first place.'

In my stillness I sat thinking. Nothing, nobody was going to take my baby. Something nice was meant to come from the horror that had been that night. If I smelled any social services sticking their beaks in, I would indeed go nuts. Nobody was going to drag my baby into the system. Stubbornness glued me to the seat for more than an hour, unmovable. Other patients came and went in the small courtyard, bringing a strong sense of mania with them but taking it back when they left.

How was I to get myself released from this strange landscape? There must be hoops to jump through that would land me at the exit. Nobody is locked up forever. Are they?

'Madison, your mum's here,' called yet another nurse with the same sense of overfamiliarity the male nurse had used at the window of the nurse's aquarium. Terrarium? Nurse-arium?

What? My mother? Nothing was making any sense. Perhaps I *was* insane.

'I'm not insane,' I told the nurse as I re-entered the building, more to settle down my own self than to notify staff.

'No, dear.'

CHAPTER 12

Outnumbered

I had never seen my mother look so out of place. She sat between two patients in the common area, her back so straight it looked like her spine had been frozen from top to bottom. Barely disguised horror was written all over her body language. It was clear even to me, that she'd rather be most anywhere else in the world than where she was.

Do you want to go outside? I asked her, and she vaulted upright, startling the patient on her left.

'Fuck!' the woman squawked, and my mother apologised before rushing for the courtyard door as if from a fire.

When I'd planned how to tell my parents about the baby, this was nothing like my imagined scenario. I'd anticipated ringing my mother and saying, 'You know how we think Nana might have the most illegitimate great-grandchildren in New Zealand and Australia? Well, you can add one more to the list.' Oh, how we'd laugh.

Instead, my mother had somehow been summoned here to a psychiatric unit and had seen my belly for herself. 'Tah-dah,' I delivered without an exclamation mark, pointing with two index fingers at my burgeoning stomach.

'You seem better today,' she answered, injecting a sigh into her tone.

'I can explain about the baby,' I said, but didn't say anything more.

'Well?' my mother prompted.

'I said I could explain but I'd rather not.'

'Madison, you aggravate me to the point of ...'

'You've visited me here?' I asked, interrupting with the realisation that she had told me I seemed 'better today,' in the manner of a visitor who'd called on me before.

'Yes, don't you remember? I was here yesterday and the day before. How do you think you got those clothes?'

I saw then, realisation smacking me upside the head, that I wasn't wearing the clothes I'd had on for my panicked rush to Accident and Emergency. 'I ... Oh. I really must be in the ... Can you get me out of here? You know I'm not insane.'

Just as I said this, a siren blew louder than anything I'd ever heard. The thick glass doors into the building gave an audible click and we were locked outside. 'What the?' I blurted.

Mum seemed about the routine of the psych unit. 'It may be Gary going off. They'll unlock all the doors when they've contained him.

Her explanation should have been reassuring but it generated further bother for me. Within my unsteady grasp on things, I didn't have a clue which inmate Gary might be. He was problematic, because it was a good half an hour before he was taken to the higher dependency unit. The doors clicked open and a bunch of people poured out as if they'd been dying to be free the whole time, which was weird, because as soon as I'd been locked out, I'd wanted to go back in. All of us contrary by nature, I guess.

'So, can you get me out of here?' I repeated the question to my mother.

'Apparently not.'

'Why not?'

'You've been scheduled and have to go before a magistrate on Tuesday.'

'What? A magistrate? I'm not a criminal. This is stupid! I came to the hospital because I was bleeding and I was scared and now I'm being locked up against my will?'

'Lunch!' a nurse called from the door. Other courtyard patients jumped up and headed toward her, but I didn't move. 'Come on Madison, your Mum will wait there for you. Spit-spot.'

She and her lunch call were a bit too Mary Poppins for me.

'I'm not hungry,' I said even though I was.

'Eat something, Maddie,' my Mum said, almost kind. 'You've a baby to think of now.'

Was I in a parallel universe? Mary Poppins is a psych nurse. My mother is kind to me. Dumbfounded into obedience, I stood and walked indoors. Stunned, I was stunned. Inside, to the left, was a group of tables where two nurses were pulling trays of food from a tiered heated or refrigerated trolley system and plonking them in front of patients. What can I say about hospital food that hasn't been said before? It looked nutritious, was the best that could be said.

'Madison?' asked a nurse holding a tray.

'Present,' I answered as if in school roll call.

Lunch was placed in front of me and I feared I was going to lose my breakfast, which was odd because I couldn't remember eating that meal. I turned various shades of green before settling into *P21F8 Nasturtium Shoot* on a paint colour chart.

'You're eating for two,' an old man sitting next to me said. 'So am I,' he added, patting his paunchy stomach and laughing. It might have been humorous, except for the little bit of food that drooled out of the side of his mouth, sliding south inside the fold of a downward-directed wrinkle. It looked made-for-the-job of draining slobber straight onto his shirt front.

The shades of green wafted over me again. I gave him a wan smile and turned away. When the queasiness passed, I tried to eat my sandwiches. With each triangled quarter I felt better, and once my stomach had settled, like a famine survivor I guzzled down a chocolate mousse.

'Who feeds the spawn of Satan?' a voice demanded.

*

When I woke up the next time, my mother wasn't there, but I did remember that she had been. I knew I wasn't in a maternity wing. I knew I was insane.

I didn't feel at all crazy. My label had come from a vote that had taken place behind my back. The doctors had voted insane, so had the nurses—my mother appeared to vacillate toward and perhaps had landed on the same nutty diagnosis. I was outnumbered and being herded into madness.

When I rose from the bed, I felt the effects of whatever drugs I had on board and the room tilted and I almost slid off the world. My bones had been filled with something large. I walked with heaviness, as if trudging through sludgy treacle.

I struggled to the nurses' station and tapped on the glass.

'Why are you trying to kill my baby?' I asked the nurses. They were staring at me like bemused cows in a paddock. One was chewing.

'Madison, we are well aware you're pregnant. The drugs you're on have been okayed for use by pregnant women. We've told you before, your baby would be more at risk if you had psychotic episodes throughout the pregnancy, and even more so after the birth.

'Okay,' I said, then I burst into tears. I didn't want to be crazy.

It was dark outside, but I went out into the courtyard and had a sob. A long sob. There was nobody to blame for my world being tilted, but I wanted to be angry at somebody. The scars on my arms called for me to reopen them—penance for my thoughts.

'Walk it off,' I told myself and stood up to begin pacing around the courtyard. 'Walk it off.'

My sobbing continued. Walking it off was more or less how this whole business had started.

Within fifteen minutes I was tired. Too tired to contemplate or execute self-harm. I trudged inside, dropped into a lounge chair near the TV, swamped by a tidal wave that was later diagnosed as depression. If you stay in a psychiatric ward long enough, you can collect quite a number of labels. I'd just begun. If it wasn't for the baby, I might have contemplated ending myself. I cried again until another patient told me to shut up. She couldn't hear her Kardashians or something. If it wasn't for the baby, I might have plummeted headfirst into the TV screen, to end the stupid reality show and also, with luck, ending the stupid unreality show I was living.

Your scheduled normalcy has been interrupted, please try switching yourself off and back on again.

Standard programmes were not being resumed.

CHAPTER 13

Fragments

The day or was it night I met the owner of the deepest voice, was the worst of times. He looked like my abuser, the demolisher of my childhood—the uncle who had taken from me things I could never replace or repair. He who had killed the me I might have been. The uncle who had died.

Only a few people attended his funeral, including my father who should have known not to. I didn't. I knew. I did not mourn.

'The spawn of Satan still grows. Kill it,' demanded the voice, now embodied but cloaked in darkness. With eyes I couldn't look into, unable to face the horrible truth they held in their intense uranium green, high lit and glowing with toxicity.

My wits were scared far away from me by his unexpected and fierce arrival. A scream, mine, erupted and I rushed into the small bathroom and locked the door. The nurses found me there, quivering on the floor, banging my head against the wall to bleed out the horror.

Alarms went off. I heard footsteps, rushing. There must have been an emergency. It took me a while to realise, I was it.

'I'm alright,' I said and struggled to stand.

'Stay down,' ordered a voice of such authority, I obeyed.

My pyjamas were covered in blood. Pyjamas, so it was night, the worst night.

*

When my head and face had been sewn back together and I was medicated to the point right before unconsciousness, I wasn't taken back to my room but placed in the higher dependency ward. In this unit I was watched at all times, while my paranoia took shape and settled into me.

'You'll never be unobserved again.'

I heard, this time from a voice without a body.

'They are watching.'

I cried until my head ached too much to cry further. Never was a brutal measurement of time. As sedation took its hold, I slept. Fragments of despair woke me, mingling with the sound of the breakfast trolley trundling into the ward. My maladjusted bearings took time to regulate and when I became aware of my surroundings, things became less fragmented. Hopelessness was now closer to a full overwhelm and a mere splinter of sharp edge remained. It might have been anger.

I stumbled across to the table in the centre of the room.

'I don't understand,' was my mumble. 'I used to be a steady human.'

'Your face is a mess,' the woman across the breakfast table told me.

'Not just my face,' I answered.

A bout of nostalgia was reminding me of days when I walked about on an unwavering floor, when my mind had not played vicious games with my sense of reality. When I had hours, even days without noise. If it wasn't for the baby, I'd had given up.

'Stop!' I yelled, at my own self. Too much burden was being placed on that little being, still growing and kicking toward delivery day. I had to keep me alive for me, not afflict a child with the responsibility of that job.

The ward observers came toward me, looking ready to dispense sedation or something more restricting.

'I'm okay,' I told them. 'I didn't mean to think out loud. As you were.'

Picking up a piece of toast I began munching on it to prove how sane I was. In time, they turned their attention elsewhere.

'You'll never be unobserved again,' I heard repeated.

*

That day, I began working with the doctors. I took the offered medication without hesitation or argument, and I began to tell them what I was hearing or seeing, knowing it was crazy talk. But I wanted the noise to stop. I wanted to go out into the world and make a nest for my child. I wanted to not see the look on my mother's face when she came through the door; some kind of weird mix incorporating love, shame, hurt, fear and empathy. It would be so nice to see my mother smile.

*

Late one afternoon I heard a patient singing, 'Pardon me boys, is that the cat that chewed your new shoes?' to the tune of that old train song, and I smiled.

I smiled. Had I turned a corner? If humour was returning I might be allowed to leave?

'No,' said the doctor. 'But soon. You've come a long way.'

It's much harder to get out of a psych ward, than to get into one.

'You can go for your ultra-sound on your own tomorrow,' the doctor continued. 'It's just in the next building. If that goes well, we'll start to plan your discharge.'

I smiled again. I'd now smiled twice on the same day. Magic.

Like a child before Christmas, I couldn't wait to go to bed so the next day could come quicker.

'Get up, Maddie,' a nurse said, coming into my room. 'Lunch is ready.'

*

Freedom has a taste. The next day, when I'd been ushered through the many locked doors and walked into the open on my own, it was amazing. The air outside was the same as the air drifting about in the patient's courtyard, but it was made different by liberty. It caused me to breathe deeply and to savour the feeling, as if I'd been drowning and was now on dry land.

After the initial euphoria, I at the same time felt weak at the knees and wracked by painful aloneness. For months my every move had been in a locked ward or with an escorting nurse and now I felt my own inadequacies. What if I lost my way, in the literal or metaphorical sense? What if the voices attacked me and I relented and did whatever they demanded? What if I couldn't be autonomous ever again? What if I wet myself? The amount of water I'd drunk in preparation for the scan was eager to reach the exit.

'Get a grip,' I told myself. 'You're just going over there.'

I could see Building G and the doorway to the Maternity Clinic. It wasn't more than 100 metres away. The effort to walk there made me breathless. It seemed I couldn't even breathe without a reminder from somebody else.

Inside the Diagnostic Lab, I tried to act like a person of efficiency.

'I'm here for an ultra-sound,' I told the receptionist, and my voice came out like somebody in control.

'Name?'

'Madison Kitchener.'

There was proficient tapping on the keyboard and slow seconds of reading time. Her eyes rounded like a startled owl. 'I'll let them know you're here. Take a seat.'

She dashed through a door. It seemed the receptionist was fleeing the scene. Ignoring the prospect of complaint from women in assorted stages of pregnancy who were observing me from the waiting area, I turned the computer monitor toward me, to see what had perplexed her. My mental health file was open on the screen. Horrible details. Labels I'd been given. Doctors' notes. I wanted to scroll down and explore, learn more about myself but the desk lady returned.

'You can go in to Change Room 3,' she began to explain. 'Change into the gown that's hanging on the door, leave your underwear on unless your bra has wire. When you've changed go through the door on the other side.'

'Sorry,' I said, as I moved, following her instruction. I wondered why I'd felt so obliged to apologise. Sorry I was snooping at my own file? Sorry I'm a lunatic? Sorry I made you feel ill at ease? Sorry about global

warming Sorry I'm bringing another child into the already over-popu-
lated world. Sorry I exist. Sorry. I'm just sorry.

In the change room I remained the same, still crazy, no change there
but I took off my clothes excluding underwear and put on the flimsy
gown like a coat, not bothering to tie the ties. Holding the thing closed
over my bump I opened the door and walked into the technician's area.

'Hello, Mrs Kitchener,' said a woman in a pristine white coat that
suggested importance.

This startled me, and I looked about, frightened that my mother, the
real Mrs Kitchener was behind me.

'Ms, not Mrs,' I said when I realised her mistake. 'Call me Maddie.'

'Oh, sorry. I've not looked at your entire file, only the relevant maternity pages.'

Thank goodness for small mercies. I wasn't a bona fide crazy person
in this room, yet.

'Let's get this started. I imagine you're dying for a pee.'

*

Afterward, after I'd peed and struggled back into my clothes I returned to reception.

'I have a small human inside of me, 'I told the receptionist. I was so
happy. For the first time I'd seen the baby as a baby; the little spine, the
rather large head, the legs, arms, everything kind of where it should be.
I'd heard the strong heartbeat; such cheerful signs of life and I was going
to be somebody's mum.

'You certainly do,' said the receptionist returning my smile, and I
felt I may have underestimated her somewhat. I'd judged her for being
judgy. Now, as a lunatic and hypocrite I signed relevant forms, made
an appointment for a final ultra-sound before the birth and left the
building grasping photographic proof that existence continues— a new
branch on the family tree, my baby as the greenest leaf.

Outside, my knees went weak again. Liberty. I could just walk away.
Walk down the street on my lethargic, drugged legs, get on a bus and

go home. The pull was forceful. It sent me zig-zagging on the path then held me at a full stop at the entrance to the psych unit, indecisive.

I waited. The outcome felt like a firm hand on my shoulder. A somatic message.

'Go home,' it said.

Sometimes you have to do what is right. I wanted to be a good mother. To do that I had to learn how to handle my mental health on my own. To do *that* I walked through the automatic doors and pressed the buzzer to be let back in. I was in earnest— somebody had to teach me how to be me before I was left in charge of a tiny human being.

'You will kill the child,' the deep voice began. I felt his shadow near.

'Oh, fuck off,' I said.

The door buzzed and unlocked. I pushed through.

CHAPTER 14

Human Just Being

A lost grip on time presupposes that at some point, you had chronology well and truly grasped, before dropping it. Not me. Time was slipping through my life in the way it always had. At intervals big chunks of it disappeared without leaving me with a reminiscence; blank spaces, unremembered places, great wads of nothingness fragmented my life cycle into mutated pieces that would never fit together again. One day I was a little bit pregnant and in what seemed like a matter of hours I was a lot pregnant, if measuring by size. Pedants might argue there are no degrees; you're either pregnant or you're not. Even so, bulk-wise I'd reached the point where my belly entered a room with me one step behind.

I had a great desire to be out of the psych unit, to be home polishing my place until it was baby-ready. I wanted to clean it from front door to back, from floor to ceiling and prepare a gender-neutral nursery of sorts. There was not much time left to waddle about and make things nice, to nestle down.

The excitement of being given a discharge day, (three more sleeps) was almost submerged under the anxiety of my actual leaving and relying on myself again. Small parts of me had been erased by the institutionalisation of my psyche. I had a frightened self who had lost confidence in her own governance system. How could I ever trust my mind again? It lied, played tricks, operated me as if I were a constrained puppet. Delusions are real to the deceived.

Once the door of the psych unit shut behind me I would have two weeks to pull everything together. My nest and my mind needed to be tidy. Lists were essential. My first list would be a list of lists I required.

Within a day, I'd created a pocket full of lists.

'I've written you a referral for the psychiatrist Doctor Sandwich, your first appointment will be on Monday at 1.00 pm,' my ward doctor told me.

'I don't think I could possibly see anybody named Sandwich.'

'If you want me to release you, you will.'

'Okay. I'll put him or is it her on my list of people I need to see.'

'Him.'

I shuffled through papers and found the correct list. Sandwich Monday 1.00 pm, I wrote. Doctor, I noted down next to the time, in case I thought it was a reminder to have lunch. 'What's the address?'

The doctor handed me an envelope with the referral inside and an address on the front and it pleased me to note it was in walking distance from my flat.

'I need a compendium,' I said, looking at my pile of lists and the envelope, before writing compendium on the shopping list labelled non-essentials.

'A nurse will come and see you at home on Friday. It'll probably be Helen.'

That was good. I liked Helen. She'd done some shifts on the ward. A kind woman but not a pushover.

'I need a written timetable, or can I have my phone to put stuff in the calendar?'

'The nurses will go over everything again on Thursday. You can put it in your phone then. I won't see you again before you leave. Please, don't forget to take your medications, and please, see Don Sandwich. I can't stress enough how essential it is for your mental well-being that you keep taking your meds. Good luck and I hope everything go well with the baby.'

'Wow,' I said, a little stunned. 'I'm leaving.'

The doctor smiled, 'Yes, you are.'

If I could put time in a bottle, the moment of that smile was a keeper.

I smiled too, we hugged and then went our separate ways as if we were going to see each other again. We never would. It had been an intense time and I almost felt I needed to be debriefed, as if I'd been to war and returned. In a way, I had. Perhaps Doctor Sandwich could help me through the transition back to ... Back to what? Perhaps Doctor Sandwich could help me through the transition forward to ...

Bugger, I don't know which direction I'm supposed to be going.

Mumbling to myself a bit, I wandered out into the courtyard. It was beautiful and warm. Summer was coming. I was leaving. The baby was coming.

I felt a twinge of back pain. No, the baby wasn't coming. It was just a sore back. About five minutes later there was another stab of back pain. Then a few more at regular intervals.

'Is this labour?' I asked myself. Couldn't be, I thought.

I watched the clock for another hour. Every five minutes a spasm of back pain hit. It was far too regular to be normal back trouble. After three more twinges in fifteen minutes, I went to the nurses' terrarium and knocked on the glass.

'I'm not certain, but I think I may be in labour,' I called through the slot.

'Woo hoo!' one of them cheered. 'We're going to have a baby.'

I let them believe there was a we because they seemed excited to be part of the proceedings. I let them order up a wheelchair even though Maternity was a five-minute walk. I let them do whatever they wanted because I was overcome with nerves. The name of my obstetrician fell out of my brain.

'Doctor somebody,' I said.

There was an argument about which nurse would stay with me. As a psychiatric in-patient I had to have an escort by my side the whole time.

'I've got the wheelchair, so I'm going,' announced Nina.

'But Maddie's on my list for this shift,' complained Rae.

'I haven't got kids to worry about so if she goes past three o'clock, I can stay on,' said somebody else.

Most of the talk flew about over me like squawking sea gulls as I slumped into the wheelchair to wait while the job was allocated.

'I need to pack a bag,' I said, rubbing my back as another pain fired up.

'Don't worry about it. We'll send some stuff over.'

The chair started moving and I looked up to see Nina had won the 'get me off the ward for a bit' prize. She dropped my printed file on my lap and waved at the other nurses as she pushed me away. We were greeted as we passed through the last exit by a blast of warm weather.

'Phew, it's going to be a hot one,' Nina said.

'Can we sit outside until the next pain?' I asked. 'I just want to make sure they're really happening. It'd be embarrassing if we had to go back to the psych unit because I wasn't in labour after all.'

A pain hit, not intense but quite real. 'Okay,' I said. 'We can go in there now.'

I waved and pointed at the maternity building like some old empress in a sedan chair.

'What are you doing here, Nina?' welcomed the maternity triage nurse, without acknowledging me.

'Delivery for you. This is Maddie Kitchener. She's in labour and can't remember her doctor's name.'

'Like he'll even turn up,' said the nurse behind the desk. 'Okay, Maddie let's get you checked and checked in.'

It turned out I wasn't advanced in dilation and my waters hadn't broken. I was also given a fast-working enema and felt empty of everything but baby. The part of the building they placed us in after I'd been monitored and measured, looked like somebody's living room. There were lounges, armchairs, a TV, even some beanbag chairs.

'I'm not giving birth in the doctor's lounge or something, am I?'

Nina laughed.

'No. No. This is a pre-birthing suite. You stay here until the baby is almost ready to come out, then it's off to the delivery room.'

After two hours I was getting quite tired of the five minutes apart back pain, but I wasn't in the agony I had been led to believe would be the indication of a baby's imminent arrival. Nina was getting bored. I was sure she thought there'd be more action.

'Just nipping into this loo,' she pointed to a door to her left. 'Don't run off while I'm in there.'

'Run off? I can't get out of this beanbag.'

While Nina was in the toilet another nurse came in. She looked a bit surprised.

'Where's your escort?' she asked.

'In there.' I nodded towards the toilet and we heard the hand dryer start up in noisy confirmation.

'Oh, good. Anyway, because of your gestational diabetes we've decided to break your waters and see if we can't get this baby to move itself along.'

'Oh. Okay. Do I have to go somewhere else?'

'No, we can do it here.'

'In the beanbag? Eww.'

'No. Up here.' She pointed to a chair and when she whipped the cushion off, it looked like an easy chair had crashed into a commode, creating some sort of hybrid.

'I can't get up.'

Nina helped me out of the beanbag and over to the chair. I sat down and we waited for another midwife to bring in sterilised equipment. It was over in a minute and I thought the baby would just pop out. But no, this was the start of ramping up the pain. It was still not agony, but the discomfort spread from my back and moved to the business area as well. There's a window for an epidural and I missed it because I thought the soreness was manageable. By the time I wanted one, it was too late.

Nina's shift had ended but she stayed on. After a further six hours, watching Nina nap through my pain and a movie on the TV, I was taken into a delivery room. Exhausted, I wanted to go home, call the whole thing off. My relationship with pain had reached a level of intensity I'd not known was possible to survive. The spasms remained five minutes apart, but as one searing pain finished another had already begun. Now, I believed birthing stories.

In the delivery room we re-hooked me up to monitors and I began swearing like I never knew I could swear. Gas was offered and I sucked in as much as I could. It turned out my body can't tolerate laughing gas and I became nauseated, puking into a bowl all the while cursing all chemists and their crappy gases, between heaves.

'Jesus, Mary and Joseph and the donkey they rode in on,' I called. 'Make it stop.'

Three hours later, my obstetrician, Doctor Something-or-Other, popped his head in.

'Have to do an emergency D and C. Back in an hour and we'll get that baby out.'

'What?'

It didn't matter anymore; I was sure death would claim me by then.

From memory, I was calling for a chainsaw by the time he returned. My mind may have grown senseless with pain, so its truth could be exaggerated. The public health system doesn't allow for a chainsaw.

Within minutes of the doctor arriving, there was a grumble about my pelvis being too small. He cut me open further than I'd already torn, grabbed some salad servers and pulled the baby straight out. There was a hearty cry from those gathered around the delivery table, and the mother and baby joined in.

'It's a girl!' Nina blubbered.

'Where's my baby? I want her.'

They'd checked the new-born over, cleaned her a bit and were swaddling her tiny form in a soft blanket. When they placed her on my chest I fell instantly, deeply and unconditionally in love for the first time in my en tire life. Tears dripped from my eyes via my heart and I felt a moment of joy and peace as I stared at my little human, who was looking right back into my soul.

'Do you have a name for her?' Nina asked.

'Micah,' I said, before starting a soft sing of Happy Birthday to my child. The midwives joined in with hushed lullaby tones and I even heard the doctor sing a few words while stitching torn pieces of me back together.

Pain was forgotten. I'd never felt happier.

CHAPTER 15

Intentions Were Good

When Nina went home, nobody from the psych unit replaced her. They'd realised I wasn't going anywhere without my baby, without my Micah. Any escape plan would be foiled by having to carry her seven kilometres home whilst bleeding out what seemed to be every drop of blood my body now thought was unnecessary.

Micah was taken to the nursery while I was cleaning up. The shower stall looked like a crime scene within minutes. Blood poured from me and I marvelled at my capacity to not die. My cleaning-obsessed inner self wouldn't let me leave the shower stall until the exiting flow slowed and I was able to leave the floor bloodless.

'Okay in there?' a nurse called through the door.

'Fine,' I answered, though I was feeling a little faint.

I'd been issued hospital strength sanitary napkins, which were so large it was like sitting astride a surfboard, but they were necessary. The nurse was waiting for me with a wheelchair and I was startled to see her when I opened the door.

'Have you been out there the whole time?'

'Yup.'

'Hope I didn't say anything too stupid.'

'I've a tendency to talk to myself aloud too, when I'm alone,' she murmured. 'I heard something about an autopsy…' She laughed as she wheeled me toward the maternity ward and my bed. 'You must be tired. That was about fifteen hours of labour.'

'Really? And Nina stayed the whole time?'

'She didn't want to leave until your baby had landed safely.'

'That's nice of her.'

The room they put me in had one other occupant, a woman who was sleeping.

'She's very quiet. Had a multiple birth but only one survived,' whispered the nurse.

'Oh. How sad.'

Another nurse arrived with Micah in her hospital crib-on-a-trolley thing. The bed part was made of clear plastic or Perspex or something non-toxic, I supposed. I could see the baby from my horizontal position, which was fine with me, for I was a mixture of wired and tired, a mix that was followed by a complete crash. My baby was sleeping and I followed her lead.

The last thing I heard myself say was, 'I'm a mum.' And another voice 'You must kill the spawn of Satan.'

*

When I woke up, my baby was gone.

My panic was ten notches higher than ever before. What a crap mother I was, to misplace my baby on Day One. Or worse. I'd been tired, un-medicated, unescorted. Had I obeyed the voices, even though I knew my baby wasn't the daughter of the devil?

My dread flung me out of the door and down to the nurses' station before anything sensible registered. I was leaking from more than one orifice, including tears of self-anger at my lack of vigilance.

'Hey, Maddie. Micah's down in the nursery. Go on down.'

'Oh, I ... I'll just, um, just put some clothes on.'

I went back to my room and dug through the stuff that had been left by my bed. There were some daggy-baggy track pants that could stretch around my belly, a maternity bra and an old sweat shirt in a plastic bag. Given the limited choices, I put these on and cleaned myself up as best I could, ran a comb through my hair and tried to look like I hadn't just given myself the shock of my life.

As I passed the nurses' station again, I mentioned my medication. They told me they'd bring it to the nursery.

The next blow was the number of babies in that nursery—at least ten, all bundled up in cocoons of blanket. For some reason, I thought maternal instinct would take me to Micah, but no. They all looked very similar and I had to scan name tags until I found her.

Some mother I was. Micah was asleep. She still had the forceps indent on both cheeks and tiny bright red veins lay beneath the marks, looking like a vague miniature map of the Sydney Rail System. She was beautiful. I'd seen some ugly babies in my time and I knew she wasn't one of those. I acknowledged to myself that I was wearing mum-goggles that pushed me toward profound bias—but she was gorgeous.

They fuck you up, your mum and dad.

'I won't,' I said to Philip Larkin, in my mind. 'I'll try so hard not to.'

There were tears then, I felt them, saw them and tasted them. I cried because I knew I'd make dreadful mistakes.

'I love you,' I told Micah, and I promised myself I would say it to her every day, so she would never have any doubt.

'Here's your tablets,' a nurse I hadn't met said, moving around the crib to be by my side.

I took the assortment and she handed me a small waxy cup full of water.

'Can I take her back to my room?' I asked, after gulping down my sanity initiators.

'Sure, she's your baby. Let Sister Mac know. You can bring baby back in anytime, when you want to rest. Some mums like to leave babies in here at night, so they can get a decent sleep. Because, you're not going to get much of it once you leave. Actually, you look like you need to go back to bed now.'

I was feeling a bit woozy.

'Have you had anything to eat?'

'No.'

'Okay, let's take you back to your room and get you some food. Those tablets shouldn't be taken on an empty stomach.'

The nurse began to push Micah out and I followed like a weak lamb. I had to admit it was pleasant to get back into bed.

The sun was coming up on a new day. Micah's birthday proper. Both of us had our first feed together. I was slamming down hospital-strength sandwiches like I'd not eaten for weeks and Micah suckled on an offering of colostrum I'd made especially. It's a mammal thing.

In a very tired way, I imagined I was the most contented person in the hospital right then.

When Micah was tucked back to sleep in the wheelie beside me, a slow tremble of anxiety took hold. It was up to me to keep this little being alive, happy and nurtured for as long as we both should live. I needed books—to know what I was supposed to be doing and when. Responsibility meant I was in charge of my response ability, if anything should happen to Micah. She looked very small, at just over three kilos, and fragile. It wasn't until I met other tiny babies that I realised she was quite a large small bundle.

With quite bizarre 'What ifs?' floating about my head, I fell back to sleep, to be woken seconds later, okay it was an hour, by a flower delivery. Pink is not my favourite colour, but it was the obvious theme of the it's-a-girl bouquet. The flowers didn't smell pink, which was a relief. I grappled for the card, trying not to wake the baby.

'Congratulations Maddie and Micah!' It read. 'You are a family! Love from the staff and patients of Ward 17!" (which was code for the psych unit).

'Wow,' I said out loud. 'That is so nice of them. And boy, they do like an exclamation point.'

Micah woke for a bit, looked like she was going to cry and fell back to sleep.

'I can't give you anything but love, baby,' I whisper-sang.

*

The next time Micah woke, it was, I think, to test her lung capacity. She hit a pitch that brought my milk in, with a flow of immediate obedience.

'So now I am leaking from every main orifice,' I told my little one as I plucked her from the crib. Mothering aptitude wasn't emerging as I'd expected—I was one gigantic fear that I'd drop and break Micah. But this time we settled in my bed and she began drinking like a champion, a greedy little champion. Motherhood had begun, in a nipple-stinging kind of way.

As she lay satiated and sleeping in my arms, I had time to examine my new charge. Everything appeared to be where it was supposed to be. Her head was covered in quite a lot of dark hair. She'd done plenty of growing before she came out. Her tiny fingernails looked as if they could do with a cut. My heart was full to a dangerous level. If it was going to break, it was going to break hard.

'Please, don't hurt me,' I whispered to her.

A group of Vietnamese women arrived to visit the lady in the next bed. She stirred, and I was relieved she wasn't dead. They drew the curtains around the bed and the chattering cacophony sounded like they were trying to cheer her up and cry with her at the same time.

I must have dozed off, because next thing, Helen arrived from the psych unit.

'Look at you,' she quipped.

'I must look a fright.'

'You look better than I've ever seen you,' Helen told me, and she smiled as punctuation. 'So, good news. You're released from 17. When you're discharged from here, you're allowed to go straight home. I've taken the liberty of putting your stuff in my car and I'll bring it on our first home visit, or if you'd rather I can bring it here?'

'I'm free? We're free?'

'Yes.'

It was stunning. Micah must have felt my astonishment. She stirred and began searching for my nipple.

'Can I have a hold?' Helen asked. 'She's beautiful.'

I nodded, and Helen picked Micah up in a confident way that made me a little jealous.

'Look at her neck straight already. She's a strong one.'

Micah took the opportunity to show the strength of her lungs as well, and cried. Helen considered this a good time for a bit of a walk around the room. The baby seemed to enjoy the movement, and quietened.

I was free. For the first time in a very long stretch, I would be able to take a walk further than thirty steps before I hit a wall or a locked door. And, I'd be doing it with a newborn. My excitement was tinted with fear. While it was repairing me, the unit had become a bit of a protective bubble. There'd been no real-world infiltration or interaction. No responsibilities. Not even a decision about what to have as a meal. I was free to mess up, big time. Yes, I was afraid.

My free-fall panic was interrupted by Micah. While on her journey around the room she had let out a liquid burp.

'I'm so sorry,' I said to Helen as I jumped out of bed. 'We both fell asleep while she was feeding, and I didn't do the burping thing.'

'No problem. You've seen where I work. This is nothing in comparison.'

Helen placed Micah in her see-through crib and I tried to clean her puke-covered shoulder with baby wipes.

'If it's any consolation, you're the first person in this world Micah's ever thrown up on.'

'A dubious honour.'

Helen laughed. It was a smoker's laugh. Or a whiskey drinker's laugh. It kind of said, 'I'm here for a good time, not a long time.'

I had been surprised by the number of health professionals who smoked. A defiance, "Yes, I know what this does to my health, but I'm doing it anyway."

Helen's laugh ended in a cough, as if to verify my thoughts.

'I'd better be getting back to the unit. All going well, you'll be out of here late tomorrow. I'll see you the next day, at home. Around ten o'clock. Here's a card. If you need to talk to anybody before then, ring. It's a 24/7 line. Don't be afraid to call it. Readjusting's not easy. We're here to help. Oh, crap, is that the time? See you at your place.'"

My place.

Micah began to cry again.

Our place.

I felt her nappy. It was wet.

'Anyway, how do these things work?' I asked her, picking out a disposable nappy from a bag on the bedside cabinet.

'It doesn't go on her head,' my mother said, entering the room.

CHAPTER 16

Dust and Cobwebs

For the first time in many years, three knots on our maternal line were in one room at one time. I was swamped by a sense of occasion, marred by my maladroit maiden attempt at changing Micah's nappy. Sticky plastic tabs seemed to want to adhere everywhere but the point where I needed them to catch on. My mother's sudden arrival made my fingers quiver with a very old sense of uselessness that smote my brain— accompanied by an over-enunciated echo. *'You. Stupid. Girl. Stupid girl.'*

'You must be extremely tired,' my mother said, taking over the nappy task. 'Lie down. Let me get to know my granddaughter. Does she have a name?'

'Micah,' I answered, collapsing on the bedside chair. 'Micah Matilda Kitchener.' I didn't know I was considering Matilda as a middle name, but it burst out of me and sounded quite fine.

'Micah,' my mother said, leaning over the baby, 'I'm your grandmother. You may call me Nan. You've given me quite a surprise today. I went to visit mummy at the other ward.'

This seemed like a loaded chat with my daughter.

I' would have called, but I was a bit busy,' I said, defensive, but I'd enjoyed being referred to as mummy.

'I'm not having a go at you, Maddie, for goodness sake.'

Stupid girl was all I heard.

My mother swaddled Micah in the soft hospital provided baby blanket and picked her up.

'She's beautiful. Doesn't look like you at all.'

OMG. Spare me.

'I mean, you're beautiful too, in a different way.'

My super-sensitivity was doing my head in. My mother placed Micah in my arms and changed the subject.

'I was bringing this in today. I made it for baby... Micah, to wear home.'

Digging into her mammoth handbag, my mother pulled out a parcel wrapped in gender-neutral yellow tissue paper. Inside was a beautiful soft satiny crocheted outfit in a shade of whitish blue. Or, a bluish white. Pearl, it might have been. I couldn't believe it.

'It's lovely,' I said, and it was.

'Unfortunately, I think her head might be too big for the bonnet. I didn't expect her to be...'

'So large? Tell me about it. Her head is pretty big. They had to help her out using forceps at the end.'

'Well, she might have inherited my brains. You'd need to have a large head to protect such a substantial intellect.'

My mother thought she was joking. I grasped that she was, against all odds, happy. I'd not seen that in a long while. If it were solid, her humour would have been covered in dust and cobwebs. If there were moving parts they'd be groaning and squeaking, impacted by rust. My baby was a miracle worker.

With a swoosh of wind and a mighty swing, one of the Vietnamese women pulled back the curtain that divided the room and passed by us, heading for the door. She smiled and we returned her smile. We fell silent and our flow of intimacy broke.

'I suppose I should be going. I've a bit to do before tomorrow,' my mother pronounced with a decision's-been-made air, rising and gathering her bag.

'What's happening tomorrow?'

'John and I are moving up to the coast.'

'What? You're moving in together? Already?' John was my mother's newish boyfriend.

'When it's right, it's right.'

'Are you selling the house?'

'It's sold.'

'What?'

This dismissal of my childhood home seemed as if my little person self-had been erased like chalk marks from a board. I'd never be able to go back and heal her now. She'd be left sitting in my old room in the cobwebs, wondering where and why everybody went. After my long stint behind locked doors, I felt like another part of myself had been blocked, locked away from me, away in the past. Unreachable. Lost.

My face gave me away. At least my mother noticed.

'I didn't think it would sadden you. It never was a happy home.'

'No. I guess not, but it was the only one I've had.'

'We're all having a fresh start,' my mother announced, her tone registering a false positive.

It was hard for me to forget that my father had crawled away to the edge of nowhere like a wounded dog, in the wake of a previous iteration of one of her fresh starts. My own starts had all been false ones. Never fresh. Never planned. I thought about it for a few seconds as she fussed over Micah, patting her cheek. This could be the day where I say aloud, 'I'm starting over too,' and mean it. What better time, than the onset of motherhood, to begin again?

'To fresh starts,' I toasted, raising an imaginary glass of champagne. My imagination had no fiscal limits—I conjured a full glass, crystal, and bubbles to the brim, the most expensive available, whatever that was. 'Could you let Matthew know he's an uncle? I still don't have my phone.'

'Here.' My mother passed me her mobile. 'Press and hold number 1.'

I did, and the phone dialled my brother.

'Hello Uncle Matty,' I said when he'd answered.

'Mum?'

'No, it's your little sister. You have a niece.'

Matthew said all of the right words. Asked the right questions.

'Three and a half kilos. In the early hours of this morning, about three o'clock. Fifteen hours. Yes, I am tired. She was worth every hour though. We're good.'

Matthew asked to speak with my mother and I gave her the phone. Before communicating, she walked out into the corridor. I was relegated to watcher, or in this circumstance, listener, back in my normal position of family fringe dweller. At least I had Micah for company now.

'Oh, Micah, your so fine. You're so fine, you blow my mind. Oh, Micah.'

Old song, fresh start.

Mum and the Vietnamese woman had a politeness stand-off at the door, trying to re-enter the room at the same time.

'You first,' my mother said and moved to make way for the wheel-chair the woman was pushing.

It looked as if my neighbour was off somewhere but from the noises behind the closed-again curtain, it sounded as if she didn't want to be going off anywhere. There was a loud, harsh squeal of demand, it must have been, because soon the women left *en masse*, pushing the reluctant but obedient traveller out of the room. I gave my roommate a weak smile, trying to load it with sympathy. I was aware it might come across more as if I had digestive troubles and would benefit from a burping. The body language of speech was not my forte.

'Can I bring you anything from the shop before I go? 'my mother asked.

'I ... No. Maybe. Cou ...Yes. No,' I answered. Speaking any language with my mother wasn't my thing.

'Well, now that that's settled, I'll be off. I'll let you know when I'm coming next. Be back and forth between houses until we're done with the moving.'

'Oh, okay.'

Abandonment issues floated to my surface and I did what all good lunatics do—I repressed them. My mother bent to kiss me goodbye. No, she didn't. She planted a kiss on my daughter's forehead.

'See you both soon,' she said and was gone.

'Thanks for Micah's outfit,' I called.

Emptiness made no response, but I looked at my baby and my heart refilled.

'We're going home tomorrow,' I told Micah.

'To expired food products and a mouldy fridge, 'I told myself. 'There'll be dust. There'll be cobwebs. There'll be signs of my mental deterioration and nothing ready for a baby. Oh, crap!' I said, and Micah startled to the point of crying. 'Sorry. I just remembered the keys to our place are probably in the boot of Helen's car. We can't get in anyway, dirt or no dirt.'

I sighed. Fresh starts. False starts. Broken parts. Mended hearts. 'The door key is our key to the renaissance.'

A nurse came in to do her obs, my obs. That's blood pressure, temperature and to eyeball me to see if I looked non-dead.

'You really should be getting some rest. I've brought you a hair dryer.'

How those two sentences connected was beyond my weary mind. 'Sorry?'

'Rest. Sleep.'

That part I understood.

'Oh, the hair dryer. After you've had your showers, it's best you dry your downstairs area with this. We don't want things going wrong with the doctor's sewing and it's best for the wound not to be moist.'

'Eww. Okay. But, doesn't? ... Never mind.'

'When you get home, it'd be good if you can let the sun shine on it.'

'I'm sure the neighbours would love that. Me spread-eagled out on the balcony.'

'Nature is the best healer. The stitches should drop out over time.' The nurse picked Micah up and placed her in the crib. 'Now,' she said, turning to me. 'You get some proper sleep.'

Proper sleep. Proper sleep? Right and proper sleep. There was much to think about. Should a baby sleep in the same room as her mother? How would I get Micah home? The key. How do I get groceries? Sleep didn't happen.

It dawned on me that having not been home for many months I would have amassed a satisfactory amount of money. Thank goodness my bills were on auto-pay, or I wouldn't have a home. Would I have to keep that appointment with Doctor Sandwich now that I had a newborn to look after? If I'd saved enough money during my enforced break from spending, should I buy a car? Proper sleep. Counting sheep. I didn't want a doctor named Sandwich. Would I be able to listen to the man? Where were my lists? What were my must-haves? Nappies. I'd prefer cloth. How many would I need? If I ...

I slept.

New dreams brought with them a new Hell. There I was, frantic in a maternity unit nursery, looking for Micah. Formica. What? Keep still mind. There were thousands of babies. Thousands, and I couldn't find her. Reading the name on each baby's ankle tag, I became more and more desperate. The newborns began to cry, and I was overwhelmed by the racket. Each cry, pitched to shatter an eardrum, triggered the baby in the next crib, like one mousetrap snapping and setting off the proximate one. Louder and louder grew the symphony of discordance. I needed to find Micah, quick, and run away before my fragile sanity was blown. The noise crowded my headspace, making rational thought impossible. I'd been trying to search the cribs in a systematic manner, but soon I was flinging about examining them at random. The babies all transformed into hungry penguins, which made them even harder to tell apart. Then I heard it, a cry that was milk-flow initiating. 'Micah?'

I awoke still saturated in fear. Micah was crying. I was at her crib before I'd left that dream-world and landed bumbling into the real-world.

'Hey, Baby,' I said, reassuring myself that she wasn't a penguin.

I needed to slow my heart down before I picked Micah up, in case my distress was able to jump from my heart to hers, drumming a beat of anxiety through our skins. Before anything for her, it was necessary to tend to myself.

'Just popping into the loo,' I told my mewling baby.

If anybody had informed me there'd be so much blood after childbirth, I would have accused them of exaggerating, pitching for sympathy.

*

After I'd fed and burped Micah, I watched her fall back to sleep. The idea of my baby lying alone and vulnerable while I took a shower had been too much for me, to contemplate so I wheeled her down to the nursery and left her with Sister Mac.

'I'm just going to have a shower.'

'No problem,' Sister Mackenzie said. 'Why don't you have a proper sleep before you come back for her?'

The nurses it seemed to me, were quite fanatical about 'proper' sleep. My nightmare replayed, vivid, like a disturbing flashback, as I walked to my room. If that had been a part of proper sleep, I wanted none of it.

My fresh start was giving me palpitations.

CHAPTER 17

Daydream Deceivers and the Home Coming Queen

Creeping misgivings. The next time I woke in horror, it was to cry, 'What have I done?' This world is not so beautiful. Should I have chosen to bring yet another being into it, out of a selfish need to love and be loved? A daughter, if things happened in their predictable order in my life up to this point, I would leave behind in abandonment caused by my death, or worse, by my unreliable mind.

My optimism had drained away, tainted by salted tears for the crying millions, to dry up pessimistic and brackish. Hate thy neighbour was underscored in every news headline. Governments needed racism so they didn't have to feel immoral about their refugee policies— and pacifists were wounded on a daily basis by man's carnages toward man. Men who had been 'othered' for ridiculous reasons. This was our planet, being eroded by hatred and climate change caused by ignorance, arrogance, selfishness and greed— and I'd dropped a baby fair into it. And to top it off, Micah's mother was a bit crazy. She sometimes referred to herself in the third person.

I could do nothing but apologise. Sorry was not the hardest word. It had lost sincerity through repetition. It fell off my tongue, useless. But I apologised to Micah, nonetheless.

When the morning light seeped in, I too became lighter.

'Fresh starts,' I mumbled, spilling coffee down my front. 'Fresh mucky starts.'

Micah was in the nursery. I'd surrendered her about 1.00 am for fear of waking my roommate. I hadn't been sleeping as much as falling into darkness and being twitched conscious by glum thoughts.

I have no skills. 3.00 am

I know nothing about first aid. 3.16 am

I've forgotten who I am. 3.42 am

I'll feel like a stranger in my own home. 3.55 am

I have, I haven't, I don't, I can't ... I. I. I.

I greeted the relief of dawn. Slinking about, I prepared for the day. I showered without waking my roommate, who may or may not have been sedated. She was a constant sleeper, perhaps on the verge of profound post-natal depression. Some people found sleep a relief from real life. For me, it was the other way around or no relief at all, day or night. Sometimes I dreamt while I was awake, a surreal-ness that came with my touch of madness. Lightmares, like nightmares, only, in broad daylight. Lightmares, as punishing and confusing as any night incubus. Incubuses. Incubi? Cue bye.

'Bye,' I said to the nurses. 'Thank you so much.'

Helen, bless her, realising she had all of my possessions in the boot of her car, including my house keys, had arranged to take Micah and me home. She'd borrowed a baby capsule from somewhere and Micah was strapped in it, wearing her going-home outfit of blue pearl, decorated with fresh spit-up. I had two plastic bags filled with baby products that all new mums receive with love from a pharmaceutical company and one plastic bag bulging with my dirty laundry and toiletries. These were added to the three bags already in Helen's car.

'I'm on the cusp of being a homeless bag lady,' I said to Helen as we loaded the boot. 'I saw a homeless bag once, from the hospital window, blowing empty along the road. It was flattened by a car at the roundabout, and I felt sad for it. Cut down in its prime travelling years, to become mere litter.'

When I'm nervous, I talk rubbish.

*

Micah was in the world. Not just in a hospital, she was out in the big, loud, scary, bright blue-sky world. The weather was warm, and this was my first taste of real freedom in a long, long time.

'Smells like liberty, I said,' pressing the button to lower the passenger side window and gulping in the air like a happy puppy.

The car ride was over too soon. Micah had fallen asleep, peaceful in the rocking motion of a pot-holed road.

'Let's see if we can manage getting up to your flat all in one trip. Find your keys first,' Helen suggested.

I rummaged through the bags in her boot until I came across a large envelope containing my wallet, phone and keys. They'd lived locked in a safe while I found my sanity in the psych unit. They felt as if they belonged to somebody else. Somebody valid, whose life I was now slipping into without anybody noticing. As if I were a doppelgänger stealing the life of my twin. Trouble was, I didn't know her very well and believed my fraud would soon be discovered.

'I'm not who I think I am,' I said.

'What?' asked Helen.

The stairs took my breath and I couldn't talk anymore. Months of inactivity had left me very unfit and I had to stop on the first-floor landing. I couldn't catch my breath, that's how unfit I was. Helen kept going and beat me to the top floor although she was carrying the bulk of the plastic bags. She dumped them and was back down to carry Micah up before I'd climbed three more steps.

'Wow,' I wheezed. 'I need to get some exercise.'

'Don't worry, a couple of weeks of these steps and you'll be fine.'

We stood outside my door for a few minutes while I fumbled about with the keys. I noticed the number four on the door had lost a screw and was now hanging upside down, looking like a dyslexic or drunken ampersand. There were three locks to unbolt— I was glad I didn't need to pee. We were in. I carried Micah over the threshold into her new life and we were hit in the face by trapped heat rushing to get out.

'Phew. Let's get some air in here,' Helen said, and began to wrestle with window locks.

After putting Micah on the table (she was still in the flat-bottomed car safety capsule) I flung open the door to the balcony and a slight breeze flowed inside with a couple of flies surfing in on the ripple. My pot plants on the small veranda were all dead. Pots of colour had turned into graves of brown, sad sunburned brown.

'Would you like a drink?' I asked Helen. 'I can offer you tap water or tap water.'

Tap water's fine, she answered, dropping or drooping into my old lounge chair.

I didn't dare open the fridge while I had a guest, God only, knew what was in there—a strong possibility of some sort of penicillin growing, as if my cheese and milk had been part of a Louis Pasteur experiment. The interior doubtless smelt all different degrees of manky. Helen took the offered glass of water and cleared her throat.

'Now,' she said, 'I'll be back tomorrow about ten, for our scheduled appointment. Will you be okay until then?'

'Yes. I'll take Micah to the shops later when it's cooler, buy a pram and a few groceries.'

'Have you had your morning meds?'

I nodded.

'Make sure you keep to your home plan. Don't try to do everything at once.'

Helen waved her hand about the room. She must have felt me itching to scour the place from top to bottom and set it to how I'd wanted it for Micah's homecoming. There was a fine layer of dust over the place. Miss Havisham, I thought, eyeing cobwebs in the corners.

Helen had not long left upside-down number 4 when there was a knock at the door. I didn't peek through the spyhole because I assumed she'd forgotten something, so I opened the door, to find a puffing delivery guy with a dolly-trolley piled with plastic crates.

'Groceries for Kitchener,' he said.

'What? I didn't order any.'

'Are you Kitchener? Number 4?'

'Yes, but.'

'These are your groceries. Where do you want them?'

'Okay. On the table. Who ordered them?'

'Here's the sheet.'

The man passed me the list of products. It had been ordered in the name of Kitchener.

'Are they paid for?' I asked, searching for the envelope with my wallet and phone.

'Yup,' the man answered.

'Oh. Well, I ... I ...

There were twelve bags, all full. I thanked the gruff fellow and he left happier than when he'd arrived, his trolley much lighter. For me, it was Christmas. Better than Christmas. On light feet, I snuck into the bedroom, where Micah lay sleeping, now on my bed with a pillow on either side even though she was too new to wriggle off the edge. Safety first. Trying to be quiet, I pulled my phone charger from the wall and took it back to the kitchen table for my phone's first charge in a long while. It displayed no signs of life, not even a weak beep when I switched the power point on. It'd be a while before the battery woke up, before I could telephone my mother to find out if it was she who had purchased my groceries.

Now was the time to tackle the refrigerator and whatever beasties were growing inside so I could house my new load of perishables. It wasn't pleasant. A lettuce had become liquid in a bag and other nasty unidentifiable mush was growing on a shelf in the door. There were eggs to be removed with care. If they broke the smell would kill me and frighten the neighbours. I removed them one by one like small unexploded bombs and placed them in an empty ice cream container lined with paper towel. I was taking no chances.

The fridge emptied, I scrubbed it out and wiped it over with vanilla essence. A job well done.

Micah cried from the bedroom that it was time for her next drink. I threw bags of fresh veg, meat and other stuff into the fridge to sort out later, and went to her.

'Guess where you are?' I asked my little one. 'Home,' I answered for myself, when it was obvious Micah wasn't going to acknowledge my question. 'You are home. We're home.'

After incarceration, home felt such an alien concept. It was as if any minute, somebody would come in and tell me I was delusional, that my child didn't exist and thrust a giant syringe into my posterior then haul me off to seclusion.

'We can come and go as we like', I told Micah as she suckled. 'Although, you have to ask me first.'

After she had fed herself into an oblivion, I walked my baby around the flat while she burped.

'This is the kitchen. That's the fridge. That's a pile of stuff I have to take downstairs to the garbage bin. That's groceries waiting to be put away. This is the bathroom. Yes, it's small, but it's mine. And here's the living area. TV. Lounge. Chair. Table. And here we are, back in the bedroom. This ends the tour. Please be sure to fill in your customer survey.'

I didn't quite know what to do with Micah while I had another shower. Cleaning the refrigerator had left me feeling grotty. So, after pacing and trying to think through a safe and reliable solution, I folded a blanket and laid her on it in the bath, while I slipped into the shower stall and washed myself free of the hospital and the fridge microbes. It was luxurious, knowing a nurse wasn't going to open the door.

Micah seemed happy enough lying in the bath, looking at I don't know what. I sang lullabies until I realised they all tended to end in death or disaster or gruesomeness.

'And down will come baby, cradle and... oh, that one's not very nice either.'

By the time I was dressed in maternity jeans and a T-shirt, I felt human. We'd been home for two hours.

'And they said we'd never make it,' I told Micah, mocking the naysayers. 'Look at us, we're naturals at this living stuff. Come on, let's walk to the shops and buy you a pram and... and things. Baby things. And be free in the world.'

I took the two levels to the ground floor one careful step at a time. In one arm I cradled Micah and in the other hand, dangled a large green garbage bag containing the rotten food, including the ice cream container of gaseous eggs.

What could possibly go wrong?

What if I threw Micah in the big wheelie bin by accident?

Worst case scenarios are my forte.

What if I slipped, dropped the baby and landed on the eggs?

By the time I'd reached the relative safety of the ground floor, I was covered in stress-generated sweat. It was necessary to put the bag down, to sit on the bottom step of the building access and to engage my recovery mode.

'I'm so unfit,' I said to the world.

My next leg of the fraught journey was to the congregation of wheelie bins in the gated area of the front garden. Here I left the bag, propped on the ground, thinking it would be easier to throw it in a bin once I had Micah in a pram. My mind was still being cruel, and as I turned away I had to check twice to make sure I was carrying Micah and not a garbage bag.

'Baby, check.'

When I reached the street, I saw a few people waiting at the bus stop. My idea of walking to the mall was right then, crossed off my plans. Walking home would be much nicer because Micah would have wheels. She stirred while I tried to get my wallet out of my handbag, I held my breath and rocked. 'Please, please, please don't be crying on the bus'. A small mercy, I had enough coinage for the trip.

The bus ride was incident free except some woman had a very, very young baby on board. The baby cried all the way to the mall. Okay, it was Micah. Longest fifteen minutes of my life. Painful, the sound—

and my inability to do anything about the obviously wet nappy. First stop once we arrived at the mall was the Baby Changing room, where I changed Micah into a happier baby. Second stop was the Baby Shop, where we test drove some of the prams. In one, Micah fell almost straight away to sleep.

'I'll guess I'll have that one to go, please. How much?'

It was the demonstration model, so they knocked a few dollars off. The price was still more than my parents had paid for their first car. I glanced at it to see if there was a Rolls Royce bonnet mascot on the front. No. After my card details went through, I strapped Micah in good and secure and we went for a slow amble home, stopping at the park, milk for her, ice cream and a cold drink of water for her mother.

Life was so much smoother with a pram. I gave thanks to the inventor of the wheel— and further thanks to the inventor of the brake. Life looked to be good. The well-behaved type of good. Able-to-work-things-out sort of good. A fate-testing good.

CHAPTER 18

Speculation and the Internal Combustion Engine

Abigail Kitchener had packed her life into boxes, literally and figuratively. Lounge room, Dining room, Bathroom, Kitchen, Bedroom One, Bedroom Two, Bedroom Three., Laundry. Love. Death. Taxes. Guilt. My mum had never meant to hurt anybody but in the end her life was divided into boxes of hurt. Some were hers, some she'd gathered, some she'd left behind, some she'd caused. Caused not through malice but through a dichotomous search for, and fear of love.

She may have been the victim of her own misinterpretation. It seemed to me, she'd mistaken lust for love a number of times, to the detriment of all. And now, here she was moving in with her boyfriend— to a new town. Like a teenager, not a confident woman of this uncertain age. The age of uncertainty is a long one. Perhaps the physical move would give a 'fresh start' feel to life for my mother.

This is all supposition. But supposition can't help but be fattened by secrecy. I never really knew what was happening growing up and Mum seldom explained or spoke in terms a child might understand. I began speculating at a young age about what the heck was going on in our house. My mother would often be fuming. Her anger may have come from financial worry, it might have been work trouble, or the weariness of an overwhelmed mother. Eventually she would snap at me. So, naturally, I came to understand that I was the actual problem—my earliest assumption. Aww, isn't that cute? Now, I understand, but back then self-hatred grew from the strange feedings it received. I could not look in a mirror because I saw who I thought my mother saw. That child in the mirror irritated me so.

And Dad? He was snoring through life, a drunk sleepwalker. Life with my father pushed mum to do things she resented. Then she resented feeling resentment and felt guilty for feeling resentful in the first place. It was a cruel cycle in hurtful perpetual motion. Mum boxed the guilt up and appeared to store these boxes in her stomach, causing biliousness that didn't respond to medical treatments. I've never known her not to have stomach issues. Her internal combustion engine is always on fire.

I can trigger nervous tension for my mum like no other can. Mum's guilt for not being close to me during and after Micah's birth would have made her physically wretched—her customary somatic response to contrition. I know this because it's more than likely a sudden queasiness prompted her to order a van load of groceries for my, and her new granddaughter's homecoming. The groceries said to me (they weren't talking, my delusions don't manifest as chatty supermarket products—although, never say never). They said my mother knew she should've been with me in person, as a sort of guide, while readily taking up her position as a hands-on grandmother. There was a little bit of "I'm sorry I'm not with you. Here, have things instead" behind the gift. Women need their mums, when they've just become mothers themselves. Mum almost certainly (I say certainly, but I don't know—I'm still feeling assumptive. There's probably something I can take for that, a panacea bought over the counter. She almost certainly-ish wished her own mother had been around when Matthew and I were born. It must've been hard for her, so isolated and so alone. Dad was at the pub, both times. But she mum mustn't remember it as so hard, or she would have felt compelled to be by my side when I brought Micah home. Which would have been a kind of nice.

I never asked, nor expected her to be with us. At some point on our shared timeline, I'd been taught by example of the safety in aloneness. If I didn't ask I wouldn't be hurt by 'no.'

I now know what I couldn't know as a child. My mother has and always will do the best that she's able. Life has been cruel, thrown things at us both to make being 'able' difficult, sometimes more shortfall than overreach. Mum's been tenacious and tried to make things better through planning and control. I, on the other hand have fallen inelegantly on my arse over and over and have spent a great deal of time trying to get back on my feet. I've never lost control because I've never really had any.

Micah's early birth had altered all of mum's neat boxes on her calendar. It displays a different highlighter colour from her basket of pens, for categories of event. The baby's ETA box was still over a week and a half away and she had cleared a few days on either side to be of some practical use. Practically perfect planning rendered useless by a lack of syncopation in the timing. The rhythm of life is quite chaotic when I'm a part of the score. How much I must have mucked up mum's well laid out schedule by having Micah in the middle of her great move.

Her moving timetable was set. Mum's boyfriend owned a truck. Not sure if that was a valuable aid to being self-sufficient or a 'boys with their toys' thing. He knew the inner workings of engines and other mechanics, and not a thing about horse racing. The vehicle would have been a plus in mum's reckoning, a benefit and a cost-cutting perk for their move.

Repeating 'Mum's boyfriend' has not made the title less odd, but I grow accustomed. I will call him by name from now.

So many changes, all at once. It made the ground unsteady. It made feelings confused.

On the day they left, I wondered how my mum felt as she closed the door on twenty years of life. Had it all been a waste? Did she wish she'd kept every calendar, to be able to look back at the highlights of twenty years in the one house? Were there any? Or would the years stack up as an endless stream of doctor's appointments and bills to pay, highlighted in the fluorescence of false importance? Birthdays that came and went. Twenty years without any real highlights.

How extraordinary are twenty ordinary years?

Shutting the front door to a house for a final time should be a sad 'goodbye.' Goodbye to the last twenty years, mixed with a cheerful 'hello' to the next twenty. Bittersweet. Sweet and sour. Pick a side already. To tell you the truth (read as, to tell you my assumption), I bet Mum was relieved and walked away with a snap of the door into place and an echo of emptiness that left no mark on her except 'gone and good riddance,' without much unhappiness at all. In our house that was never a home, there had been no death, but there'd been no life either.

Did Mum think of my Dad at all, driving away from our shared history, on the freeway at one hundred and ten kilometres per hour— away from twenty years of imperfect yesterdays? Did she hope he found happiness way out west?

More speculation. Mum would never tell me anything, especially about relationships. We keep our own shallow or we'd both drown, or tire of treading water and drift apart. It's best for both of us, a safety measure.

Dad always said Mum had known from day one that their marriage was ill-fated, but it had taken her a very long time to say it out loud. I don't think it was ever said to me or around me. Denial and circumstance kept them together for nearly two decades. Admitting a mistake was admitting failure and this was difficult. Not me, failure is my forte. It's the one thing I can do quite well. My father had been happy enough. What is enough? He'd witnessed his marriage as if seeing it from the outside might and had been the one most hurt by the collapse of the pretence of its ability to continue. In the bliss of ignorance, he'd not realised he'd been living behind a façade. Dad wasn't one to study things too closely, except the Daily Horse Racing Form Guide. The newspaper page that lived in his back pocket. From the outside my parents had been a normal couple, whatever that means. From the inside, the pairing was murky and troubled.

But don't look. Why risk further exposure to the dis-ease? Shield your eyes and your heart. Best to get well away. I learned that, back there.

For Mum, the easiest way to deal with her history was to jump into John's truck and drive well away. Maybe she took a quick glimpse in the rear-view mirror as the twenty years and its house disappeared. More to make sure it was going, rather than to dip into fleeting nostalgia.

Made me want to buy a car.

CHAPTER 19

The Art of Darkness

When I looked down on Micah sleeping, I almost cried again from that deep hurt of love. Hours I spent, just looking. Unbelieving. I struggled to accept as true, something so beautiful was mine. Not mine as in property, but mine as in kinfolk. Mine as in blood. Mine as in heart. Never had I fallen in love at first sight before. I'd not felt the sensation of love at all. When I opened my eyes after sleep and saw her, I fell in love again. Falling again and again. Happy bruised heart. Behind it all was a very unnerving notion that somebody might take her from me.

Living with this persistent thought wasn't easy. It was like existing with a small spike impaling my brain in a syncopated rhythm. I'd be all happy and doing what needed to be done when my thoughts would tear open and fears would drop out. Some nights I'd wake in horror and have to check that Micah was breathing. I may not have believed in a benign God, but I seemed to believe, without evidence, in a malignant force that was going to bestow evil upon me and break me.

Micah did her best to allay my fears. She maintained a normal breathing pattern and tended to stay where I'd put her. If I left her in one room to get something from another, she was always in the same place when I returned.

Nights were hardest. When the world quietened my worries grew louder. The what-ifs noticed my weakness and took advantage. I dreamt of tsunamis swishing Micah out of my arms. I'd wake, panic having pre-readied my flight responses, and would find myself already halfway across the room. Lying down again I'd be watchful, on the verge of ready. And self-berating. Fool. Stupid girl. Echoes.

In the early hours I saw the lights from car headlamps sweep across the wall and I'd be thoughtful. Is light the absence of dark? Or is dark the absence of light? I don't know why my mind chose to chew over the unanswerable. What if the sun just explodes and dies?

It was never long before my mind went apocalyptic. Death began to preoccupy my conscious mind and it was a morbid, weird kind of self-harm, because it frightened me, yet I couldn't stop.

What if gravity just disappeared?

'Oh, do shut up,' I'd say, out loud in an accidental and unsettling mimic of my mother.

What if North Korea decided to nuke Australia?' was my unhelpful reply in my head.

The worst one of all was, what if I have a psychotic episode and never come back?

In the early hours, I needed reassurance that nobody could give me. Not Helen or the doctors. Love doesn't conquer all. My love for Micah could not guarantee sanity. Not one person on Earth could be guaranteed sanity. Depression bowled people over when they least expected it. People who have fought a life-threatening illness and come out on the other side shocked, but alive, can find themselves depressed and suicidal.

That's how nonsensical and arbitrary mental illness is.

My what-ifs were based on questioning my own ability to be a good mother. The fears, although ridiculous, were real. Plague proportioned; they needed heavy chemicals to eradicate the Queen. All the worker fears could be dealt with on a one-to-one basis but the Queen, she was indefatigable. Industrious at all hours. A bitch. My Queen was the fear of losing Micah—by illness, death, abduction or taken away from me by authorities 'for her own good.' This Queen fear was not unrealistic. That's why it scared me most. Haunted my happiness. Made it fleeting/tentative and hard to enjoy.

'You bitch,' I'd say to it, in the dark.

My mind was a mess, but not delusional. It would be chewing on a stupid procedural plan to keep Micah protected, when I'd hear myself say something like, 'You can only be over the weather in an aeroplane or on a high mountain.' What? Somewhere, behind my back, my brain had been contemplating the saying, *under the weather*. What? Why? These type of leaks from my subconscious made me a little paranoid. My own brain was having discussions without including me. What else were these privileged brain-sharers talking about, using my grey matter? Would there be some sort of coup d'état to take me over? Dump my core self into complete darkness? Was I even necessary? Would the assassin come back with his 'kill the spawn' mantra? This thought quaked my interior.

'Hello lightness, my old friend,' I would say when dawn drew silhouettes on my curtains. Then I would sleep until Micah cried out. I called it sleep, but it was my collection of fears in a different weirder realm. Sometimes I fell with Micah in my arms. On my way down into the dark abyss, I had to decide whether to let her go. She would land less heavily on her own, maybe survive if she landed on me. What a relief when her cries woke me before we crashed at the bottom.

'You need to reschedule an appointment with Doctor Sandwich,' Helen would tell me on her home visits. If it doesn't happen soon...'

She left the ending off so my imagination could finish. *They'll take Micah off you.*

'Okay. Okay. But, I'm not happy about it.'

'Why not?'

'I don't know.'

'Ring now, while I'm here. Make an appointment. Make it for a Thursday and I'll take you and Micah, and I'll look after her in the waiting room.'

Under duress and with a vague awareness that I was being hounded *for my own good*, I made the appointment.

'Thursday the 12th,' I told Helen when I'd concluded the call. 'At 2.00 pm.'

With a bit of sulkiness, I set an alarm in my phone for the appointment.

'Anybody would think you don't believe I'm coping,' I said to Helen.

'Not true. You're doing well. But, have you looked in a mirror lately? You've lost too much weight, too quickly for a breast-feeding mother. Plus, you look like you haven't slept for a week.'

'I think sleeping for a week would be classified as a coma.'

'You know what I mean. Now, show me your medi-pack.'

Helen like to see that I'd been taking all of my meds. I knew it was her job, but it seemed I wasn't to be trusted. I showed her the half empty blister packs.

'I'm an adult,' I mumbled, a sulky inner child operating me, with little resistance.

'So, you say. Come on. Let's take Micah to the park. You could use some air and I could use a lunch break in the sun. And, I think you ought to have yourself a hamburger with the works.'

That was a prescription I could get behind. Before long, I was also behind the pram, and we trundled down the street the park to meet Helen who was finding a place to park her car.

The town's small central parkland had been wagon-trained by a bunch of cafes as the suburb gentrified with the influx of developers, hipsters and economically unsuccessful but coffee-drinking creatives. I included myself one of the latter tag. I'd been known to flick a paintbrush about in splendid spurts of artistic endeavour. Works that were skilful enough, but not splendid enough to rate the tedious effort involved in the clean-up afterwards—or arranging for frames. This told me art wasn't my true vocation.

There's disappointment in having an artistic temperament but no talent. Like loving to sing but unable to hold a note where it's supposed to be held. Sometimes I just have to sing for the joy of it. Or maybe get my paint supplies out and start messing about with colour, just for the fun of it.

It was another sun-burning day. The type that could make you forget how cold you'd been the previous winter. Christmas, and the summer school holidays were fast approaching through the swelter. I could almost taste glitter in the air as shopping centre tinsel went up. The world was turning bright, although the temper of some drivers seemed frayed. Afraid at a pedestrian crossing, I had to wait a few minutes before I dared step out onto the white stripes. There was no way I was going to push a pram onto the crossing and hope for the best. When cars stopped, I scuttled across. Micah enjoyed the breeze and because of this, I kept the pace up, looking like somebody with an important errand to run. Scuttling and running errands— grown-up occupations. I was halfway there.

Micah's first Christmas. Was I supposed to put a new-born into shopping centre Santa's lap for a photo? Parenting protocols weren't clear on this question. If I didn't, would there be regrets? Or if I did?

I flopped under a tree in the park. From my vantage point, I could see Helen's car parked near a coffee shop with crap coffee but the excellent burgers. There was no sign of Helen.

'Here's your burger and a cold drink,' she said coming up from behind me, and I startled. 'Sorry,' she added when she realised I'd been alarmed. 'I came around via the post box. Had to drop in a few Christmas Cards so they could get to the UK in time.'

'I'll be all right in a minute,' I lied. It'd be more like five. 'How much do I owe you?'

'Nothing.'

'Yes, I do. How much was lunch? Don't treat me like some ne'er-do-well. I'm, at the very least, a sometimes-do-well.'

'If it so hard for you to accept a free lunch, then its eight dollars.'

Helen sat down beside me on her health care cardigan spread like a flattened torso, while I ferreted about for the money.

'Here's ten, I offered. Buy yourself something nice.'

*

'The daughter of Satan will be dead by Christmas,' a familiar boom-ing voice proclaimed.

I was hardened blue by the cold comment, the pleasantness burgled from the day by the message.

'I'll never be safe. Micah will never be safe,' I whined. 'My terror is portable.'

'Sorry? 'Helen asked, her mouth full of burger.

CHAPTER 20

To Trust a Thief

Lucidity comes. Lucidity goes. Lucidity comes again, in the sky with diamonds. It frightened me how close I came to madness—its pit was deeper than death. There was no full stop. Just uneasy respite. My interior was whimpering but I didn't let the sound out because I was a grown up, a mother, responsible.

Thursday came and I grew glum. To see a psychiatrist was to admit that I was a little bit mental. To admit that the fight couldn't be waged alone. It was to accept a label that would be worn for life. Label. Tag. I'm it.

Doctor Sandwich already knew more about me than I knew about him. A copy of my hospital discharge papers and other letters were in a brand-new manila folder on his desk, my name in an easy-to-read font affixed to the vertical edge. There was a red dot stuck on the top right-hand corner and I wanted to know what that dot meant. Was it a colour code for my degree of mental illness? Did it mean I was new here and nothing more? Red is the universal signal of danger. Was I dangerous?

This all left me at a disadvantage. There was no folder for me to read about the doctor. The interview would be worse than applying for employment. At least at a job interview I knew a little bit about what the heck I was doing there, and beforehand, I could rehearse words to say to avoid sounding incompetent.

'What brings you here?' the doctor asked.

'It was a 'who.' Helen. She brought me. I didn't want to come.'

'Why not?'

Your surname suits a food stuff, not a human. 'Because I don't think you can help me,' I answered.

'You don't give me much credit for my twenty years as a doctor.'

'I think what can be done for me is already being done. I take my meds. I'm compliant.'

'Then tell me a little bit about yourself.'

'I have no story to speak of.'

'Everybody has a story.'

'Okay. What's yours?'

'My story has little to do with your illness. I'm the doctor here.'

Fail. All you had to do was say something minor like 'I was born in blah blah.' Earn some digging rights. Treat me as an equal, even if you're faking it to get information. It seems I'm a bit of a Socialist, at heart. Egalitarianism.

'I imagine most of my story is in your notes. I can't add any more, except, since then I have become a mother.'

'Why are you here at all?' the doctor asked, maybe with a touch of exasperation.

'It was a condition of my release.'

'What if I was to say most people who seek advice have suffered some sort of trauma in childhood? What if I was to say I could help you process that trauma so that you might be able to move forward on surer ground?'

'I'd say, that might be okay.'

Red dot. Stop.

'Tell me, did you have a good childhood?'

'Tell him nothing,' said the voice of the assassin.

'It was fairly bland.'

'Okay, what brought you to the point where you had to be hospitalised?'

'I'm not sure. I went to seek treatment at Emergency for some bleeding during my pregnancy and I guess I went mad, because I woke up in the psych unit.'

'You talk too much. There will be consequences.'

*

That first appointment didn't go very well at all. For some reason, I wasn't open with Doctor Sandwich. If I'd told him I couldn't hear much of what he said because there were voices and threats going on in my head, he might have been able to help. But I was wary of his Sandwich super powers. He had the authority to throw me into the psych ward whenever he thought it necessary. Who could deal with that sort of power? If I'd been honest with him, we may have dealt with the voices then and there. But he scared me.

He scared me. He scared me? Was it that simple? I was afraid of men? Was that my story?

I'd buried the fear under the guise of ridiculing the doctor's name, and a generic mistrust of authority, but in truth I was scared of him. I was scared of men. Or everybody? Perhaps it was a gender-neutral fear of everybody? Hell, I scared myself.

The main ingredient, I imagined, to any successful patient-doctor relationship would be trust. I had none of that. I didn't have the basic recipe for how to concoct it. I was certain trust has to be homemade from scratch. It's never seen for sale in shops.

The one being in whose company I could relax was Micah. She could trust me and so far, I trusted her. This could be the base to start trusting again, if I didn't let it crumble.

My fear of men, I thought in a quiet moment of space in my noisy brain, might be harder to transcend than trust issues. It was counted among my oldest fears. Fears are fascinating, are they not? For instance, I'd always had an acute phobia of snakes. A phobia, I didn't know I had until the first time I met a snake. I'd seen them on TV, pictures of them in books, and two-dimensional snakes did not bother me at all. The first time I came face to face with a live three-dimensional one I had panicked myself into a state of shock. A farmhouse, a living room, a DVD cabinet and an unsuspecting lone house-sitter. I'd reached in to pull out a couple of DVDs to watch and there was the snake, curled up behind the row of movies—and not even behind the horror section. Flight responses were engaged. My fear was doubled, maybe tripled, by the snake not being where I'd expect to find a snake.

Men. Men are quite different to snakes, unless you're thinking metaphorically or psychoanalytically with a Freudian twist. You can't pretend men don't exist. Unless you live in complete isolation you see them every day. They're where you expect to find them and, on occasion, where you don't. Dissociation is my key to day-to-day functioning under these circumstances, or else life would be dreadful. Dread-filled. I try to confine this constant dread inside myself. A dreadlock. Lock it down and away so my surface remains intact and shows calm to the world. If I screamed every time I saw a man, the way I did when I saw that snake, I'd be screaming without end. That's not acceptable behaviour. I could find me and my locked-in fears, locked-up. Fears within fears. Double locks.

So, I had learned to live with the fear of men, or it would kill me.

'How was it?' Helen asked, after I'd seen Doctor Sandwich.

'I don't think I can do it again.'

'Why not?'

I shrugged, and we began walking toward Helen's car in the carpark around the back of the doctor's office building.

'I think Micah and I will walk home,' I said to Helen. 'I need to mull stuff over.'

'Are you sure? It's pretty hot.'

'I'm sure. Thank you so much for bringing us and looking after Micah. You've gone above and beyond.'

Our walk home became an internal argument about whether therapy would be of any benefit. Half of me thought I should continue on with Doctor Sandwich. Half of me thought it was all bollocks. Half of me was undecided, and the mathematician in me, counting halves, walked off in a huff.

Do spiders pee? What sort of question was that? Now and then I could understand where some of my thoughts came from, but this one was right out of nowhere, and I wasn't curious enough to seek an answer. The question of a spider's waste remained unanswered, as did my yes or no to therapy. I'd been once. Was that enough to fulfil my obligation and satisfy the conditions of my release from the psych ward? Did I need to go and rehash my childhood traumas and let free my secrets? Secrets are important. Private. Mine. I didn't want Doctor Sandwich stealing my secrets. I'd held them so long. They were a part of me. Like scars.

Micah broke my thoughts. She was peckish and grumpy. A few weeks old, and she'd acquired hangry tendencies, my little crabby prodigy. Her miniature cries were heading toward maximum frenzy. I detoured into the park and we sat under my favourite tree while she fed. I dreamed of coffee and stared a jealous stare at people leaving cafes with their take-away cups, while I drank tepid water from a bottle.

Children were playing on nearby climbing frames and swinging on things like they were riding a bunch of unsynchronised pendulums. Their squealing was not pleasant. I would need to avoid the park until the long school holidays were over. There'd be plenty of squealing in my future, when Micah reached that age where her legs worked and stuff. She'd climb. And fall. How brave mothers are, to not wrap their children in bubble wrap before they climb things and ride things and go out in the world.

You need your therapist to be a woman.
Women are brave.
At last, sensible thoughts.

CHAPTER 21

21 Personal Growth Excision and Regeneration

At the baby weigh-in that week, I was told perhaps I didn't quite have enough milk to satisfy Micah. In the end I chose to abandon breastfeeding. Sterilising bottles came into my life. This also meant I could bring alcohol-filled bottles back in. It was summer. There was beer.

What was I thinking? Well, I was thinking, it's summer and there's beer. Yes, I was taking prescribed anti-psychotic drugs. Yes, I had a very young baby. But I figured it out this way; my mother asked me to bring Micah and visit her for a couple of days on the coast. I knew that was no excuse to take up alcohol again. It was, but not the best one. There is no best one. What's a cuse anyway? Why and how did it become an ex, an ex-cuse?

Changing the subject is my way of creating a logic pathway where there isn't one.

If going knowingly into a circumstance that I knew would make me uncomfortable equalled an opportunity for personal growth, I was going to grow enormous. I wasn't sure I liked the idea of personal growth so close to Christmas. Time with my mother was the sort of overwhelm that could weaken an immune system. The surprise of the invite gave me temporary brain arrest and I agreed to visit the coast before its thinking part had time to revive.

I would be catching a train to personal growth. My mother said I needn't pack anything for the baby. She'd set up a nursery with everything I might need for Micah or John's grandchildren. I could travel as lightly as somebody travelling with a baby on a train for two hours could travel. Micah cried for more than half of the trip and I felt like crying for the other half. But two hours later I pushed the pram out of the train and onto the platform of a strange town. It gave me a sense of alienation mixed with a touch of wanderlust. Also, a sense of capability. Travelling with a small baby takes competency or stupidity. Perhaps a mixture of both.

There was a lift up to the main concourse and we rose up to find my mother waiting at the ticket barriers. She smiled when she saw us and gave a little wave. The station guard opened the large barrier to let me and the pram through.

'Hello, Micah.' my mother's voice was high with excitement as she leaned over the pram. I was an interloper.

'How was the trip?' my mother asked, and I didn't answer because I thought she was still talking to Micah.

'Well?' my mother asked. turning to face me.

'Fine, thanks. And you?'

'No. I meant I was waiting for you to tell me how your trip was.'

'Oh, sorry. It was fine. Micah was a bit grumpy, but she settled down by the station just before this one.'

This was meant to convey with humour that it hadn't been the best trip, but my mother did not find it funny or she wasn't listening.

'Well, let's get home,' she said.

Home. The word still seemed to be able to bite me—sting a little. It was magic how home rolled over my mother's tongue and out, like/as if it was not an alien concept.

I couldn't call my own place home. I understood there's no place like it, but my next-door neighbour's flat was the same design as mine. And, the one above me and the one below me were also replicas. At that point, I recognised that home was what the dwellers brought into a space and I had failed to be 'at home', to make a home. Most of my mail was addressed to The Occupant. That's all I was.

Before we'd reached Mum's car, I'd added my inability to be a home-maker to my long list of life failures. At least I remained a very successful failure, even if I was a life occupier, not fulfiller. Mum's car. Mum scar.

No matter how I'd been adult-ing in my own occupied territory, the minute I was back under my mother's roof things became peculiar. She showed me about her new home like the Queen might show Balmoral to a friend. Relaxed, but still the Queen. Compared with the suburban boxes we'd lived in while I was growing up, this was an absolute palace. The living room had a view of the beach, a very impressive and expensive vista. Not everyone could afford a front row seat—from their living room—to a panoramic show called the seashore. My mother had become one of the select few. The house was new, in mint condition, all shine and light. I was a stain. Afraid to move in case I ruined the new. The carpeted areas were plush and light beige, just waiting for me to debase the unspoiled.

That visit was when I met beer again. Beer was my friend. The reason I hadn't reunited with beer earlier was the wrongness associated with wheeling a pram into a liquor shop. I had some standards. They were changeable or flexible, but nonetheless in place and would fade a little over time rather than disappear altogether.

It was obvious to me that I was not going to relax until I forced myself, with chemicals, to lighten up. My mother must have felt the same because, after the tour she headed straight for the refrigerator.

'The sun's over the yard arm, let's take some beers out onto the veranda and enjoy the scenery. Put Micah in the crib and grab the baby monitor.'

Micah had nodded off in my arms during the tour. I don't think she'd made it to the third bedroom, which was where my interest had dwindled too. It was an awesome house and I was maybe jealous or perhaps sensitive, or over-sensitive about my no money-ness. Fish out of water? Round peg, square hole? Sober?

'You have no breasts,' my mother stated to me, accusing. As if I might not have comprehended that my inexcusable well-documented carelessness was behind their disappearance. Was I reading too much into four words?

'They kind of just fell off after I stopped breastfeeding,' I told her, defensive.

'You've got even less now than you had before your pregnancy. You'd better not have any more children or they'll end up concaving and poking out of your back. Actually, joking aside, you're far too skinny.'

'I was glad she'd said "joking aside" or I wouldn't have grasped that she was in fact, joking.

'How much do you weigh?' Mum added, interrogation slipping into her tone.

'Forty-eight kilos,' I answered, believing/hoping honesty would be the best policy. Else she'd march me up to the bathroom and make me step on the scales.

'Maddie! That's horrible. We'd better fatten you up. Oh! I hear John coming in. Wait here. I want to show him my granddaughter sleeping.'

There was a beer with my name on it so I remained at the table, compliant and battered. The baby monitor told me they had slipped into the nursery and were admiring Micah. I smiled.

'Isn't she brilliant?' my mother whispered to John.

John must have answered using body language because I didn't hear him react.

They both soon appeared at the glass doors and I stood up to say hello. John threw himself at me in an open-hearted bear hug. Hugging to the point where I believed my spinal column might snap. He held on in a manner that led me to fear incapacitating back injury. I held my fear back.

'You're right,' he said to my mother, letting me free. 'She's way too skinny. Let's be having some of your world-famous pikelets.'

My mother had world-famous pikelets. They both disappeared into the kitchen and I sat down with care, expecting my back to crumble into small pieces causing the rest of me to melt onto the decking in a puddle of un-scaffolded skin. My skeleton was stronger than I expected, and I remained in an upright position. My fear calmed. Down.

My mother came back outside with a plate of pikelets, each one piled with a small hill of cream and strawberry jam.

'If you don't like the topping, just lick it off.'

I laughed out loud. Really.

While I was still processing the idea that my mother had a sense of humour, John brought me a fresh beer.

'We ought to get some black beer in,' he said. 'That'd help build you up.'

Before I could answer in the negative, Micah announced she was awake via the baby monitor.

'I'll go,' my mother said and was up and off before I could pull myself into the take-off position.

'Thank you for coming,' whispered John, passing over his gratitude once Mum was out of earshot. 'It means a lot to your mother.'

This was a strange pivotal moment in the story of my mother and me. It was dizzying, a pivoting, a rotation of my core beliefs. My spot in the family had always felt tacked on, as if after the birth of my brother the family had been completed. I had arrived by accident, unplanned and had to be pinned onto the family in a makeshift way. Like names written in a Christmas card, "From Peter, Abigail, Matthew and Maddie." Three on one side and me on the other.

Now, in my mother's new house with my new daughter, I meant something. Even if it was as the maker of my mother's first grandchild, I had a more valuable position. I wasn't sure how to allow myself to be appreciated and thanked. My instinct was to curl up and wait for a harsh blow. Like the type I was used to receiving if or when I let my guard down.

'You've got a lovely home,' I said, forcing the conversation back to a superficial level.

'Your mother has great taste,' John said. 'Well, she must have, hey? She chose me. That pretty much proves it.'

John laughed at his own humour and watched as my mother came out, carrying a very alert young lady.

'Look at Micah taking everything in. She's as bright as the proverbial button. The sea air must be doing her some good. Do you have a bottle made up, or do we need to mix some formula?' my mother asked me.

'I've one ready to go in the cooler. I'll go and heat it up.'

When I stood up, things went a bit spinny. If I was going to drink, I did need to eat more. As I passed to move indoors, I grabbed a pikelet and licked off the topping to amuse myself, before popping the bottoming into my mouth. It's the opposite of topping, I thought, so why not call it real?

All of the interior doors were the same and I was dazed by the maze but found the door to the nursery and grabbed Micah's pram and pushed it into the kitchen. There, I took a bottle from the cooler and settled it into the brand-spanking new micro-wave, to be spun about until heated to the preferred non-baby scalding temperature.

On the veranda, Mum, John and Micah were having a chat. I handed my mother the heated bottle, so she and her granddaughter could continue their bonding session over a drink. We all grew silent, on the verge of awkward for me. But the beers had kicked in and I took my tension down one notch to semi-strained, and slammed down another world-famous pikelet while I still had an appetite.

Misgivings tapped me on the shoulder then. There was I, drinking, eating, with no tangible cause to be sad. It was summer. There was beer.

Your father's sitting alone in a bed-sit no bigger than this veranda.

Stupid voices.

A covering of sadness, as detectable as a blanket, drooped over me. This sudden gloom; for something invisible, was unfair, heavy.

CHAPTER 22

Shifting Gears

There was an unbearable sense of fairness and guilt, mushed into a tired remorse that pushed me into inviting myself way out into the middle of nowhere to visit my father in his little bed-sit on the edge of normality. It was an edge. A cotton town—not made out of cotton but through its profits. A cyclical town that breathed in and out by the swelling and abating of seasonal workers filling all of the spare accommodation during picking season. There was a rough gentleness to it. Some guys would brawl with relentless savagery in the gutters outside the pubs—there were three pubs—then tend to machinery, coax it, bandage it, weld it to stay together until the bailing was done. The season would end, and the town would relax again as the last ute, with mandatory dog in the back, drove out past the old closed-down drive-in, and away. The dust would settle.

After a horror nine hours in a train, Micah and I fell out into the red and found my father waiting by a ute under the shade of an old tree that had been alive there longer than the oldest citizen. We hugged like family is meant to, but there was an awkward self-consciousness about us. A grey cloud had followed me from Sydney and there was a light shower that did not cool the earth.

'Brought the rain with you,' my father said, and I noted how his words came from him in the slow country way. There was no trace of his kiwi accent.

'Yes. I thought it'd be more suitable than flowers or chocolate.'

By the time we were settled into the ute the rain was hard, dust-smearing drops, audible on the windshield. It proceeded to rain for eleven of the fourteen days that I was there. The town rejoiced. I was miserable.

There was no baby capsule in the ute, forcing me to hug Micah, wrap her in my anxiety during the short drive to my dad's flat. Turned out the ute wasn't even his. My father left me in the bedsit while he zoomed the car back to its rightful owner.

I didn't see him again until after the pubs shut. An ancient anger was awakened in me, but I held it still, feeling my resentment burning my innards fury-red. The exhaustion of the long train ride caught up with me, so I tucked Micah into her pram and flumped onto the lounge. The place was no bigger than the average motel room. The benefit that set the three tiny rooms above prison-cell status was the front and back doors that opened to the outside world. Still the rain would become my gaoler.

My father was in his early sixties now and had very little to show for his half-century of adulthood. A three-quarter sized wardrobe held everything he owned. On top of it lay a battered old blue suitcase that looked the same age as its owner, weather-beaten and worn.

So very difficult not to be sad. Sad for my father and sad for myself. There was I, one thousand kilometres from my residence, sitting in a small bedsit with the used-to-be fear of my Dad coming home and the equal fear of him not, resurfacing like a longstanding and persistent enemy. I wanted to go back to Sydney.

The rain had turned torrential. Micah cried.

It was very difficult not to be sad.

When my father swayed in, the baby was asleep and I had made a bed for myself on the sofa.

'You're supposed to be in the proper bed. You're the guest.'

'This is fine, I said. And I'm shorter than you.'

'Why didn't you cook the dinner?' he asked from the tiny kitchen. 'It was all ready to go.'

'I wasn't hungry.'

'Well, I'm cooking now. Little one's a good sleeper, then?'

'She wore herself out. Your neighbour banged on the wall.'

'Ah, don't worry about her. She likes to complain. Gives her something to do.'

My father wavered over the stove hob, frying some sausages. I worried that he'd tilt too close.

'Is that shirt polyester?' I asked.

'Probably. Why?'

'I'm frightened it'll melt into your skin.'

Micah woke again. Cried. The neighbour tapped on the wall. Dad replied with some loud banging with the kitchen tongs. It was hard not to be sad. A fortnight of this, plus rain.

The dark man, the assassin, sat at the table across from my father who was eating burnt sausages. But the dark man was looking at me. There was promise in his eyes. He promised pain. Without speaking he told me Micah was his. He would reclaim her. Soon. Very, very soon.

My baby was crying again. Had she felt the threats? A hot night despite the rain and so, after a bottle, I gave her a relaxing bath in the kitchen sink, looking over my shoulder now and then, to make sure the assassin wasn't there.

Dad was unconscious and snoring in the single bed by the time we were done. My insides were chaotic. The dark man, not real, but there he had been, radiating animosity— sitting shrouded in black at my father's kitchen table, in a bed-sit, in the middle of nowhere Australia. Why? Why must he follow me? To this place, where my Hell had been all of those years ago. Because my Uncle the predator had also lived in this town. He'd died in this town, but not soon enough. His bones lay now uncared for, and the grave marked with a handmade cross fashioned out of old fence posts and two rusty un-matching screws, his named burnt into the wood much as his poison had burned into me. A marker of his infringement remained in my skin.

My uncle's wife had made it clear that she didn't want to be interred with him when she died, or even laid to rest in the same cemetery grounds, less they seep together during periodic flooding. My father would die later in the year, in this town, and I would return with Matthew for the funeral. Dad was buried in what ten years later would become my auntie's cemetery and then we left town. A sad quickness to the end of my father.

Nothingness was now necessary. An empty space to sort out my thoughts. It was never peaceful enough during those thirteen days to do the sorting. My brain hit overload and coherency was prone to stumbling. I loved my Dad, that's why stuff hurt. Thirteen days with him was okay. Thirteen days in this town was not.

The next morning, Day 2 of the 13, I wished a fresh start to the visit. Pouring with rain it was, and the dampness took a fair hold of my mood as I boiled five-minute eggs, plus toasted soldiers for dipping, while I was trying out assorted bolstering thoughts in my head. My father was as sober as he could be, and he met Micah over breakfast.

'She's got a decent set of lungs.'

*

After an 'if you can't beat them, put the stick down and join them' decision, I agreed to go to the pub with Dad for lunch. The bed-sit was shrinking because I'd opened my back-pack and clothes had discharged across the room as if they'd been so compacted that they were desperate for release. They'd never fit back into the bag without a struggle. I needed space. The clothes needed space. In desperation I opened the front door so that I might see sky and let the grey in. I knew there needed to be a shift in my mind-set gears or depression was going to drop me to the ground and render me useless.

'Let's get ready to go,' my father said.

'It's only ten o'clock.'

'We'll beat the rush.'

A sigh escaped from me, I heard it and assumed my mother had taken possession of my moral codes and reconfigured them based on her own specifications.

'Okay. Mikey, what do you want to wear for your first ever visit to a pub?' I asked in an attempt to curb my new uptight inner censor.

'Has she got a check flannel shirt?'

As I went sighing into the bathroom, I hoped my father was joking. A face appeared in the medicine cabinet mirror when I stood in front of it. I didn't like the look of her. She looked judgemental. I made her smile and that was a tad better.

'Give me strength,' I said and swallowed my morning medications.

We managed to walk up the street in the interval between rain inundations. Straightaway I knew why my father left at such an early hour. He had to talk to everybody we encountered. Show them his grandchild. Discuss the rain. In time, we were in the beer garden of the middle pub. Many larger country towns have a top pub—the one at the top of the main street, a bottom pub and a middle pub, all nick-named after their main street positions. My father had been banned from the top. He wouldn't tell me why. So, the middle was his next choice.

The beer garden was basic. A large pot plant—hence garden—some tables and bench seats in a quadrangle covered by a see-through corrugated roof which was managing to keep the rain out. I was ready for a beer by then. Panting for one. My father went inside to the bar to buy us the drinks and I settled on a bench with Micah close beside me in her pram. She was awake but not fractious. Glad to be out of the bed-sit and its cloying walls of inoffensive Housing Commission beige. By contrast, I was still a bit fractious.

Dad came out with a beer in each hand and a smile on his face. We sat together and talked about nothing important for a while. In the time-honoured tradition, I bought the next round, feeling happier in a beer-heightened way. After half an hour or so, my father went off again, to order us lunch and buy more drinks.

He didn't come back.

CHAPTER 23

Slur and Repetition

In the beer garden, I sat for fifteen minutes before I began to consider I had been forgotten. Had my father become involved in the horse-racing blaring from the pub television? Had he met a mate inside? I was staring at the solitary pot plant wondering if it was the Australian bush everybody talked about, when I decided to enter the bar and see what my father was up to. It'd been half an hour since he went in.

Aside from the barman, there were two other men, neither which were my father.

'Do you know where Pete Kitchener is?' I asked the barman.

'Up at the hospital.'

'What? Why? What happened?'

'He knocked himself on the door in the men's toilet and peeled the skin off his arm like it was an old onion. You could see bone. Bob took him ta hospital'.

There was me standing at the bar dumbstruck, with Micah in her pram beside me.

'Oh,' is all I said.

The barman handed me the landline telephone. 'Press six,' he told me. 'It's the speed dial for casualty.'

A pub with hospital emergency room on speed dial. Who needs European vacations? I pressed the number six. After a wait, I was told Bob was going to drive my Dad home once the wound had been attended to and wrapped. Bob was a good man. I would need to thank Bob.

Everybody my father had chatted to on the way to the pub, stopped to talk to me as I headed back to the bedsit, trying to push the pram and hold an umbrella up at the same time.

'Sorry to hear what Pete's done to himself,' was the average comment.

It seemed the whole town knew already about my father's mishap. There I'd been, sitting sipping a warm beer in the beer garden as uninformed as a garden gnome while the information was sprinting its way down the street. I guess, if you have to be a garden gnome, a beer garden gnome is high-quality employment—perhaps talked about with awe by unemployed garden gnomes having a chinwag of an evening. If I hadn't been so out of practice about my father disappearing, I would have asked at the bar sooner.

The spare key was hidden where I'd been told to find it and I let myself into the oppressive little bedsit. Although it was raining I opened the back door and left the front one gaping to give the illusion of space, while creating a small wind tunnel that blew dusty stuff about, from under things and out into the open. This gave me the urge to clean.

The safest place for Micah was in her pram. After a bottle and a burping, she lay in there quite content, watching what I imagined was a blur, rather than her mother flashing about in a cleaning frenzy.

It should have been no surprise that my father didn't come home until after the pub shut, full of slur and repetition.

'Your dinner's in the microwave,' I told him, tiredness in my voice, reminiscent of my mother's sighing resentment back when she had been his cook.

His behaviour made me hate myself. Twelve days to go. Why on earth had I decided on two weeks? One week would have sufficed, wouldn't it? It would have proven I had no parental bias. It would have made me a good daughter. Meanwhile, the sound of my father eating almost made me throw up. My senses had been heightened to an uncomfortable level by the instability of the day. Sleep was needed.

*

A community nursing sister came each morning to change my father's outer bandage and inner dressing. His skin was so frail it could
not be sewn or glued. Nature had to do the healing at its own pace.
The next day, after the nurse had been and gone, on our trip up the
street I purchased a small radio and headphones. My survival instinct
had kicked in. I also bought a pair of gum boots, a clear plastic weather-
proof cover for Micah's pram, a light raincoat and a small backpack.

'We'll meet you in the pub for lunch,' I told Dad as I left, between
rain showers. 'Try to remain intact,' I joked, but was unsmiling on the
inside. 'Ring my mobile if you need to. Micah and I are off to see the
sights, or sight.'

I wasn't sure if there were any. There weren't many, as it turned out.

And that's how Micah and I spent our holiday days; traipsing about
in knee high mud, slipping from one small island poking out of the
flooding plains, to the next. We saw The Old Courthouse. The Old
Mill—everything on the high side of the river, everything that had The
Old in front of it. We went to the sodden Agricultural Show too. Sod-
ding agricultural show. I left a gum boot there, perhaps it's still at the
showground, trapped near the best-in-show cow pen. Still sticking out
of dried mud today, perhaps for the rest of time, a monument to the unknown stumbler. From then on, we kept to The Olds. They tended to
be less muddy, some with concrete paths, and didn't smell so much of
saturated, mouldy agriculture.

At night my baby and I began to get to know my father, in small in-
crements. He started to arrive home before dinner, almost sober. Micah
would lie on the lounge feeling the cross breeze from the open doors. It
was still hot even though we were surrounded by water. It was a wonder
the puddles didn't boil during the heat of the day.

More than a decade older than my mother, my Dad was showing his
age, combined with the effects of long-term alcohol abuse. His hands
trembled. Anything he had to read was laid on a table or flat, stable surface so it might remain still. I thought his life was gloomy, but he seemed
happy. Having taken early retirement and living in this small cubby,

Dad had more money than he could spend— as long as he kept away from slow horses. He'd built his days around pleasant routines that he could do on autopilot or drunk. He wanted for nothing and said he thrilled to have a grandchild to love.

One afternoon, when it was plain too wet for Dad to venture to the pub, he pulled out an old box of photos. Or a new box filled with old photos.

'I've been saving these for a rainy day,' he said. 'To sort 'em and write on the back of 'em. For after I've kicked off.'

'Dad!'

'Well, a bunch of photos with nothing on them will just end up in the bin when I'm dead. These are all I have to say I was ever here.'

'You have us.'

'You don't want to be the human archive of my life. Besides, your memory's crap.'

'True.'

We turned our attention back to the contents of the box. Among the curling, fading pictures were some war medals. Dad looked at them. Held them in his trembling fingers. Sighed.

'War is the stupidest way to solve anything,' he said. 'It broke more people than it mended... There's no glory. Just guts. Courage and in-nards spilled all over the place.'

My father sighed again and wrapped the medals back in their paper towel and handed them to me. They felt heavy, coated perhaps in his post-traumatic stress.

'Keep these as a reminder of people doing the wrong thing for the right reasons. A reminder that to be human is to be ... I don't know, a mess.'

'Well, we've both got the hang of the mess part,' I said to lighten the mood some. 'Who's that?' I asked, pointing to a photo of a young woman while I tucked the medals into my pocket with the other hand. I wondered if I was up to the responsibility of a human archive.

'Ah. Let me tell you about Sonia.'

There were plenty of photos of women in his collection. My father had been a bit of a player back in New Zealand. Until he met my mother. What a collision that must have been. It had knocked them both senseless. As he gave me the information I wrote the names, vague dates and a bit of each woman's story on the back of the photos.

'Now, let me tell you about Maureen, my father said.

*

Our visit out in the far-away ended in the same soggy way it had begun. Dad borrowed a four-wheel drive and drove Micah and me to the train station. This time we had to board a bus—the train line had been closed by raging, rising waters. In the bus, I waved to my father as we waited to leave. I waved even after it felt awkward. The bus began to move and I waved again. The ride would take us around the edges of the flood plain and to the first train station on the other side of the water. From there, another eight hours on a train.

It was a very, very long trip home. I saw my father just one more time before he died.

I missed him in odd pockets of melancholy and to my shame, sometimes I forgot he was ever there.

CHAPTER 24

Fears and Fresh Fruit

Travelling long distances with a baby was never going to be on my to-do list again. It felt like folly without a back-up person, someone capable for when I wanted to curl into the womb position, trying not to cry while the rest of the folk in the train carriage drank alcohol they'd paid an extortionate rate for. By the time I reached my front door, I must have looked like a tornado survivor.

The rush downstairs to retrieve my backpack, after I'd dragged and pushed Micah into my flat, did me in. I galloped down and up the stairs again, as always with the fear that some unforeseen horrific accident would hurt my baby while I was away for those few minutes. An anvil dropping from the sky or something like that. These things could happen. I'd seen it in documentaries. Okay, they were cartoons.

My recurrent anxiety was built by a news item showing witnesses and neighbours asking over and over, "where was the mother?" I was troubled by possible judgement by people I didn't know and would not encounter as a rule. I tried not to encounter anybody as a rule. It was one of my Cardinal Rules.

Neuroses were never in plain sight (another rule) but they propelled me to think of worse case scenarios. Living like that was no laughing matter but I smiled at my own inadequacies. Keep Smiling —yet another rule. I also told myself often, to shut up about the stupid rules.

I had accepted that people like me never advanced very far in life due to the continual exhaustion of my Judgment Day prepping and worst-case scenario assemblage. I was tired.

So very, very tired.

Micah and I slept through the night and I jumped up to check on her the minute, the second, the nano-second my eyes opened, because... Well, worst case. But my daughter was fine. We had both slept through an entire night. That triumph over interrupted sleep made me feel like I'd won something and I ran around in small circles with my arms raised Hallelujah style. Until I crashed over my unpacked backpack.

'Yay,' I said from the floor.

A success was a success. Although I wasn't going to spend twelve hours travelling every day, confined, uncomfortable, in a small space, if that's what it took for us both to sleep through a night. A line had to be drawn somewhere between victory and torture.

An interrupting text arrived on my phone during Micah and my shared ablute in the bathtub. Morning ablutions tended to be easier that way. The beep from my telephone annoyed me. Made me over-think things when all I wanted to do was enjoy a cleanse. Yes, I wanted to know who the text was from, but I didn't want to get out of the bath.

'I suppose we should start the day,' I told Micah.

The text message was from the Acute Care Team to remind me that Helen was scheduled for a visit at ten o'clock. That gave me two and a half hours to make my place not look like a crazy person lived there.

'There's no fruit!'

When I heard myself say this, I was bemused but troubled. What inner recess in my mind reasoned fresh fruit proved sanity?

'Bananas,' I said, and commenced a cleaning whirl.

By the time Helen arrived I thought I'd set a decent rationality ambience. Although I couldn't get the assassin to move out of the kitchen corner, near the sink.

'Would you mind dreadfully, fucking right off?' I asked him.

'Call me Dolofónos,' he said.

'Whatever. You're not real. Leave me alone, Dolly ... Dooley, McBugger Off, or whatever your name is. Leave me alone!'

He didn't. But there were no threats either. That was better.

My bravado would last a somewhat unsatisfactory length of time. It always expired before my expected *use by*. Now that I was away from my father and wasn't impelled to act holier than thou, I craved a beer to knock the edge off Dooley's visit.

'Hooley Dooley,' I mumbled when the doorbell rang.

'Hi,' Helen said.

'Gidday,' I answered, because I'd been to the bush.

'Hey, Mikey,' she said, almost knocking me out of the way to go and see Micah, who was lying in the vacuumed living area on a clean blanket, beneath a disinfected, colourful swinging mobile that made me a bit woozy to look at.

'You haven't come to see me at all,' I said, shutting the front door.

'Of course, I have—in my official capacity. I'm seeing Micah in my unofficial capacity.'

Helen sat down on the lounge and put on her serious face.

'How are you? How was the trip?'

'It was both lovely and not. Do you want a cuppa?'

I hoped not, Dooley was still lurking in the kitchen, like a film-noir villain.

'No thanks. I've just had a coffee.' She reached out and waggled her hand at Micah, catching her tiny fingers. 'Keeping up with your meds?'

'Yes, ma'am.'

'You look a bit jittery to me.'

'Well, I not long ago spent twelve hours on public transport with a baby.'

'You deserve a medal.'

'I brought some home.' Helen looked confused, which I thought was not good. 'My father gave me his war medals for safe keeping,' I added. I didn't want to sound weird.

I was trying too hard.

'Oh, that's nice. Anyway, we have to find you a new doctor, if you're certain Doctor Sandwich is not for you,' Helen said.

'I don't wish to sound sexist, but I'd prefer a woman. There's stuff I have a lot of trouble talking about, at the best of times. Men scare me.' There, I'd said it again, so I repeated it. 'Men scare me. I don't want them to, but they do. Women kind of scare me, as well,' I added. 'But not to the same degree. People,' I said. 'People scare me. Could I maybe just talk to a puppy?'

'Puppies don't come with a prescription pad.'

'Do I really need meds? 'I asked, thinking of Dooley loitering with intent in my kitchen. Medication had not rid me of him.

'Don't even think about discontinuing your medication,' Helen barked. 'I remember what you were like when you first arrived at the hospital, even if you don't. You're much better on your meds.' She turned to face me, still holding Micah's fingers. 'There's one, only one woman psychiatrist within a fifty-kilometre radius of here. I've taken the liberty of making you an appointment. Unfortunately, the waiting list is long—four months. In the meantime, you have me once a fortnight. Or on the phone, if you need me.'

'People, people who need people, are the luckiest people ...'

'Sarcastic singing will get you nowhere.'

'I'm glad you noted the sardonic tone. It's hard to pull off while singing. But you know I've always considered myself a lucky person. Just most of it's bad.'

'Well, I can't sit around admiring your little baby all day, I've got sick people to see.'

'I'm sorry there wasn't any fresh fruit.'

'What?'

'Nothing.'

'Sometimes I get the feeling you're having a different dialogue with people I can't see.'

'I know, right? It's like there's people listening to my every word as I speak.'

'You're an odd goose. But promise me you'll at least text me if things are getting out of control. As I've said before, these episodes are much easier to prevent than it is to carry out repairs afterward.' She got to her feet, unwrapping little fingers from her own as she stood. 'I might see you next week. I'm not sure you're being upfront with me.'

My mention of the lack of fresh fruit had screamed insane. 'I'm okay, but a little worn out by two parental visits in one month. I promise I'll behave.'

'I'm still coming next week. I need my Micah fix.'

I didn't think Helen was being upfront with me, either.

'Intruder!' complained Dooley from the kitchen.

'Yes, you are,' I said to him. 'Do,' I added, when Helen looked at me with an eyebrow raised. 'Yes, you do need your Micah fix.'

When I closed the door after Helen left, I was scared. Too close to the edge. Scared the authorities would take my baby from me. Scared that this was my life. I should have called Helen back, had my medication tweaked. But I didn't.

'Come on, little one. We need to go out and buy some fresh fruit. And beer.'

*

First we went to the local library. I told myself that education and fresh fruit were the keys to sanity. There were mountains of books about craziness. I wanted to find accounts about people who had come out alive on the other side of psychoses and had moved on to enjoy proper, well lived, unafraid lives. There weren't many. None.

It was a small library. Instead, I went to the check-out to borrow a book on toddler taming. Turned out my library card had expired, or gone dormant, or suicided. Anyway, it was dead. There was a wait while a replacement was issued.

'You've got a way to go before you'll need this book,' the library assistant said, nodding toward Micah as we stood waiting for the computer system to spit out a new card.

'I like to be prepared,' I told her.

'Knowledge is power,' Dooley said, startling me. I almost jumped the counter.

'Sorry,' I told the librarian. 'My phone's on vibrate in my pocket. It went off.'

My real mobile phone then began to ring, from the carry bag on Micah's pram.

'Goodness,' I said, preparing a lie. 'Now, it's my work phone.'

I checked the number. It was my mother's.

'Aren't you going to get that?'

'No. I'm sure I'll be needing to sit down for this one. I diverted the call to messages.'

Lying made me feel ill. Dooley beside me made me feel ill. A phone call from my Mum made me feel ill. I was finding it hard to get a grip on the day.

Once I had my new library card and the borrowed book, I pelted out of that library like it was on fire. I thought that if I didn't keep still, Dooley would never catch me.

'We need to buy some fresh fruit,' I repeated to Micah, a little out of breath as I rushed toward the main street. 'It's become essential.'

CHAPTER 25

Level Crossings

On a subterranean level, my thoughts seemed opposed to my feelings. On the surface, I was quite happy. My baby lit up my life in a way no other had. In a good way, no arson. Thoughts fell onto the floor of my mind, unreconciled with emotions, and this detachment seemed to pull me apart a little. When Micah smiled at me, I was awash with delight but within the same time frame I heard my thoughts drop and spill into speech, one by one:

'Nobody can live like this.'

'This will only make things worse when the shit hits the fan.'

'How can I care for a baby?'

'I don't know what love is.'

'I'm never going to amount to anything.'

'I want to die.'

Was Dooley attacking from within, even though he appeared to be standing in the kitchen most of the time? Was he throwing me down metaphorical stairs, where on each step our thoughts became darker? Could Dooley be in two places at once?

'Shut up,' I told my own head. And Dooley.

Micah was able to roll over, and it wouldn't be long before the square of blanket on the floor was left behind. She'd be rolling all over the place soon.

'You'll lose her.'

I made a management decision and opted to purchase a portable baby pen so I'd at least be able to go to the toilet and not come back to find Micah had rolled under something and was choking on dust bunnies. The purchase, after buying formula and baby stuff, left me with twenty-five dollars to last for two weeks. So began my love-hate relationship with instant noodles. For the fourteen days until my next crazy person's pension, I ate so many pre-cooked noodles, my pee started to smell like M.S.G. But it was worth it for a piece of peace in one part of my mind.

Another prompt for the purchase was the telephone call from my mother, which I'd thought would need to be taken sitting or lying down. I hadn't been wrong.

'We're all coming here for Christmas,' she said, when I'd found enough courage to call her back.

I wasn't sure what that meant. Wasn't my mother already there? My silence must have encouraged her to explain, not customary in her dealings with me.

'Matthew and Carey and John's kids, and their kids will all be here for Christmas.'

I was glad I was sitting down. Was I expected to go, too?

'And, of course, you and Micah.'

'That's great,' I said, but was ready to put my head in an oven.

'The others are just coming for the day, but you can stay over.'

'Because I'm so special?'

'What? No. Because you won't want to be travelling on public transport over Christmas. Lots of drunk folk and weirdos.'

That might have been a description of my Christmas Day survival plan—to be both drunk and weird.

'So, I suggest you come up on Christmas Eve and stay a week or so.'

Suggest meant expected in Mum-speak. And *expected* meant *be there*.

When I ended the call I was overcome with resentment. There's an anthem for people who aren't all that excited by Christmas. Kevin Bloody Wilson. I began to sing it.

Ho Ho Fucking Ho, what a crock of shit ...

'Looks like we're going to your Nan's for Christmas,' I told Micah. 'Your first Christmas.'

Micah blew a little bubble and I wasn't sure if it was a raspberry of disapproval or a drool of delight. For me, it meant instant noodle on-set and stressing about having enough money for gifts. 'It's the thought that counts,' I told myself, but I couldn't think. Dooley didn't comment, for once.

*

'Are you losing more weight?' Helen asked on her next visit.

I hadn't told her about my all-noodle diet. I didn't confess I was eating them every day because Micah needed stuff. I also didn't mention that part of my eating-disordered self was impressed with forty-eight kilos. I shrugged and worried that there was no fresh fruit on the kitchen table and that Dooley had kicked his threats up a notch. His presence was like I imagined it would be to live with a terrorist. The fear of what he might do was hideous enough, without any of his threats coming to fruition. Fruit. Fruit was turning up in my words but not in my reality.

Fruition is a strange term. If bearing fruit would complete Dooley's tasks, that would be helpful. Nuts. Nutty as a fruitcake. Fruity as a nut-cake.

I shook my head as if my thoughts were written on an internal *Etch A Sketch*™ and shaking it would erase them all.

'Okay?' asked Helen.

If I came clean about Dooley, would she be able to...? 'I'm seeing things,' I blurted.

'Is it any wonder? You're looking so run down. Healthy mind, healthy body. Are you feeling safe?'

'No.'

'How about you come into hospital and let the doctors tweak your medication?'

'No!'

'Just a couple of days. You can't go on like this.'

'Kill her!' yelled Dooley from the kitchen. 'Or I will.'

'Oh, fuck off.'

'Hey. There's no need for that.' Helen sounded hurt.

'No. No. Not you. I was talking to him,' I said, pointing through the kitchen door.

Dooley was sharpening a kitchen knife, the best one. The keenest one. My world tilted on its axis and his and other voices tore at my ears.

'Sorry,' I heard Helen say through the noise.

She picked up my mobile phone and I heard her. I heard her betray me. I heard her ring my mother, telling her to come to Sydney and pick Micah up from the hospital. I heard my heart break, wide. Then, I didn't hear anything else but my own yelling. Although I couldn't understand my personal babble, I felt the meaning might be obvious underneath it. Dooley was shaking hands with somebody.

Helen was pleading with me to take some medication. I complied because—because all was lost. Swallowing drugs without knowing what they are is not recommended, but in my mind, my life was over. Failure was stamped, branded with fire on my soul and continuing on would do more harm than good to Micah. She was still young enough to forget who I ever was.

As I was about to take the knife from Dooley, I was slam-tackled by a policeman and bundled up by paramedics. Where these men came from, I didn't know. Maybe they weren't real. I couldn't tell the difference any more.

Next thing I knew for sure was waking in seclusion, aching all over and with my shattered heart spiking me in the chest with triangular shards. The next level of consciousness revealed I was restrained, my wrists secured to the bed. Dooley was in the corner, laughing with his new friend. If Dooley was my shadow, his buddy was his shadow. In my mind I began to call him Shadow Man. He and Dooley both had a penchant for Goth's cloths of black. Rhyming brought a stupid grin to my face. Perhaps it was the medication. Thioridazine smile. Dooley, Drooly (me) and Shadow Man. I couldn't tell if I was drooling but it was possible, even probable.

'Hey?!' I called out toward the busy-ness of the nurses' station.

'You're awake then, Maddie?'

'Not all of the way.'

'Can I take the restraints off? Are you going to hurt yourself? You've got quite the black eye already.'

This news horrified me. What had I done?

'Did I hurt anybody?' I asked, very afraid I had. My voice sounded as if it was coming from elsewhere. I shook my head again. *Etch A Sketch.*

'No. No. Only yourself. So, the restraints? Do you promise not to hurt yourself?'

'I haven't got the energy.'

'You certainly burnt some calories yesterday,' the nurse said, unbuckling my wrist restraints.

Yesterday? Let's do the Time Warp again.

'It's just a jump to the left,' I said.

'Pardon?'

'What?' I waved my freed hands in front of my face. 'Are these mine? They don't feel like mine.'

How disciplined are psych nurses at not rolling their index finger clockwise around their ear (the universal sign for cuckoo) or sing-saying, 'woo-oo-oo;' in the manner of a clown's slide whistle going up and down a scale? Such control. You can say anything to a psych nurse without them batting an eye. Batting an eye? Is that right? Eye lid. Phrases were floating about, and I was trying to understand idiom while it tied my brain into knots. All the while I was endeavouring to reclaim my hands.

'Let's go and get some food and water into you before you're blown away by the next big wind.'

I liked the idea of being blown away by the next wind—riding each zephyr until death blew me to pieces like a tropical cyclone might. *The answer my friend* ... What is the answer? What's the question?

'Where's my daughter?' I asked. That was the question.

'She's gone up the coast with your Mum and step-dad.'

Step-dad surprised me. I wasn't used to seeing John that way. But, I guessed that buying an expensive property as a couple was a commitment as solid or as fragile as any marriage. Mum and John were in an allegiance of funds. That showed their confidence in the longevity of their commitment, financially at least.

I was both relieved and frightened Micah was safe. What if the happy couple wouldn't give her back? What if they spent their combined income in having the Courts find me useless as a mother?

'She's my daughter,' I said like a sulky teenager, to nobody.

'She's mine,' Dooley answered me, with cruelty.

I comforted myself. At least if the Shadow Man and Dooley are with me, they can't be anywhere near Micah.

CHAPTER 26

Readers of the Lost Dark

There were days of daze and then I began to seep into reality one bit at a time. It was horrible. Reality was horrible. Unreality wasn't that good, either. Whenever I thought I was gaining traction, I slipped into a bruising, confidence-dismantling fall. I wanted to hurt someone but the only person I didn't fear was myself. So, I took everything out on my self, I had the conversation with the she in my crowded head. *If you've been scheduled into a psych ward once, you might be able to fool yourself into thinking it was a one off. You're not mentally ill, you're just worn out. Denial is a friend. But when you've been scheduled twice it's time to start accepting that things might be more permanent. So, accept.*

I didn't want to accept. Many families have at least one member on the lunatic fringe. I didn't want to be that person. The one who nobody wants to sit next to at gatherings. The aunt who allowances have to made for. The one people speak to in exaggerated volume, because they think all disabilities need over-enunciation. Keep her away from the children, they say to each other at the table. They whisper about her. There might be another aunty the children are shepherded toward for a greeting. Kids would be distracted away from me by protective parents. I would become nothing more than the label affixed to me by doctors.

With one toe in reality, testing the waters, I was allowed to move into the open ward. Open but locked, nonetheless. The open part was the walled-in garden where I'd spent much time during my previous hospi-

143

talisation. There was a patch of sky above and if I laid on the grass, looking up, I could be free.

'Come in Maddie! It's raining,' a nurse yelled from the glass doors.

'It's okay, I'm waterproof.'

The look on the nurse's face, sent me scurrying inside for fear of being returned to seclusion.

'I'm compliant,' I said. 'Nobody's more compliant. It's a warm rain.
Refreshing. I thought it might wash off my sad mood.'

'Go and towel off,' the nurse ordered.

I complied, deciding to have a shower first, because I could think
for myself now. Wasn't rational autonomy the desired outcome of treatment? In my bathroom I'd wash off the sadness, as long as I could get
Dooley and the Shadow Man to keep out. It was too creepy when they
crowded in to the tiny space.

As I walked past the nurses' station, I saw a thumb tack on the floor
near their entry door. In an effort not to dive straight on it, I moved over
as if to get out of the way of pedestrian traffic and squatted down, feigning an adjustment to a shoe. It was empty of laces, so I played around
with the tongue, damp from the rain, grabbing and secreting my prize
with my other hand. I'd done it all before I knew the plan. As I continued toward my room, there grew an odd animation beneath the drug-
induced, thick molasses torpor that coated my being. In my hand was an
emergency exit.

It wasn't to be my death so much as a hope for some sort of rein-
carnation as a new flawless soul. When doctors typed more labels into
my records, they didn't consider the life sentence they were authorising.
Each diagnosis without excellent prognosis or complete cure told me I'd
reached 'as good as it gets.' It was nowhere near good enough. If this was
life now until death, it made sense to shift death closer and get it done.
Disappear before Micah had a chance to learn what a fucked-up unit I
was. Before she had time to look on me with fear, dissatisfaction, pity or
regard me as a heavy burden attached to her life.

There had been a time when I held potential in my hand rather than a thumb tack. But before I was barely alive, the possibility had been stolen. The little of me my uncle had left untouched had been further damaged by the rape— and what remained was of no use and had been rendered beyond fragile by brain chemistry gone awry. I loved my daughter so much it hurt, but if the meaning of my life was to give birth to her, I'd already fulfilled my destiny. In fact, I was gifted to have achieved the anticipated creation so early. There was nothing left for me to do. Apart from being tarred over and placed on a road as a speed-hump I had nothing additional to offer the world.

Missing Micah occupied my life, but would it occupy my death? In the end, there is only the end, I thought. It was annoying that people wouldn't be able to say, 'she died doing what she loved.' Nobody loves sitting in a shower fully clothed (I didn't want them to find me naked) hacking at their ankle with a thumb tack. I wasn't sure where the major artery was, but I thought I'd faint too soon if I hacked at my wrists and if my arm tired, I wouldn't be able to swap hands.

I missed any major vessels due to a lack of anatomical knowledge and the difficulty of gouging skin out with a tack. If persistence counted, I should have been dead. But I'd hewed in deep before my bathroom was stormed by the troops. They turned the water off and I watched my blood swirl down into the drain.

Safe travels, I told it.

'What the fuck, Maddie?!'

It was Helen's voice. Maybe not happy about having taken a day shift on the ward.

'Sorry,' I said. 'She knows not what she does, or at least how to do it.'

They wrestled the bloodied tack from my closed palm and a towel had been applied to the wound.

My resolve hadn't gone down the drain. I would bide my time and try again. If they ever let me out of seclusion.

A doctor was called to tend to my injury. He brought into the treatment room an air of anger. His already busy day had been interrupted by an insignificant 'cutter.' A nurse brought him everything he would need for sewing and left to help deal with some sort of hostile patient irruption near the TV. The doctor decided he didn't have time to mess about with local anaesthetics and he inserted nine stitches into my wound, each one more painful than the first. It was the treatment I deserved and I said nothing, holding screams inside myself until I felt my chest wall might rupture. They are inside still, those screams, and one day they might emerge. No, perhaps not. Maybe they've decayed within the essence of me, adding to my overall toxicity as a being.

I didn't see Helen again. She stayed in the open ward while I sat a dejected, sad little pile of excrement in high-dependency seclusion, wishing I'd found an important artery to sever. Sometimes sadness slips deeper, a dark, bleak hold takes your heart firm to the point where even your breath is shallow, without vitality. Depression was underlined in my list of ailments and I was fed more medication. Dooley and the Shadow Man sat on the floor, their conspiring quietened by my lacklustre imagination.

It was nearing two weeks I'd been away from Micah. Missing her was an ache that never let up. It also was my failure. If permission to die was denied, I had to get back to the thing I was able to do with some success—be Micah's mother. Nobody else could be more mother-y than her biological mother. It was decided somewhere within me, to pull it together.

Becoming together wasn't easy. The opposite of easy is hard. Oddly, the opposite of hard is soft. Depression is physically heavy; it's not for the soft. You have to be in strong shape to carry it with you and function at the same time. Extra strong shape. A triangle is a strong shape. Standing with my legs wide apart, I could manage a hint of triangular construct. Unfortunately, I wasn't a very hefty triangle. A pyramid would be better. My form needed bulk. I began to eat again.

Dooley and the Shadow Man rose to their feet, glad to be back to their regular undertakings. My phantom menaces began to discuss tactics to get to Micah. Grave diggers—whenever I tried to feel sane, they dug away solid ground from beneath me. It was like walking in a bouncy castle without the laughter.

'Fresh fruit, I need fresh fruit, please,' I said to the nearest nurse, ignoring the shadowy collaborators behind me.

CHAPTER 27

Inanimate Objections

There were ups and really downs. Being without Micah was an amputation. It left me limping. By ups I mean I was upright most of the day, rather than horizontal. Caught in lethargy, my mood remained low. Voices buzzed into my head, annoying as mosquitos in the night. I slapped at my face in a similar manner, when things grew too loud. My thoughts were like mice on an exercise wheel, doing a lot of moving, ticking over too fast to stop. Yet I remained in the same spot. Not quite stagnant. revolving in a pool of my own whirling noise. I sat at times with my hands over my ears even though logic told me the voices were coming from my own mind, not elsewhere. The unintentional ventriloquism was making me the dummy.

It was decided to try a different anti-psychotic, but it was necessary to be weaned off the usual ones first. The details of that process are not pretty. During the ugliness my ankle wound had to have a few new stitches in to replace the angry doctor's mediocre sewing. With some local anaesthetic that time. I had split his work open during a chair kicking fury. It was best for inanimate objects to keep well out of my way.

At last, after what seemed like years, I became constant in mood. Enough to be relocated back into the open ward, and to begin again, my attempt to be dead, or new and improved. The anti-depressants had kicked in and although I was down, I was not out enough to sustain a death wish—so new and improved could become my daily lived intention. Besides, the amount of medication I was on was a death in its own listless way. My personality was subdued, stolen, and I couldn't summon up the full-blown resentment I knew was down in me, deep.

Killing me softly, I sang in a mumbling, couldn't-be-bothered' kind of way.

'It's a shame,' I told the doctor. 'That nobody likes the real me.'

'What do you mean?'

'I'm not acceptable as myself, so I'm drugged into submission or this near-death experience.'

Before I heard any reply or reaction from the doctor, I walked out of the interview room, cracking my left shoulder on the door jamb as I passed.

'Sorry,' I said to the door post. 'I'm unbalanced.'

That was a belated attempt at making my peace with inanimate objects. I knew how they felt, now that I was their equivalent. Outside, I drooped under the big tree and melted into the midday heat.

'Don't let the sun get on you!' a nurse called from the doorway. They were always yelling at me from the doorway. 'The drugs you're on make you very photosensitive.'

'Of course, they do,' I said, the four words dripping acrimony. 'I've always been a bit sensitive about having my photo taken, anyway,' I added, in a struggle to strengthen my up and down sense of humour and clear away a spikey bitterness that I could taste.

'That's not what I meant,' called back the nurse.

'I know,' I said, without mustering the effort to be heard, and moving over in a show of compliance, to lie shaded by the tree.

My next plan was to sleep there until I was cured and ready to go home.

*

I could tell my plans were not always practical but I plotted anyway. If I took to my bed they would ramp up my depression treatment, perhaps offer electric shock, so bed wasn't an option to help put hours behind me. My melancholy, although ongoing and unpleasant, didn't require such powered management. In a psych ward environment it was more acceptable to sleep outside under a tree in daylight hours. Less so at night. I was forced indoors when it darkened. Dooley and the Shadow man followed but they were bored and tried to do things that might elicit a reaction from me. At dinner the two of them went around the tables sticking their fingers in other patients' food. Not very noir of the dark pair; I felt no such cheekiness. I couldn't understand/capture/ their motive and it was difficult to ignore the behaviour. They scared me. If their operating system was coming from my mind, why didn't I have a clue? Had I built some sort of artificial intelligence into Dooley and the Shadow Man allowing them self-government? If I'd lost control, they might be able to get to Micah without me.

When the pair weren't in my room the next morning, I panicked. They'd found a way to get to Micah. My heart palpitated to the point of audible and its thumping took my breath away.

Dooley and the Shadow Man weren't outside, either. I paced around the quadrangle, expletives flying. It was a beautiful day outside of me. Inside was dark turmoil. On the boil turmoil. *Shut up, you insane piece of shit.*

I didn't realise I'd said that aloud until, Jim, a male nurse with a Kings Cross bouncer's build tapped me on the shoulder.

'Madison?'

'I need to ring my Mum. It's an emergency.'

'You can use the patients' phone.'

'I don't have any money.'

'Here.' He pulled some coins from his pocket and offered them to me.

'I'll pay you back, Jim. Honest.'

There was a woman on the phone. I paced in a small circle near her. She'd have to be blind not to realise I wanted to use the phone.

'Hang on,' she said into the receiver. 'There's a weirdo hovering. Do you mind giving me some space?' she asked me.

'Could I just use the phone for one minute, please? It's kind of an emergency.'

'I'm talking to—'

'Please? I need to ring—'

'Sorry,' she said again into the receiver. 'I can't hear you over this fucktard beside me. Where were we? Then, he said...'

I pressed down the doo-dad that cuts off the call.

*

When I woke up, I was in the treatment room with folded gauze taped over my right eye. Jim was there, and Helen.

'What happened?' I asked.

'Jenny happened. She hit you with the phone.'

That reminded me of my need to call my Mum.

'I just wanted ring my Mum to make sure Micah's okay,' I said, my panic re-growing.

'You're going to have to get a stitch or two over your eye,' Jim told me.

'Here,' Helen said and passed me her mobile phone.

'I don't know the number.'

Helen took the phone back and scrolled through her contacts, pressing call when she reached Abigail Kitchener, before handing me the phone.

'Hey Mum, it's Maddie. Is Micah okay?'

'Of course, she is. Why wouldn't she be? And hello to you, too.'

'Is she awake?'

'Yes.'

'Can I talk to her?'

'I suppose so. Although, she's not saying much, given she's only a few months old'.

'I know, Mum.' My heart was slowing down. 'I just need to be near her, to hear her.'

My mother put the phone next to Micah's ear and I heard her little baby breaths.

'Hey, my little baby. I miss you. I love you,' I said and began to cry, rendering further speech useless.

Helen took back the phone and spoke to Micah too, before asking for Abigail. There was a short exchange and Helen put her phone in her pocket.

'Micah's more than okay,' Helen reassured me. 'Now what's this all about?'

We were interrupted by the on-call doctor's arrival. Thank goodness it wasn't Angry Doctor. This time a proper local anaesthetic was administered before three stitches were sewn into my eyebrow. All the while I was feeling jealous that Helen had eased into my other world, that my mother's number was now in her phone. Paranoia trickled into my already crowded mind. There was discomfort with the notion that people were talking behind my back. Discussing me without me. How rude.

Helen found me later in the garden.

'So?' she said, in an ask-y way.

'So, what?'

'Are you going to tell me what this morning was all about? We've got to fill an incident report and whatnot.'

'I asked to use the phone. Jenny said no, in her own way.'

'What was the emergency?'

I knew the words were going to sound ridiculous, but I said them in the best way workable.

'My ... um ... visions ... left. Were gone this morning. I was frightened for Micah's safety. They've been threatening her since before she was born.'

'You realise it's a good sign that they're gone?'

'No.'

'Of course, it is! It means the medication's working.' She turned, ready to go back into the building, hands in her pockets. 'Now, I have to get back in to fill out accident and incident reports. You must let me, or any nurse know if you develop a headache or vision disturbances. We can't rule out a head injury after the thump you took, and you lost consciousness as well. Please take it easy this arvo. And maybe steer clear of Jennifer.'

'Vision disturbances are a constant in my life.'

'I meant blurred or double vision or dark spots. Not your beasties.'

My beasties.

I smiled. 'Beasties' took much of the dark brothers' fear factor away. Although, I remained uncertain if their absence was not them making their way to the coast to find and take Micah from me. It took an average of two hours to drive there. I didn't know by what means my beasties travelled, so I decided to ring my mother again in two and a half hours to check on Mikey. As long as Jenny was not on the phone again. Two and a half hours was ample time, unless the beasties were forced to walk or float in a breeze or something.

It felt bizarre to look up and not see Dooley and the Shadow Man skulking about on my horizon. Their absence was both good and bad. I knew it'd take me a while to adjust. My uneasiness bothered me, but I watched the clock. Vision disturbances. Where had all my beasties gone? Long-time passing. Two and a half hours of it.

CHAPTER 28

Nobody Should Be Afraid
of Optimism

This time my discharge came a panic-inducing week before Christmas.

'You may as well come straight up to us,' my mother suggested when I talked to her on the phone.

Way to trigger my suicidal ideation, Mum.

The trouble was the suggestion made sense. Micah was there already. When I hung up the phone, I turned to see Jenny waiting. My flinch was reflex.

'Sorry,' she said. 'I over-reacted. You know? That time?'

'So did I,' I replied, rubbing my eyebrow scar in a way I hoped made me look thoughtful, even though my mind was drugged to emptiness. 'Have a nice Christmas,' I said. It was a stupid thing to say— Jenny wasn't allowed out. I walked away before I said anything else idiotic.

The longest part of release was waiting for medications, prescriptions and the slow wheels of bureaucracy to rotate as far as opening the door. A point was reached where I'd think it was never going to happen and next minute I'd be on the footpath outside with a plastic bag or two full of my crap and my heart filled with fear.

At the train station there was a short wait for the coastal train. I sat in bewildered disarray. In the psych ward patients can't wait for liberty; the build-up is intense. Once freedom arrives it's very disconcerting. Did I have 'just released' written on my world-weary face? I'd already stood in front of the hole in the wall like a goose, trying to remember my bank PIN so I could withdraw enough money for my trip. In the end I had closed my eyes and let my fingers punch in the numbers. They had better recall and the cash spat out, feeling strange in my hand. There was a jagged alienation from reality after more than three months in an institutionalised environment. I wobbled as if I were just off a yacht after weeks at sea. Solid land didn't feel solid.

The world was a loud place. The train squealing to a halt at the platform did my head in. A window seat on-board was vacant but it caused me to spend the bulk of the trip being afraid somebody might sit next to me and I'd be trapped. Once the train reached Hornsby I relaxed a little. People didn't often join the train trip beyond the city's edge.

I was lulled a bit by the rhythm of the train, the rock, the roll, to be startled by the announcements over the PA system. My nerves were jangling by the time I reached the destination, where the train terminated, ready to turn around and go back to the big city. There was my mother waiting by the exit barriers. Alone.

'No Micah?' I asked, knowing her absence was obvious.

'I thought it'd be easier to leave her at home with John.'

It was an agonising fifteen-minute drive to the house. Neither of us attempted conversation. John greeted me with his signature crushing hug and I thought I might snap in two before he released me.

'Where's Mikey?' I asked as soon as I had enough air back in my hugged-out lungs.

'Nursery,' John said, handing me the baby monitor.

I rushed in. My baby was sleeping. Micah looked so like herself that I began to cry for the want to hold her to myself, to my heart. I missed my baby so, even though she was right there.

'Go on,' my Mum said. 'Pick her up. You know you want to. If you wake her, you wake her.'

As I leant over Micah's eyes opened. I swear she smiled.

'Hey, baby,' I said, tears still sliding.

*

There were a few firsts ahead. Micah's first Christmas. My first Christmas with John's family, as well. The first time I went to a shopping maul—sorry, mall. Some people live to shop, I would rather have died. Starting my Christmas shopping on the third last day before Christmas was awful. The sights, the sounds, the horror. I was no Ebenezer Scrooge, but I found myself missing the organised uncomplicated life of the psych ward. That told me I was even crazier than I'd thought. Mental. I was freaked by the label but realised it wasn't the ward I missed, but the insular security, not to be confused with selfish life. I knew I could get that sanctuary at my own flat, as well. I just had to survive the crowded days of Christmas.

My mother had gone into super-hostess mode and I became her unwilling but compliant assistant. I wasn't proud of the tactic but I used alcohol as a buffer. John was on summer break and holidays meant drinking could start at lunch time—if there was a certainty that driving for the day was over. It was wrong, very wrong, to mix alcohol with the potions prescribed to me, but I was drowning while pretending to wave. Survival was all I hoped for while crossing days off an imaginary calendar until I could take my baby and go to my own place and see what it was like to be me again.

The Christmas upsurge wasn't all bad. There were times Micah and I escaped to the water, weighted down by our sun-sensitive attire. I could get lost in the blue and ignore life for a while—sometimes minutes. My Mum took to hanging a big red towel over the balcony rail when she wanted me back at the house. Any red towel became the signal of feeling summoned. No matter whose house or hotel I was in.

I held up for the duration. Christmas morning, I met John's children. I met my brother's wife for the first time. She was heavy with child and was missing alcohol. This activated much empathy from me. I made her mocktails and she got mock-plastered from the sugar, while I took the edge off my nerves with a few beers.

I found John's six adult children intimidating; but my fear of everything was well enough documented. They were large, boisterous and had opinions—three features I lacked. Beside them, I was a minute bundle of deficiencies. It was useful that I had hostess assistant's duties and cleaning to throw myself into. I was already used to finding myself in the kitchen at parties. Micah was most excellent at being the centre of attention and I was pleased to be planted as a wallflower. The food was excellent and abundant, almost to the point of decadence. The weather was hot and stereotypical of an Australian Christmas. After so long inactive, I was exhausted by three in the afternoon and instead of putting Micah in her room, I settled her in my bed and we both had an afternoon nap.

Stillness wrapped me in disquiet when I rose. There was a post-apocalyptic quiet about, and as I carried an alert Micah into the empty kitchen I called a gentle 'hello?' Nobody echoed. The house, aside from Micah and me was a large emptiness. After some aimless wandering through empty rooms, I found a note on the refrigerator letting me know that Mum and John had gone to a neighbour's house for drinks and nibbles. That surprised me. My mother hadn't been one for neighbourhood friendships.

That part of the day was how I liked Christmas. Festivities over, when all was done, relaxing was a sanctioned activity and I could survive on the debris of the lunch table for days. While Micah's bottle heated, I grabbed some leftovers from the fridge and made up a small plate to take out onto the veranda for dinner. I was surprised by how hungry I felt, given the amount of food I'd packed in over lunch.

As I sat out in the warm evening, my mother's laughter floated on the air from next door's open window, over the fence and landed near me. I hadn't heard that in a very long time, a musical lightness absent for many years. It gave me a sense of peace and optimism.

And that scared me.

CHAPTER 29

The 5 Rights to Happiness

As Told by an Uneducated One

Micah's first Christmas was done. I was done, or undone. Mum drove us back to Sydney because Micah had scored big time from Santa. I stared out of the window in a post-Christmas daze. My interior landscape remained a disaster zone. I groped about, disliking the unpractised feel I had about life since my autonomy had been handed back on discharge from the hospital. Self-rule atrophy left me second-guessing all decision making. Being in charge again made me, if it were possible, more uncomfortable in my own skin, not less.

Blundering about as if it were the first day of a new job, I couldn't find anything in my own kitchen. I couldn't so little as decide what to have for lunch.

I was relieved to be in my own space again. Instead of acting like myself, I could be my-self— or as self as I could be. Selfish. Self-ish. It took Micah and I a few days to remaster a routine that was suitable for a lone adult with a baby.

Just as I began to feel like I was home, not just at home, I received a phone call from Dad. He needed to come to Sydney for some vascular surgery. Could I put him up while he recovered enough to travel home? Feeling guilty about little acknowledgment over Christmas, I agreed straight away.

'Sure. No problem. I can put you up, but I'd never put you down. That's a job for a good veterinarian.'

As I hung up the phone, it occurred to me I'd grown up. I was now going to look after my father. Not vice versa. He should hope I did a better job than he'd managed with me, I told myself as I prepared Micah's bottles for the day. As a caring man, my father didn't like to force himself upon Matthew and his wife because, you know, he'd muttered, they had lives and a baby on the way. And a spare room, I'd added in my head—but said nothing.

As a fledgling but reluctant martyr, I would give up my bedroom and bed down on the sofa for the duration. I washed the linen and made drawer space in preparation for my Dad's recuperation.

'S'pose Dad will want to be fed, watered and amused,' I said in conversation with Micah.

My father had not eaten an instant noodle in his entire life. He was a leftover from the meat and three veg days.

I settled Micah into her pram for a voyage to the supermarket. The stretch spent in hospital had provided time for my bank balance to build up a little and even after Christmas, I had enough funds for one hundred dollars' worth of sustenance, plus home delivery. Somebody else could do the struggle up the stairs with the load. I tried to buy light things but gave up and bought kilos of potatoes. We would have them boiled, roasted, mashed. We would have them sliced in a cheese sauce, gratin style. We could have them ... *Oh, do shut up.*

Because Dad had sold his old car when he moved north west, needing funds while awaiting his superannuation payout, train was his mode of transport for the nine-hour voyage to the North Shore. He would travel straight to the hospital and I would visit him there until his surgery and subsequent release. Although I lived in a suburb of Sydney, getting from one end of the sprawl of the city to the other with a baby was not easy. Each step brought me closer to my disinclined martyrdom goals. Gaols. Martyrdom could be my gaol, if I let it stifle me. This martyrdom of mine hadn't come with resentment, but it had come with a type of exhaustion that made my legs sluggish.

'Is this the Continental Shelf?' I asked the food-stacking staff member at the supermarket. He was standing in front of soups. It was a question I raised for self-amusement, for my tired-out sense of humour. The look I was given by the teenaged packer person I would file under dead-inside in the pictorial dictionary of emotive faces.

'What?' he asked, unamused by geological punning.

'Nothing,' I muttered, disappointed by my poor audience.

I pushed the trolley past him and stopped speaking to staff members.

When considering food for other people, I found it funny how much more effort I put into choices. It took me far longer than usual to reach the check-out. Very surprising to see the sun still out when I reached the outdoor brightness. Turned out it was midday and baking hot, not midnight after what seemed like a whole day nomadic in the aisles. I walked the many blocks home, sweating out half my weight on the way, while trying not to go barking mad. Arrived, in one arm I held Micah while I dragged her pram behind me up all of the stairs to our flat. The groceries had beaten me home and I was excited and relieved to see the bags stacked at the door. I wanted to lie on the floor with them, but the ice cream was still near solid. I threw frozen food into the freezer and cold stuff into the fridge all willy-nilly. Micah was demanding a drink in quite a vocal manner. It was imperative I quieten her down before her mother's head exploded. As a single parent without staff, I would have to clean up the brains if my head did explode. I wasn't up for that.

We both fell asleep during the feed and I woke up all murky and deranged. Once I'd rearranged myself into human, I packed away the rest of the groceries and flopped on the sofa a.k.a. my soon-to-be bed, to prepare for a late afternoon cleaning spree. The place hadn't been cleaned since I'd been in hospital and the grime had dust on it. Dad wouldn't be judgemental, but that didn't matter. I was judgy enough for both of us.

It was a three-beer clean-up and in my defence, it was very, very hot. I peed or sweated out the beer before it had a chance to impair anything, although I felt less inclined to be critical by the last beer and decided washing out the range hood filter could wait until another day. That's how reckless I became on three beers.

The next morning, I began preparing for our first trip to Royal North Shore Hospital. It took more planning than a trip to the coast to see Mum. A couple of trains. Then walking around in small circles until I worked out which direction to go from the station. Three bottles in a thermos carrier for Micah. A bottle of beer for me. Kidding. Although, I wished. Trying to find the right ward. Hating hospitals. It was all energy consuming.

'Hi, Dad,' I said after the three-hour adventure to get me to his bedside.

'What are you doing here?'

'Just happened to be in the area. What do you mean, 'what am I doing here?' I'm visiting you.'

'I said not to worry about that until it was time for my release.'

'Here's some chocolates and fruit,' I said, feeling the disappointment that my mammoth effort was unappreciated after I'd just spent time on a train with a crying baby and frowning co-passengers.

I plopped down on one of those vinyl hospital chairs that are never as comfortable as they look. Dad's carotid endarterectomy was scheduled for the next day. He didn't seem to know much about the procedure and didn't appear to care enough to find out. I took my cue from his nonchalance and burbled on about nothing, until boredom attacked my attention-deficit mind. It hadn't taken long.

'I guess I'd better get going before the commuters take over the trains. See you tomorrow,' I said, trying to act like I'd rather stay.

'Don't come. I'll be unconscious most of the day, anyhow.'

I couldn't gauge if this was martyrdom or truth.

'We'll see,' I said and kissed him on the head, hoping next time I saw him, he wouldn't be dead. There's a limerick in there somewhere I thought but shushed my restless brain.

The two trains and the walk home from the station did Micah's head in too and she was screaming like a cat with its tail caught in a closed door, by the time we arrived home three hours later, hangry and done in.

When I'd fed her, the world was a much quieter place and she was content to roll about in her play-pen. I took the hush time to do a quick stocktake of my purse. Thirty-five cents. There's nothing like an empty purse to knock any feeling of adequacy from anyone's self-esteem, mine included. Poverty, like insanity, takes away the right to happiness. In an unwritten book I carried around in my head, a human had five rights that form overall happiness. They are the right to:

1. Considerate parenting (especially during the first years of life)
2. An income enough to sustain
3. A sane mind
4. A healthy body
5. Love, as in giving and receiving

I'd thought up an addendum to Number 3. In addition to the right, we should have the power to say no. Healthy self-esteem is part of sanity. My lack of it had handed me a false understanding—that I didn't have the right to say no. To anything. With each withdrawal of one of the five, the ability to be happy diminished as far as I knew.

For the time being, I was living on the giving half of Number 5. Too late for Number 1. Numbers 3 and 4 came and went as if they were tidal.

And Number 2? Not having $2.50 for a train fare made me feel physically and mentally ill.

'Fuck,' I said.

Micah looked at me. Seemed it was time I began to swear less. My baby might not understand the word, but the tone had prompted a reaction. Her bottom lip trembled, and her little face crumpled. I held her and patted her back. Slumping again on the sofa I calculated Micah's rights to happiness using my fictional order of requirements guideline. Three out of five would be good, if that's what I could achieve for her— but it would not be enough. I wanted the best for my daughter.

'I must get a job,' I told Micah, showing her the almost empty purse. 'You deserve the best.'

The next half hour was spent searching for $2.15, in and under things, to make up enough for a train fare. Shrapnel gathering is a common activity for people without Number 2 on my list of rights to happiness. The unhappy also take to spreading coinage about the house when we do have it, so there can be successful shrapnel gatherings in the future.

CHAPTER 30

Balcony

The surgery was successful. They cut Dad's throat from ear-to-ear and spent much time scraping out mucky plaque. Plaque is full of fat, cholesterol and other gunk that clogs up an artery. It's not the type of plaque on which a commemoration might be inscribed before affixing it to a wall. Don't ask a doctor what was written on the plaque. He looked at me with one finger on the security button.

Because of the distance Dad had travelled for the surgery, he was given a regional patients' type of stipend that could be used for a taxi from the hospital to his place of recuperation. This was fortunate, because Dad's skin sallowness gave him a look of near-death, and I didn't want to be on a train with him and a baby if he chose that moment to terminate. I wanted the taxi-driver to be top-of-the-class proficient at C.P.R.

Life-saving procedures weren't necessary. When it came to the stairs at the flat, I don't know who needed the pram most, but after some rest stops Dad and Micah were inside Number 4 and in their respective beds. This gave me a few minutes alone to bring my anxiety to a manageable mass of mess. Helen, wearing her Home Base Treatment Team badge, was supposed to drop in later and I telephoned her to say it'd be best if I just rang her each day until Dad went back to beyond. Avoiding a visit wasn't because of discomfort about being mental, but more so my awkwardness about letting Dad see me receiving treatment for my illness. I was able apply 'mental' to myself, but nobody else should. I say the words with gentle understanding.

As hostess, I went into my room to give Dad a cup of tea. He was gone. Not dead, just missing.

'Dad?'

The smell of smoke wafted in from the balcony and I found my father out there, having a cigarette. The balcony was bleak. After Micah's birth, I'd had a dreadful feeling that she would develop climbing ability before anything else, but still topple over the top and plummet. I hadn't been out on the balcony since.

'You ought to get yourself some outdoor furniture. It's nice out here,' my father said to me when I'd return from the kitchen with a chair for him to sit in comfort while ruining his health further.

'And you ought to give up smoking,' I said.

'Yeah, I will. One day. It's pretty easy. I've done it many, many times.'

'I've done it three times,' I told Dad.

The last time seems to have stuck. There are no cravings. But I still smoke in my dreams. Weird, eh? I get the best of both worlds. But in the real world, the smell made me feel a bit green.

'Nothing worse than a reformed smoker.'

'Paedophiles.'

'What?'

'Paedophiles. They're worse than a reformed smoker.'

'You got me there.'

We fell silent.

Then we fell further.

'I'm sorry,' Dad said.

'What for?'

'I think I walked in on my brother molesting you.'

I fell deep and hard.

'What do you mean?' I managed to ask.

'I'm sorry. I was drunk. I didn't know if I'd seen right. I just left you there, in the garage.'

My father began to cry.

I walked back inside. Dooley was in the kitchen. I didn't care. Micah was still asleep. With care, I transferred her into her pram and wheeled her into the bathroom, where I undressed and sat in a warm shower for a very long time. For part of it I was back in that garage. For part of it I was in the now, scrubbing the past off me with a soapy nail brush until my skin bled.

There was a passive knock on the bathroom door.

'Are you all right?' my Dad called through my nightmare and right through to the auto pilot operator who had taken me over to help me function.

'Just washing my hair,' called the operator, via my mouth. 'You should be in bed. I'll start dinner when I get out.'

'Okay.'

I heard Dad shuffle back to bed. Micah began to stir. My heart did rend, but I pulled it back together and turned off the water. There was no place to put my mix of feelings, except inside myself.

'Hey, baby,' I said to Micah and soaking wet, I hugged her to myself and tried to be anything but anger.

Anger aside. I had to put anger aside and tend to the ill old man, with his throat already cut, and a death pallor to his complexion. He needed food and caring.

'I hope you're back in bed,' I called, as I carried Micah to her playpen and prepared to prepare dinner.

My need for beer was immense, but this new knowledge of my father drunk, leaving the child me, undefended amid brutality, untidied my mind. Would having a beer in some way be hypocritical?

'I don't care,' I said, taking out a beer, drinking most of it in the first guzzle, standing in front of the opened refrigerator.

Dooley had departed, his brief visitation leaving extra unease. Something was building. Something unpleasant and almost too real. Although there was no time to delve into matters of the past, what with potatoes to peel. My anger had to be put away, stored until I could examine it later. If I was going to be angry, I had to know what I was angry about.

Without the rage showing, although I carried it with me, I cooked dinner, had a meal with my Dad and sent him back to bed. Once Micah had drunk her final bottle for the night, I spread along the sofa, alone, with horrible flashes of the past flicking at me. I was prepared to deal with them but again and again rushed my thoughts away to somewhere benign.

It had been betrayal, I thought, that had scorched my reminiscence and added heat to my anger when hearing my father's tearful apology. The idea that he had not intervened at a time that might have been enough to save my childhood, just ... just made me want to ... just. Tears ran down my cheeks although I couldn't feel the hurt. It was too big to let loose. How could a father turn his back on a child in trouble? His child! Even if he thought his befuddled, drunken mind was playing tricks, couldn't he ... couldn't he have fought, for me, for my innocence? Couldn't he have rescued me from ... from what? Damn it, I couldn't remember everything. But I knew it had been something horrific and I knew it had become an annual ... fucking. An annual holiday fucking.

The memory was so close, I was scared again and I wrapped myself in my sheet, even though the night was hot. And I tried to be unafraid. I was a grown up now. An adult. A mother. A mother who would go into battle for her child. Die for her child. Not walk away, drenched in alcohol to let her child move broken into adulthood.

I asked myself a whole gazette of questions, lying there on my sofa. Is it better or worse to remember? To relive? To feel somatically your recollected pain? To experience the giant aloneness again? The hurting, which has gradually morphed over your lifetime to this point, into a crushing sense of worthlessness?

My questions were with me throughout the long night.

After intermittent sleep, I woke before Micah and put on some coffee. A pot full. Lack of sleep had me feeling ill, but it would wear off, unlike the sadness. For my father, I didn't have the energy to re-muster any anger. The remnant, vague sadness plus indifference, were contrived, I supposed, to keep me from telling a frail man that his drinking had damaged me more than it had harmed him. Frail man, my father. Too frail for the truth. I heard him rise, slide open the door to the balcony and begin the cough triggered by his first cigarette of the day. Then I heard him talking. To himself?

I began to prepare a breakfast.

Dad came into the kitchen smelling of cigarette and illness.

'That neighbour, her of the next balcony, here's me with my throat cut, barely alive and she bangs on about her long list of ailments like it's a competition. You'd have to be dead to beat her.'

'I've never met her,' I said. 'One egg or two?'

I was back in that garage.

'

Are you okay?'

'What? Yes. What was I saying?'

'Nothing, I was telling you that I've booked a train for Thursday.'

'Oh. All right. Do you think you're well enough to travel?'

'I haven't felt this good for yonks. Amazing what a bit of oxygen to the brain can do.'

*

I waved my father off at the train station that busy Thursday morning. Every Sunday I would talk to him on the phone (without speaking truths) but I would never see him again.

I wished we'd been more.

CHAPTER 31

Mopping Up

Happily, the next few weeks after Dad's visit were humdrum. I knew from watching others in the psych ward that Adrenalin junkies—people who filled their lives with noise, would call those steady weeks boring. For me, boring was a life goal. I pursued boring, was happy to lie in it and let the ennui fairy dust pattern of it/tranquillity of it wash over me like a gentle rain. When life was monotonous, it meant that nothing was going on. Going wrong. No crises. No issues. No issues, no tissues. No tissues, no cry.

But I knew to never let my mind know that there was space left blank. My mind adored a vacuum. It created/left/opened up extra room to fill with chaos—like a spare room designated for guests but instead it is crammed with excess stuff until there is no place for people. I began to fill my unused head space with grief. My father's docility had caused my heart's death. I could never become the person I could have been; she died under my uncle. I was the detritus of my gone self.

I did not wish to reflect on this, but my father's confession and its outcome plagued my thinking.

Who might I have been without the damage?

I did not wish to think about this.

But I did.

I grieved for my lost self, in the boring days where there was an empty room in my head.

169

I grieved until I became used to it, as if it were a wart on my hand. It was fresh and I was raw, and my sorrow stung like lemon juice in a scratch. A sad realisation grew. I was too passive to ever let my father know how much hurt remained beneath my surface. Passivity in my case was genetic, or had become so ingrained it was irreversible. Genetic. Generic. Generous serve. Same Same.

I knew that if I ever caught anybody assaulting Micah, I would kill them. Or try to. I would not creep away and pretend nothing had happened. A lioness lived within me.

I also came to know, in those weeks, that I could not hate my father. I sensed my way forward might have been simpler if I could, but -?? it seemed a waste of my energy/I thought of him more as weak and lost in his alcoholic fug. I had not hate left for him.

After his death, someone said, 'Peter'd give you the shirt off his back. Never do a thing to harm anybody.'

They were right. It was his not doing that did the damage.

I forgave myself It was of no use to burden others with the unchangeable. Not my Dad, not anyone. I knew what had happened. I also knew what hadn't happened. None of it could be altered. Damage control. *Wipe that hurt off your face and move on.*

I grieved still.

Too still.

'Let's go for a walk, Mikey. I have to move.'

*

A new year had begun. It was an appropriate time to let bygones be goodbye-gones. A bright new calendar—unblemished weeks, spotless days ahead. I wanted a fine year, one not rotten beneath its unspoiled skin. I might find a job, I told myself. *Part-time at first.*

Micah smiled up at me from the pram as I headed toward the front door and I wondered if I could ever leave her with strangers, even for a few hours while I was gainfully employed. My mind registered maternal guilt, thinking about placing Micah in child-care.

As I opened the front door to escape my own thinking, I walked into Helen.

'Did you forget I was coming?' she asked. 'Or, were you trying to flee before you saw me?'

'The first. Sorry.'

I reversed back into my flat and put the kettle on, while Helen had a chat with Micah.

'How's Mum been?' she asked the baby.

'Micah's been sworn to secrecy,' I said when my daughter failed to speak—as I'd learned babies tend to do.

'How was your father's visit? Really, how was it?' Helen asked, turning to me. At that very second I spilt her coffee on the carpet during a slight stumble.

'That kind of sums it up,' I said returning to the kitchen for a cloth. 'There was spillage and mopping up'.

The carpet was a vague coffee colour anyway, so the damage was minimal. I cleaned it up and made Helen a coffee of the un-spilt sort.

Helen wasn't going to leave the enquiry unanswered. 'What happened?' she asked again, when I'd settled into a chair opposite her, with a coffee of my own.

The silence while trying to formulate an answer that didn't trigger me into childhood remembrances was long enough for Helen to say, 'Something happened, didn't it.'

I wanted to tell her, but didn't want to tell her, at the same time. It was too harsh to just blurt, 'According to my father, he walked in on my uncle molesting me and walked straight out again without doing a thing.' It would be awful to even form those words. To say them. To hear them. To make them existent.

'No,' I said, not from rudeness but from lack of ability.

'I'm calling B.S,' Helen responded.

'That's the right call, but I'm not sure I'm ready to talk.'

'Come on now, you're a jittery coffee-spilling mess. Are you sure you should keep what's upsetting you inside?'

'Sometimes talking about stuff kind of stops the processing and it becomes another not-quite resolved thing. I'm still brooding about it. If I talk about it now, and if you have an opinion, I'll take it on as mine. I'm a feelings plagiarist.'

'I won't have an opinion. I'll just listen.'

'And not react? Because I'll assume your reaction is the right way to react and I'm doing it wrong.'

'Goodness, you're bloody hard work,' Helen said with half a smile. 'But if you're not ready to discuss it, you're not ready.'

'I don't know what I am. Anyway, Dad's visit was nice enough. He was always chatting to the neighbours here and I'm barely past nodding at them.'

'Okay. We'll leave it at that till you're ready. By the way, here's a new referral to a psychiatrist for you. She's new to the area—has a good reputation and is taking on new clients, although I think I'm supposed to say customers now. P.C. muck. I've made an appointment for you on Wednesday. If you like her, we'll send your hospital notes on.'

'What's her name?'

'Doctor Vivian Brooker.'

'Thank goodness. I can deal with a name that doesn't sound like food.'

'You do realise my surname's Tucker, don't you?' Helen asked.

I laughed. 'No!'

'As a rule, mental health care workers don't share their surnames with patients, clients, customers, consumers, crazy folk, in case stalking becomes an issue.'

'Will I have to speak to her straight up?'

'No, Doctor Brooker will be happy just to gawp at you for an hour week after week, for bucket loads of money. Of course, you'll have to speak to her! The first session will be office work— questionnaires and details. If you're lucky you'll just have to say hello and the rest of the hour will be filled with procedural things. Name. Address. Phone number etcetera. You can ease into stuff when you work up some trust.'

'I guess it won't kill me.'

'It shouldn't. Questions will be asked if it does.'

'What about cost?'

'Medicare should cover most of it. That'll be discussed on Wednesday, too ... Look at the clock! I best be off.'

'If you haven't got time for the rest of that coffee, just throw it over the carpet.'

Helen gave a laugh and gulped down the last of her drink, taking her cup back to the kitchen sink before saying goodbye to Micah.

'Bye, bye, best baby girl ever,' she said, and my heart swelled a little with a happy lump of pride, even though Micah's latest nocturnal habits were leaving me sleep deprived.

*

After Helen left, I did some over-thinking. Was I right to be hurt now by my father's inaction two decades ago? Should I blame the alcohol and forgive the drunk? Did there exist a correlation between my mental illness now and the childhood trauma, or would I have been a fucked unit whether incest had happened or not? Chicken and egg stuff went back and forth in my brain without scrambling or poaching or forming anything solid. I figured it might all be about the egg. I'd been broken from day one. A damaged egg. In the interest of minding my eggshell-thin self-esteem, I didn't go as far as to label myself a rotten egg. But chefs know, adding an off egg to anything ruins the whole feast. Could I have been repaired earlier, I asked myself? If my father had said anything, intervened, rescued me, slain the dragon, would I have recovered?

Should I still go for that walk? The one question I could answer with a definitive yes, was the last. But

the best baby girl ever began to cry, and the walk was postponed until such time as she was fed and in a fresh nappy, plus a clean spit-up-free pink singlet. It was too hot to be dressed in anything more. I'd have been happy to walk about in such a minimalist outfit myself but remained in shorts and a lose T-shirt. For our refreshment, I packed a bottle of water with a teat on top and one without. I shrouded the pram with a light sheet, less the sun dared attempt to fry my baby, and off we went. It felt okay to have no destination in mind. Although sometimes, I wished I had an end point. It gave purpose.

After a good airing out in the world and a five-kilometre hike, I returned to Number Four—I still couldn't call it 'home'—having resolved to go back to school.

'For some book learning,' I told Micah.

She slept on, oblivious to my momentous decision.

CHAPTER 32

Exits

It was suddenly May. Not many days after I had a triumphant battle in cyberspace and won over the frozen-screen-syndrome of my new second hand state-of-the-arctic desktop computer, to enrol in an online course aimed at acquiring university entrance, my phone awoke shrieking on the bedside table. It was blinking my brother's number, frantic in the half-light of dawn.

'Hello Matthew,' I answered, my heart rapid from the vicious awakening.

'Dad's dead,' he said, without softening the blow in any way.

'Shit,' I replied, not as an expletive, more as a sweary 'oh, no.'

Somehow, Micah was delivered to Mum's and before I had time to gather myself, Matthew and I were sitting on a small plane heading north west. It wasn't a shock. My father had seemed near death as long as I could remember. Either his heart or asthma or pneumonia or ... the list of ailments was extensive, and his main occupation had become sitting in his doctor's waiting room. But I was surprised that he'd actually done it.

Died.

Matthew and I vanished Dad off the Earth, except for one small plot of land in the cemetery. We made his possessions disappear, aside from a few keepsakes. I even cleaned the last of his bodily fluids from the bathroom floor, where he had dropped suddenly and so finally. It was sad to bring our father to almost nothing. There was so very little to show for his concrete existence. He had left his mark in DNA, is all. It was nice that Micah had a little share.

After emptying the bed-sit and scouring it clean, Matt and I closed the door on that little Housing Commission flat and would not have been surprised if somebody moved in before we'd left town. The local charity shop truck drove away with most of my Dad's chattels and furniture inside. I felt the whole thing as a brutal erasure, but what else could we do? At least his clothing and furnishings would help any locals down on their luck. They had it all, except Dad's best suit. That would be going with him.

Matthew and I shared a motel room on the other side of town from Dad's empty bedsit. Arranging the funeral was amusing, from a gallows humour approach. The address of the funeral parlour led us to the door of the local hardware store on the main street.

'This can't be right,' Matthew said, but we walked in anyway.

'Can I help you?' asked a man standing at the cash register.

'We're looking for the funeral parlour. Is it near here?' asked Matthew.

'You'll be wanting Normie, then,' said the man. I'll get him.

'What?' I whispered. Where...

A tall man strode toward us, looking sombre, except for the cheerful badge he was wearing. 'Hi, I'm Normie. Deacon's Hardware.'

Normie saw me staring at his name badge and slipped it off.

'If you'll just follow me,' he said.

There was a room out the back. Funeral Directing was the focus in there, although there was a bit of spill over from excess hardware stock scattered about. We discussed coffins and other arrangements. Matthew would return later with the suit and a few odds and ends to put in the pockets. A photo of Micah and Jo, Matthew's first-born. Some coins, you know, in case. ID, also in case.

'Would you like to see Pete, er, your father? He's at the hospital.'

'No, thanks,' Matt and I said at the same time.

'We'd like to remember him as he was,' Matthew added.

We both erupted into a nervous tainted laughter, once we were outside the hardware store, half an hour later. All of the funeral arrangements had been agreed upon with 'Hi, I'm Normie.'

'That was surreal,' Matt said on recovering some decorum.

'Normie was very knowledgeable about flowers,' I remarked.

Somebody might have warned us about Deacon's Hardware Slash
Funeral Parlour. I wasn't prepared mentally for that, at all.

In the afternoon, back at the motel, Matthew struggled with writing
an appropriate eulogy. We were both troubled by how little we knew
about our Dad. After much trying, we managed to track down his other
daughter in New Zealand and phoned to let her know. Being unfamiliar with Anna only added to our feelings of disconnectedness to the
'goodbye' process. We'd missed the 'hellos.' Our parents' head-in-the-
sand policy on much of the past left us ill-informed about so much.

'Best we go to the pub and you make yourself known to the folk
there. They'll probably tell you some stories.'

To be honest, I was struggling again with being in this town. The
town where my Uncle once roamed. The town where I'd died a little
more on each childhood visit. It wasn't a large town but it did have two
cemeteries. It seemed there were more occupants underground than
there were up top. My father would not need to be buried near his
brother. He would be five kilometres away from his sibling, in the 'new'
cemetery. In my mind, I called Dad's one the 'good cemetery.'

In this town, at this time, on this mind, I struggled with self-destructive urges. There was a fight against the need to self-harm. I kept losing
time. I kept losing self. I was missing Micah. In this town I was more
damaged.

'I could do with a beer,' I added, feeling all of this.

There was difficulty deciding which pub would hold the best story
tellers.

He was banned from the one closest to here, last time I visited. I
never found out why.

Head-in-the-sand policy.

Hmm.

'The end pub, closest to his place would probably be best,' I said. We can do the middle on the way back, if you're still needing input.

I may have walked very fast to the end pub. Matthew soon found himself surrounded by mourners and story-tellers. A country pub isn't always woman friendly. I had two beers, purchased two stubbies (small bottles of beer) to go, and left Matty to intel gather.

The next thing I know, I'm sitting in the church. It's full. I'm surprised at the number of people. The service is in full swing. People are crying. Matthew gives a very moving and humorous eulogy and I'm adrift. Outside, as the coffin is placed into the hearse for my father's last ride, I burst into tears. They hit me without warning and were over as quick. It's hard to know what the trigger was; a little bit of everything.

It was typical Australian outback weather. Winter but not. A few had brought umbrellas to shield them from the sun. The cemetery was red and white dust blowing in small curls about our legs, pinging a little sting on the bare legged with small sharp bits of earth caught in the gusts. An aged, solemn RSL representative was waiting by the graveside. As we circled and stilled to quiet about the hole, with the coffin held over it as if by magic, the returned serviceman pressed 'play' on the oldest cassette player I'd ever seen outside of a museum. *The Last Post* drifted out of the crackling little speaker and I found it very hard to remain sombre. It became hard not to giggle. Next, the Catholic priest went through his set pieces and as he stepped back to prepare to anoint the coffin with Holy Water, he lost his footing in a new still subsiding, occupied, grave. He did not skip a beat or miss a word as he recovered from his stumble, holding his opened Bible outward as balancing ballast in one hand, and the anointing whatsit swung about in the other, anointing anybody within range. I may have tittered like a school girl. My father would have laughed out loud. When tragedy collides with comedy, you can't help but smile a little.

At the graveside, after the internment, I shook hands with Normie from Deacon's Hardware and thanked him. It was over. There was to be a gathering at my Aunt's, where she had prepared a post funeral se-lection of fine finger foods. My natural reticence left me clinging to the wall there, and I watched my cousins catch up with Matthew. Strangers were around me mourning my father and guilt told me I should have been more upset. I ate a cucumber sandwich and worried about how fast we'd sent Dad away from this mortal realm. With a tempered by beer wretchedness, I thought of the empty bedsit with little sign left of Dad's tenancy. Barely a stain. How could a person come and go so, with-out leaving a trace? And why was Dooley hovering by the tea urn? Not in a malevolent way, but I jolted in alarm, nevertheless.

With wall-sliding stealth, I moved to be beside my aunt, hugged her, thanked her for the support and slunk away from the house, which was easing with increasing volume into a departed party vibe. Back at the motel, it was impossible for my disarrayed mind to remember if I'd taken my medication. To be on the sane side, I swallowed my prescribed dose, sent my brother a text informing him of my whereabouts, and slid into bed. Tomorrow we would fly away and this town, this damaging town, would be in my past forever. That's from the head-in-the-sand so-ciety's lexicon. Traces of my father. My dispatched father. He was gone.

I slept.

When next I was aware, Matt and I were buckling into aeroplane seats for a bumpy flight to Sydney. Neither of us were talkative. Given, I was now beginning to deal with childhood trauma during sessions with Doctor Brooker, I felt safe in the possibility that it would at least be twenty years before I began to process my Dad's death. I had the pro-cessing speed of an old Commodore 64 with chronic RAM problems. Matt was eager to get back to his wife and very new baby. After a two-hour train ride, I would be reunited with Micah and my now widowed, but living with another man anyway, mother. Exhaustion was produc-ing some unkindness in me. I was able to nap on the train ride to the coast and my temper was lulled down by the time I reached my mother's car, where she was waiting with Micah.

From there, in a head-in-the-sand way, we more or less acted as if my father had never existed. And in a heart-breaking way, he never really had.

CHAPTER 33

The Suppress Way

These are the time passages.

Micah's first word was 'no.' She meant it. It came with a determined shake of the head. I was dead proud, and at the same time a tad annoyed my daughter would no longer do anything without argument.

Bath time.

No.

Tick, tock.

Time for school.

No.

If you don't get dressed for school right now, I'll strip naked and drop you at the gate while I'm nude; except I'll have your photo hanging around my neck, so people will know exactly whose mother I am.

No!

It was rare that I needed to do more than undo a few buttons of a shirt. Once, was I about to unhook my bra.

Tick.

Micah is five at this point. She is a great talker. I master the art of listening while writing essays for my degree courses. A great conversationalist, and it's not long before I let Mikey do most of the talking for me.

'Ring Nan and see how she is.'

We have great chats lying on my bed. Nothing is off limits - yet. There's a strength about Mikey, but also a vulnerability that shakes me a little.

I see Vivian Brooker once a week. After four years, I've come close to the amount of courage I need to tell the doctor of my childhood. It may well be quicker to recite the story to Micah when she turns eighteen and have her in turn tell Doctor Brooker for me. Vivian, I call the doctor now; because she's seen me at my very worst and very best. It's a first name basis for anybody who's witnessed me fighting demons. Vivian has observed pieces of my damage that nobody has ever seen. It's probable that I've post-traumatically stressed her to the point where she might very well want to crawl under her desk and cry. But she doesn't. The strongest of women.

Also, I think Vivian is amused by me, whether I'm meaning to be funny or not. Every week I say to myself, 'Today, I will tell Vivian what that man did to me.' Every week I hedge around the story, sometimes even lurch at it full on, before retreating, afraid. If I say it out aloud, it'll become true. Sometimes, I'm returned there, in the hurt, and the flash of the flashback blinds me into panic. One time, I rushed in unsighted terror out of the office and down the street, oblivious to everything but my secrets. A hand grabbed mine, just as I would have sped without thought into traffic.

Maddie, Vivian had said, with the authoritarian tone one might use on children, and perhaps I had been a child, but the voice brought me back. You're okay now. He's dead.

Tock.

One of my secrets was a pocket knife. The strange account of the pocket knife and its ending will come later. I had always carried that knife with me. Always.

You're a little worse lately, Vivian had told me when we returned safe to her office. I think perhaps you're being triggered more often because Micah has reached the same age you were when you...

Were damaged.

Micah is five at this point and I see what a child is supposed to look like and how exposed she is to the world before being quite ready for it. Parents, by necessity, must run interference. There are things that might wound. If I can get my daughter to a certain point on her journey without harm coming, I'd call it a win. I'm also fearful that I might be or do the harm.

As Vivian's patient, I find she is very patient with me. It's a yin yang balance thing, this patient and patience equilibrium. One day the doctor might smack me fair across the side of the head and scream, 'just let that shit out, for goodness sake! It's eating you alive.' But until then, I remain reticent. It's not intentional. Mine is a big powerful hurt. I'm frightened by its supremacy. It can't be unleashed before I am strong.

Tick.

Vivian has scheduled me into the psych ward twice by the time Micah is five. Sometimes my body grows immune to the medications. Dooley and the Shadow Man reappear and fill me with panic. Other times I have the sudden urge to end myself; to save Micah from growing up with me as her parent. I'm poison to her. Times, I'll grab something sharp and rip at my skin to just release the pressure. Fuck. It can be too much. Old pain is not dulled by the years passing, it mutates into sporadic torment.

On occasion, I think I've invented the rape and incest. I am a fucked unit. News reports about false memories scare me into further doubt. I refuse to validate my past. If my father had stepped up earlier, it may have helped. His doubt at what he'd seen became my doubt at what I'd lived. Anger pours out of me and then turns back to hammer my body black and blue. It's an internal domestic violence relationship with my own self. Who wouldn't schedule such a mess?

Vivian wears hearing aids. A deaf therapist with a patient who can't speak. In her office, after a while, my hyper-vigilance relaxes, and my body remembers. Vivian doesn't need to hear. She sees. I feel. Too much. Then not enough. Vivian sees me. I feel her eyes drill into my soul and my soul might be speaking for itself. Sessions exhaust us both.

Tock.

When Micah's at school and I'm not working on university assignments, I clean houses for extra cash in hand. It made me cry with fatigue, but I grew enough money to buy a cheap car; an old Toyota. Clutch starting became a periodic thing and I turn out to be quite proficient at roll starting. It brings back an odd old memory of my mother chasing a VW down a street. There's a necessity to always park facing downhill. In due course, I save for a new battery and then can park anywhere I wanted, within reason.

A car is not necessary in Sydney. I bought it to visit my mother on the coast. Our relationship had eased into something approaching mother and grown-up daughter. She still pushed my buttons like no other and there was so much I would have liked to say, but never had the nerve. I come from chicken stock, and perhaps laughing stock; my stock pot brews a peculiar mess. This less strained relationship with my Mum wasn't a dishonest relationship, just new. Mum was a good grandmother, although we had always to visit her. Us mountains kept dragging ourselves to Muhammad. This mother/daughter relationship seemed safer, happier, at a superficial level; both of us could be raw beneath a protective shell. So, it became obvious to me that I had trouble telling anybody anything, except Micah.

'I love you,' I'd say often, lest she forget.

'I love you, too,' she'd answer, trying very hard to not punctuate the words with a sigh. A sigh that might mean, *how often do I have to say that to this needy woman?*

Was I reading too much into one small sigh? Neuroses. New roses. I didn't mind if she never said 'I love you' back. It was very important to me that Micah knew she was loved without a doubt. Nobody had said the words to me. I was deficient. I knew the consequences of lack.

Lack made me take in a cat. Micah needed more in her life than school, a few friends and mum. We named the cat Liquorice. She was a jet-black stray kitten, who mewed in a way that left me weak with empathy. She was roaming the car park near the Chinese Take Away. As I opened my car door to drive home after a lunch time food pick-up, the kitten jumped in. Unlike Micah, I couldn't say no and shake my head. Liquorice came home with me. She followed me up the stairs. She made herself at home in a way I never could. After, I'd walked up to the school to collect Micah, cat and child met. It was instant love.

'I love you,' Micah said to the cat within minutes. I sighed.

Tick. Tick tock. Time is all over the place. Okay. I'll stop that now. No more tocks. No more ticks.

Micah, at five, was enjoying language acquisition. She was never afraid to try out a new grown-up word.

'We're going to Nan's for the weekend,' I told her. Pack Liquorice's stuff.

The cat always came with us.

'Will we be taking the suppress way or the specific highway?' asked Micah, not quite getting the words right.

'The suppress way. Definitely,' I answered and gave a smile. A far more appropriate word than 'expressway' when travelling to one's mother's house. We'll take the specific highway (the Pacific Highway to most folk) next time.

'I like the suppress way. It's easier.'

Truer words were never spoken.

CHAPTER 34

Wanting

The unbearable lightness of seeing. When each day began, there was a darkness in my soul and I had to search for brightness no matter how much it stung my eyes to tears. Fighting depression is a full-on deployment. It's a war. If I could choose between psychosis and depression in a mental illness unlucky dip, I'd choose psychosis. That's a mad choice, isn't it? But psychosis, for me, felt less holistic than the overwhelm of depression. It seemed to affect and be in my head (except those times when hallucinations, both auditory and visual, scared the poop out of me).

Depression took over every cell in my body, when it hit. Physical and mental, the blues depleted life, emptying it from me via every pore. Pore, pore, pitiful me; oozing melancholy onto everything I touched. With a smile faked onto my face, I would walk Micah to school then begin a slow devolve into a crawling amoeba by the time I'd returned to the flat. All my cells would unite into one single celled wretchedness; a blob of shite. The cat sat on the blob.

I was happier than I'd ever been in my life. A beautiful child, a crazy cat, a roof over my head, safe - but my mind was a betraying partner. It filled me with anger, this lack of control over my head space. Happier than I'd ever been in my life, yet closest to carving the razor blade in deep. Nearest I'd ever been to contentment, yet so desolate in the darkness. Content meant a dysfunctional brain. Content-ment. Content may contain nuts.

My mother telephoned one Sunday.

'My friend Sue and her husband have a property on the Parramatta River. Their last tenants left it shambolic. If you want, Sue's willing to rent it to you at the rent you're paying now, just so they know they have decent tenants. The property is their retirement fund, so they're happy for you to be a kind of live in property caretaker until they retire and sell it. What do you think?'

'I... I.'

'You'd be silly not to.'

Within weeks, we were living near Five Dock. In a house. A house! Because I'm not 'silly.' It was a split level, with a veranda out the back, looking over the water. There was a bush reserve on one side and quiet neighbours on the other. Brilliant. It was beautiful. Good for my soul, yet... Malcontent. Stupid, stupid, depression.

Much of the time, I sat on the veranda, with Liquorice. Micah loved her new school, but not so much the children in it. Poverty was noticeable in the playground. Children wore designer label shoes. Some had nannies. The kids were miniature snobs and Micah was teased for the most ridiculous reasons. I wanted to go into the school grounds and shove a brioche up their quinoa eating ar... ah, me. The colour green. It's not easy being envious.

'It's okay, Mumma,' Mikey said about the teasing.

'Is it, Micah? Is it? Teasing can be a form of bullying. You know the school's policy on that?'

'Yep. There's a zero tolerance to bullying.'

'No. It's, *We shall ignore this and hope it goes away.*'

'If it doesn't go away, I'll tell Mrs Ross.'

Micah was over the subject.

'Okay. Why don't we go to the park and do a bit of roller blading? Forget about school for a while.'

I'd bought two pairs of inline skates. Cheap ones, and we were trying to remain upright on them. Neither of us were amazing at it. The first-time Mikey tried hers, she fell in less than one second. I rushed to help her and my wheels ground to a halt in some gravel and I landed on my knees. Both of us were laughing and maybe crying a little as we pulled bits of gravel from our skin. Soon after, I bought some elbow and knee pads.

'I'm going to try the half-pipe!' I yelled in a gung-ho manner once we reached the park and slipped into our skates.

No, Mum!

Up I went, doing well, until gravity and other laws of physics, vicious, asserted themselves and down I came. On a hip.

'Mum!'

As Micah rushed to me, she face-planted in the half pipe. We never skated again. The Salvation Army op-shop ended up with two, used, pairs of inline skates. Helen laughed when I told her the story. She visited now and again as a kind of friend rather than as a psych nurse.

'What were you thinking? You can barely stand up without skates on,' she said.

'Ha, ha.' I limped inside and went to make us some fresh coffee.

'Will you be going back to Uni, next semester?' Helen asked, when I'd returned carrying two mugs.

The last time I'd been hospitalised, I'd just made it through my classes; although I had kept up a distinction average. At the end of that tiring, trying semester, I'd deferred my coursework for a while to try and deal with the great depression and other mental health issues. Issues, or, as Carrie Fisher had been known to put it, I was what psychiatrists call, *bat-shit crazy.*

'I suppose so,' I answered Helen. But I've kind of lost momentum.

'Just do one or two classes a semester. You don't want to throw three years away.'

'No, ma'am.'

'These biscuits are nice. What are they?'

'Micah and I call them dog-bog biscuits. They look like a fresh turd on the baking tray before they go into the oven.'

Helen put her biscuit down. Maybe to get that image out of her mind before she continued to eat.

'Eww. Nice. You ought to write a cookbook,' she said. 'Dog bog biscuits and other poop-like treats for humans.'

'Well, Mikey, gets teased at school if the kids see her eating these at recess.'

'Kids can be little prats.' Helen gave an audible happy toned sigh. 'Goodness, it's so peaceful here. I don't want to go back to work.'

'What time do you have to start? Micah would love to see you. I'm off to get her soon.'

'Oh. Shame. No, I have a three o'clock start. Tell my girl I'm sorry I missed her. I'll come over and see the pair of you one Saturday.'

'She plays netball now. On Saturdays. You know, because she's so athletic, like me.'

'Ha! Maybe I can come and watch one Saturday. Text me the details. I'd better get moving.'

Later, I stood by the school gate waiting for Micah. It was yet another place where I felt like an imposter. The other mothers, nannies and one or two fathers, all seemed to be at ease clustered about the gates. They had the confidence of belonging. Some were chatting as if talking to people you didn't know was easy. It became obvious that it might be beneficial to invest a little more of my time into the school so that Micah and I both developed a sense of community. The bell rang, and the volume turned large. People and noise grew. Squeaky children everywhere. Kindergarten boys as high pitched as the girls. Did anybody else have a fear that they wouldn't recognise their own child? An old nightmare gripped me, of frantic searching and loss. A small panic chewed away at my nerves. What if I lost my mind in front of the confident people?

'Mumma?'

'Oh, hi, baby. Who's your friend?'

'Josh. Can he come over to our's and play?'

'Sure. Josh, ask your mum if you can come after school on Monday'.

Josh dashed off but didn't come back. Micah and I stood there until it was clear everybody had left, except a few dedicated teachers.

'Maybe he'll tell you on Monday,' I said to Micah.

'Most probably.'

People will say there's no class structure in Australian society, but there is. There's the super-rich, rich, middle class, poor and very poor (aka Bogan). I sat on the cusp between poor and Bogan. It would be sad if Josh's mother or father had ushered him away because they felt Micah wasn't 'good' enough to be a play mate.

'What are you having for dinner, Mumma?' Micah asked, sitting down at the table for tea.

'I've had mine,' I lied, funds were low because I'd had to register the car, so I was scrimping on food for myself. 'Would you like fruit salad for dessert?' I asked.

'No, thanks.'

'Oh. But I bought it today. It's not like it grows on trees, you know. Okay, some of it does. But you don't want to get scurvy or the galloping consumption or something worse, do you?'

'Will it be with ice-cream?'

'Yes.'

'Okay, then.'

Micah couldn't fight me when I brought maladies from the Middle Ages into an argument.

'Could I really get scurvy?'

'It's not out of the question, if you don't eat the right food.'

'Can I really get rickets?'

That was the disease I'd used to get Micah outside only recently. Away from watching her 'Rock-A-Doodle' for the hundredth time. Shifting her off the couch hadn't been easy.

'No. Unless you don't get enough Vitamin D, fresh air and stuff.'

'I don't think I'll get the rickets. I'm out in the playground every day at school.'

'You're probably right.' I didn't want a hypochondriac born of my need to amuse myself with ancient disease names. 'But fresh air is good for you.'

'And netball tomorrow. I'll be in the fresh air at netball tomorrow.'

'And I'll be in the fresh air watching you. Only, I'll have a nice warm cup of coffee.'

'I wish I didn't have to be goal attack all the time.'

Netball is a cold season sport. Kids, most often girls, running about oblivious to the freezing temperatures. Whistles, with a hysteria to their tenor, chirruping, very close to a pitch that could provoke me into a crazed whistle killing spree. There were about twenty courts where Micah played, all with games going on non-stop. It was not a time for quiet contemplations. Although, sometimes Micah 'went off with the fairies' and I'd have to give a shout if ball play was heading her way.

The coffee, although substandard, was cheap and hot. Parents huddled over their cups as if they were small heaters. You could not expect more at seven thirty in the morning. The sausage sandwiches after the match were worth the prolonged sit amid arctic blasts.

'Put your jacket on,' I told Micah the minute she came off court.

'I'm not cold.'

'You'll end up with the pleurisy.'

I noticed Mikey's sneakers were looking a bit tattered and perhaps her big toe was ready to break out of the tops. It would be back to house cleaning for me, depression or not, if I wanted to keep up with a growing child's shoe expenditures. What a fatiguing thought.

Trauma is stockpiled in the body. Exhaustion is the obvious outcome. Crying while cleaning OP's (other people's) houses is an unpleasant secondary effect. Dragging a vacuum cleaner up a flight of stairs in the huge house of a stranger hurt in all manner of ways; knowing I'd left a pile of dishes in the sink at my own house, for instance.

I want to go home, I would tell the universe, while in a mental and physical mess at the top of the stairs. Home. Not to the house I lived in, but to a place of serenity and rest.

CHAPTER 35

Behold, the Unchosen

Wake up. New day. Vaguely familiar are days. There is mischief, in the corner and I try to avoid its gaze. It's drawn me in before and taken me on crazy rides that I haven't the sense to enjoy; full of fear as I am. Crazy rides. Voyages to the mighty edge of lunacy. Cabbalistic places where everyday garden variety reality is the enemy. There were battles, of which I was not a part, but still, I became the defeated. Fairness then, is about skin tone, not justice. Defeated. Left in shreds.

So now, in the new day, what price, life?

Blows a wind about the head. Clothing is selected, not for propriety or warmth, but for camouflage. What colour invisible? Mischief calls loud my name and I walk away like a child ignoring its mother. 'Not today,' I murmur, faking an inner strength.

The rip tide, the tear that pulls me apart; wrenches pieces of me toward damage. 'Not today', I repeat, but resignation poisons the validity. Defeat. Imminent defeat. Mischief howls my name and begins to move from the corner. Envelopes the world. Cries havoc.

I wander in small circles until impetus shoulders me through the door and once out, there is the electricity of escape. This jolts me everywhere and nowhere until nothing is familiar. The noise makes me small. I am trodden on. Mischief has sent me outside without defence. My identity lays on the table still, while I flee about with no name and not the money for a bus fare.

There, in the quietest part of the noise is a bench. To call everything to a standstill is combat. But sit on the bench I do, vibrating with battle fatigue. Glorious are the colours skimming my edges, except the joy of seeing is stolen by apprehension. It stands in the way like a blindfold against peace. Moving seems to be the singular resistance against mischief and before I can breathe the quiet of idleness, I am hurled into a din so much louder than reality, that I am impelled to move on. In my hand, clenched tight was the pen-knife.

I hear my interior crying apologies to all those who thought I had won for good that old conflict. I keep running, forgetting from where I came, and not comprehending to where I moved.

Moved toward sorry. I am, and was, so sorry.

'You don't seem yourself,' Vivian said later. What's going on?

'Sorry.'

How to answer such a question? Words are too simple to clarify what my head was executing. Executing. Execution. I held fast the knife. Vivian noticed blood seeping through my sleeve.

'Show me.'

'No.'

'Let me see. It might need stitches.'

'No. It doesn't.'

'What do you have in your hand?'

I struggled to unclench the fist holding the knife. The fingers had been clamped shut over it for a long time.

'Can I have it?' Vivian asked, on seeing the pen-knife.

'No. I will put it in my bag.'

I didn't. I was having trouble making my body obey instruction. In the unmoving silence, I heard the clock march off the passing minutes at a regulated unending pace. Relentless trudging ticking.

'You're not moving.'

'No.'

Move. How does one move? Frozen. I'm freezing toward statue. At last, I managed to slip the knife into my handbag. I was uncomfortable without it. Vulnerable. In response, my body curled over itself, much as my fist had curled over the knife; my head resting on my knees as I sat.

'What's brought this on?'

'I wish I knew.'

'We have to do something about your bleeding. You're going to bleed on the carpet.'

In the end, I showed Vivian the cut running up my arm.

'I'm not going to hospital,' I said, inflexible and stubborn. I was nearly frozen stiff. Unbending.

'You should have stitches.'

Vivian's receptionist rushed down to the chemist while the session continued.

'How's Micah?' Vivian asked, to try and get me talking, I supposed. Once started, I might ease into truths.

'She's fine. But she asked me about her father the other day.'

'What did you tell her?'

'Nothing.' This short answer seemed curt. I extended the explanation. 'I told her I'd tell everything she needs to know about her father when she's a little older.'

'Was that enough for her?'

'No. But Liquorice the cat began to throw up a hairball, so we rushed her outside and I allowed the subject to drop.'

'What will you tell her when she is older?'

The subject curled me up again.

'The truth, probably,' I answered.

'What is the truth?'

I hadn't actually told Vivian about the rape. Nobody knows, except my body. In my mind, Micah was never linked to that horrible evening. Also, I didn't want to, even in a subliminal way, connect her to it by talking of that night, when all that remained of me nearly died, while thinking about her.

'Can I tell you a story?' I asked, after a while of silence.

'Sure.'

I narrated, in third person, the story of a stupid young girl who had stomped off from home and walked far into the night. So far into the dark, that she almost never found her way out. On the journey, the stupid young girl met a man who offered her a cold beverage for her thirst. In the man's mind, accepting the drink meant accepting the consequences. He then raped the stupid young girl as payment for the drink. The stupid girl was never young again. Stupid girl. Stupid woman. Stupid me.

'Micah was born nine months later.'

That was the last I managed to say during the session. Vivian suggested an upping of my anti-depression medication. Compliant, I nodded agreement. The receptionist returned from the chemist with antiseptic, steri-strips and large Band-Aids. Doctor Brooker tended to my wound, and I left, with the pen-knife still in my possession. Four steps down the road and I had it out of my bag and into my pocket. I needed that knife close. At hand.

Where was mum? I was on a car ride with my uncle and nobody else. Not even Matthew was here. The car stopped. We were watching kangaroos. He sat me on his lap, so I could see the roos better. It... He... Where was my mum? He did stuff. When I cried, he gave me the knife.

Next time I do that, you stop me by sticking me with this. If you don't stab me, it means you don't mind what I do. It means you love me. I have the same knife, only bigger, see? If you tell anybody about this, I will use this knife on Matthew.

The knife.

The fucking knife. All this time. At hand.

In the park, I was near a bin, but I couldn't throw the knife away. I required its protection. I wanted the way out, a bloody end to everything, that the knife could provide. Right now, I needed to cut a hole in myself and bleed the bastard uncle out of my core. Ring Vivian. Ring; ask for help. I don't know where to put this new info. He gave me the knife! The knife I have carried for over 20 years in a bag or a pocket. All this time. How did I not remember until now? He gave me the knife.

I needed to cut a hole deep in...

'Could... Can I... speak with Doctor Brooker? Please? I... It's Maddie. Madison. I... Yes, I think it's...'

Words were disappearing. I ended the call and held my mobile phone tight. It rang, and I dropped it, like it was hot. When I managed to gather it up, the battery cover had fallen off, I was relieved to see Doctor Brooker's personal number still flashing on the screen. I answered, even though Dooley told me to ignore the call.

Vivian drove me to the hospital herself. Helen was happy to collect Micah from school and my mother was on her way to pick Mikey up from Helen's. My head was bursting with noise. Vivian had the knife. The fucking knife. It was in her brief-case. As we waited for admission to be finalised, I couldn't tell Vivian from where the knife had originated, even though the information felt vital.

Before anything, I was sedated and Vivian's steri-strips, they had not held on during my agitation, were replaced with stitches. Whilst they sewed, I heard Vivian say goodbye to the staff and leave. I felt deserted and drenched in my failure.

'You're in Room 7, Maddie.'

I fell on to the bed and didn't rise again for three days. There was a pile of uneaten sandwiches and unopened drinks on the bedside table. But I wanted something hot to eat; to heat the dead cold within. This warmth hunger was the motivation to come lurching out of Room 7 and look at the world. It was a quetiapine hazy world. When I saw the Shadow Man near the locked exit door, I froze further, but not solid. Where was Dooley? Was he after Micah again?

I've told you a thousand times; you're not real! I yelled at the Shadow Man from across the wide expanse, on a verge of side-effect's fog. Either is Dolofónos. Leave me alone.

Medication was delivered quickly to where I was standing.

I'm not crazy, I assured the nurses. I know they're not real.

Take them anyway, they'll help.

I was a fan of help, so swallowed the two offered pills.

Swallowing, wallowing, I said. There's my plans for the day.
It's 4.30pm.

CHAPTER 36

The Rhythm of the Waltz

Room 7. Were I to die in this room, on this day, it would be a relief; but I would die a failure. We have two major jobs on this planet. To be kind (to the Earth, as well as its inhabitants) and to live. I'm not so good at the living part. So, the occupant of Room 7 listens and sees the wait and hears the coming of the end and remembers the defiance that never left the interior. It screamed just do it, just do it. Kill me, kill me and the fist came down, but it didn't end. Minutes go on and on with a poison so toxic inside that it sours all tastes. Can you feel the fear that spasms the stomach and steals the breathing? Can you feel that need; that one must just get the blade and be done? Be ended?

Nothing is solid.

Even knowledge that was once absorbed, retained, has disappeared. Zero remains within, except a discord that is unrelated to reality. I wish the noise would just go away and the stench and the fear that's not mine but is, go with it. The fear belongs to the child me who has long since perished. The fear did not die with the child. Damn you, fear. Room 7 has abandoned fear left in it. Left for me to absorb and take as my own. Something. Something is knocking again at my core. Can you feel that? Is it more anxiety? Exit quickly and quietly. Do not panic.

Can we get somebody with a smudge stick to go in and purify Room 7? I asked the doctor during our morning meeting. It's full of distress.

This request may have added a few days to my incarceration. You have to be careful what you say to a doctor, even in semi-jest. Although,

I would have been happy with some sort of ritualistic exorcism of Room 7, if for the Placebo Effect. So sure, was I that it was the room, not my-self, with the issues, I would enter 7 to sleep and use the bathroom. If night-time meds didn't knock me almost unconscious, I would have baulked at setting foot in there at all.

Each morning, I awoke and there was no Micah. Her absence from my life shouted 'failure' at me. I'd walk to breakfast with my hands over my ears. As a mother, I thought I had been doing okay, but now, again, failure. My slump, my unfortunate cycle of parental intermit-tency would mess my child up for sure.

You should have let me take her from the start, Dooley said.

You were going to hurt her.

I was going to save her.

I lost my shit.

Liar. I yelled. Fucking liar!

Nurses approached.

In the High Dependency Unit, my temper evened out. It is difficult when your mind plays tricks on itself, but when an entity, that your mind has devised, also fabricates false truths, well, it's a double de-ception; two delusions. A double disillusionment. Double disillusion meant treachery; a betrayal of the worst kind. While I grew better in the HDU, Room 7 was given to somebody else. Days later, once I was allowed back onto the open ward, I was assigned Room 11. It was far more restful than 7.

Vivian came to visit me in my sealed in place. Room 11.

'You look better,' she said.

'Do you still have my knife?' I asked, dispersing with pleasantries, as I appeared to have no control about what words flew from my mouth or when.

'It's locked in a drawer in my office. Why?'

'I couldn't,' I said.

'What?'

I said, 'I couldn't.' This is the trouble sometimes, when your therapist is hearing impaired.

'No, I heard you. I meant; you couldn't do what?'

'I couldn't stab him.'

My whole interior was sobbing but, on the surface, there was left the deadness of the unexpressed. I wanted to rip the sobs out of myself. I needed that knife; craved to be bled back to basics. It was understandable, the ancient practice of bloodletting. It felt right to eliminate the illness, to let it free. I wanted to cry. Whether it was medication or inability, the sobs trapped inside left me frantic; the slight grip I had on life made more tenuous by panic.

'Breathe,' said Vivian, like it was simple.

Part of me wanted to yell, 'what a fucking good idea,' but the polite, real me, began an attempt at breathing in a normal, less gaspy, way. It wasn't easy. The need to sob held me rigid and pre-explosive. Breathe, damn you. In my mind, I began to waltz. Breathe, two, three. Breathe, two, three. In came the music, Strauss' *Blue Danube,* to help. Breathe, two, three. In my mind, I waltzed. In real life, I can't walk in a sensible even rhythm.

'You couldn't stab your uncle, because you are a normal human being. Violence is not in your nature,' Vivian told me after I stumbled through the story.

'Don't you see? I should have stabbed him. It would have saved me.'

'No. It would have brought about a set of different circumstances, and you would now be trying to deal with them as an adult. You remained true to your non-violent nature. That's a strength of its own.'

'Did I do it by choice? I don't know. I could scarcely move, let alone stab somebody. I couldn't hurt anybody, even him. It feels like a weakness, not a strength.'

In a strange arrangement of timing, a fight broke out in the patients' lounge area. It was verbal and loud enough to hear from Room 11. Doors began to slam, signalling nurses entering the fray.

'Should I go out there like Gandhi and call for non-violence?' I asked.

Vivian laughed. 'Best not.'

We couldn't continue our conversation until the fight was over. Vivian had trouble hearing me at the best of times, as I was prone to looking at the ground when talking; a habit many invisible people take up. Low self-esteem shrinks people unseen and bestows the belief that nothing said is worthy of an audible voice.

The verbal fight outside wasn't helping the internal commotion and I began to waltz again. Breathe, two, three. Hands balled into fists and fingernails were digging small ruts into my palms. My jaw was tense enough for teeth to hurt. Breathe, two, three.

'How's Micah?' Vivian asked, knowing full well I'd drop self-absorption, once my daughter was a topic.

'She's going to a school near my Mum's. Says it's nice and nobody cares what she wears. I've fucked her up, haven't I?' I asked, having fallen back into me, me, me with me. 'She'll feel abandoned and other stuff that inhibits robust mental health, wont she?'

'No parent escapes blame,' Vivian said.

The fight in the common area quietened down and now there was a lower volumed post-mortem of events being discussed. It was a 'he said, he said,' scenario that soon bored me enough to end my eaves-dropping.

'So, parents are damned if they do, and damned if they don't?' I asked.

'Yes.'

'Bugger.'

Later, I talked to Micah using the patients' telephone. The communication devise which had once been utilised in knocking me into a semi-coma. Uneasy now, I surveyed the area, like an assassin's target. If anybody came near, I finished conversations off and sped outside, to sit with my back to the wall. It's hard not to catch a form of paranoia in a psych ward.

'Hey, my baby. How are you doing?' I asked my daughter.

At minimum, my five-year-old was honest.

'Nan makes me eat all of my vegetables. I hate it.'

Mikey was going through a stage where she didn't like to eat anything coloured orange, including oranges. She would subsist on frozen peas if allowed, still frozen. In an attempt to get nutrients into her, I was forced to puree vegetables and sneak them into sauces, although, Micah was fond of mashed potatoes and they remain her comfort food today.

'I used to fill my dressing gown pockets with food and throw them over the back fence later, when I lived with Nan.'

I didn't mean this to be a life hack, but Micah took it for one.

'What a great idea.'

'No. Oops. At least eat some of your veggies, you know, for good nutrition's sake. You don't want to get a case of wandering womb.'

'Mum! I don't know what that is, but it sounds ridoubtful. (Micah's word for a combination of ridiculous and doubtful). I miss you. Can you come and get me soon?'

Mikey may as well have kicked me in the stomach. My sense of screwing up her young life swelled to pain my already irritated guts.

'I'm sorry. I'll be there to get you very soon, I promise. I love you very much.'

'I love you too, Mumma. Got to go. Nan wants me to feed Liquorice. She's screaming.'

'Liquorice or Nan?'

'Liquorice.'

'You'd better go then, my baby. I'll ring you tomorrow'.

'Okay, Mum. Bye, bye.'

We did a few seconds of 'No, you hang up,' before I left the building to brood about my constant failings to the tune of an old K. D. Lang classic, sitting rounded in a disheartened ball, by the back wall of the bricked in garden. Sobs lay beneath my skin, aching for release.

'Please release me,' I asked the doctor.

One week later, there came permission from officialdom granting leave, under the proviso that I visit Doctor Brooker twice a week for at least one month. I rushed out of the hospital as if the structure were well alight, hurried back to the house for my car, and drove as fast as I could in a legal way, to reach Micah.

CHAPTER 37

The Mechanics of Living

Like the sands of time scattered over the kitchen floor after you've dropped the egg timer, my life was looking a bit of a mess and making a crackle noise underfoot. Dooley and the Shadow Man were gone but not forgotten. It was hard to relax into their absence, when I had no idea if they would return. *They're not real,* I say to myself, often. *Their impact is too real,* I say as often. After leaving the hospital, it was as if I were a freed hostage, knowing full well my kidnappers were plotting yet another abduction. Any shadow spooked me. Even Micah, every so often, frightened me.

Driving home from Mum's one Sunday, I left her in the car for a few seconds, parked at the bowser to go and pay cash for petrol. I returned. She was gone. Liquorice was making herself comfortable on Mikey's booster seat and I hurtled into full-on panic. In the conflagration of that instant, I'm not sure if I screamed. After a few seconds, elongated to minutes by dread, Micah emerged from under a blanket in the foot well of the front passenger's seat, laughing. In a way, taught to me by my mother, I erupted into an angry release of tension and scared my little one.

'Don't you ever do that again!' I yelled.

Mikey began to cry causing her mother to feel like excrement. There was a near puking from the leftover terror blended with relief.

'I'm sorry for scaring you,' I apologised, when I could talk again. 'I thought someone had taken you. I didn't mean to go off'.

'It was just a joke,' explained Micah, tears still tracking down her face.

'Yes, I know that now, my baby. But, please don't ever, ever do that again.'

My heart hammered all the way to the house, like a clunky old engine after too many miles uphill. We'd driven the last five kilometres in silence. Now, parked in the driveway all hushed and moody, we took our time unpacking the car. Micah was sulking a bit, and I was weary from heightened vigilance. For the first time, in a long while, I craved a beer. Shades of my father. Drink it away. Even if you're not sure what 'it' is.

During the seconds of alarm at the service station and following, it struck me: If Micah was taken from me in a permanent way, I would not want to live. Struck me hard. No pressure, Mikey. My daughter was not my one reason for living, but now I had her, I didn't want her to go. Micah would leave one day, for an independent life, but if either of us was to depart life, I had to go first. It's a simple rule. I don't ask much of the universe. Except, to die before my child. For any woman who has lost children and survived, I have nothing but admiration. What courage. What pain they must endure.

That was a darkness that fell on me after the 'service station incident.' Not only did I have the irrational fear that somebody would take Micah from me, be it the universe, the authorities, the Shadow Man and/or Dooley, but also there was unsolicited apprehension surrounding death. Fretting I would outlive Micah, was a ridiculous waste of time and brain power, I knew. Nonetheless, it would drop over me at unsuitable times. It still does, right up to this very second. Any time is unsuitable for such wretchedness. Lack of control over thinking, was an entry on my extensive list of failings.

The list was added to frequently, sometimes with humour, other times with grimness.

So, I can't cook soufflé.

Cryptic crosswords aren't really my forte.

Failed video gamer. This, after managing to trap *Lara Croft* in a solid wall. She's still there, no matter what I do with the △O□X buttons on the controller.

Well, skiing's not my sport. After pelting down a slope unable to stop. Being forced to fall over in the ski-lodge carpark as a means to discontinue, momentum sliding me under a parked bus to skid to a graceless halt, emerging to receive generous applause from onlookers, as I slithered out covered in damp. You live, you learn. You live, you might bruise a little.

Okay, I'm not the best daughter. On not wanting to visit my Mum on the coast.

Wallowing away in failures, I never looked over to see an accomplishment list increasing. No. I was blinded by the blight. ‖◇♪◇♫ You've got to accentuate the negative. Eliminate the positive. (Sing it, sister.) Latch on to the damaging. Don't mess with Miss Exploding Spleen. ♪♫◇◇‖. (That's right, one's spleen explodes if you don't vent it using appropriate means). Accomplishments should be celebrated at the time, not in retrospect, and perhaps fuzzed, in your dotage. It would take me a long time to change this way of perceiving life; and realise I wasn't an over-all and absolute failure.

It's true, I suffer from intermittent third eye blindness; a fact-ular degeneration of sorts. Although, I'm not a glass half-empty person. Nor am I glass half-full. I'm the line around the middle. Neither up nor down but touching both. In reality, failure emphasis is a metaphorical wall I smack into, bruising my ego on a regular basis. Seeing failure, is a ruinous tendency to habituate; slips your cogs, grinds your gears. Which is why I find myself craving beer on occasion. It's an inner workings' oil.

After that hideous petrol station scare, Micah nevertheless continued to frighten me. She'd learnt never to make it about vanishing. It was now more about appearing. Suddenly.

'Boo!'

'For fu... funk's sake! Don't do that. You'll not forgive yourself when I have a coronary infarction in front of you.'

My hand, in reflex, had jumped to cover my heart.

'Sorry, Mum. I was just checking to see if your feet leave the ground when you get a fright.'

'Jeepers, that kind of experiment could kill me... So, do they'?

'Yes.'

Life went on, like life is intended to do. Micah grew older, taller. She still experimented with grown up language, sometimes successful, but most often she was a typical seven-year-old. Another Spring came. Liquorice had enjoyed being the only cat about town, but that Spring a male ginger tom cat, ugliest moggy I'd ever seen, began to hang around. In pre-emptive defence (don't judge my slackness) Liquorice went off to the Vet's to be de-sexed. Although, not soon enough. We found out she was pregnant. The surgery was deferred, and we watched our cat grow rounder and rounder until the day five little babies appeared.

'Can we keep them?' Micah asked.

'I'd love to, but people call you crazy cat lady if you have more than two cats'.

'Can we keep one?'

It didn't take much nagging for me to concede. I'm a sucker. The difficulty for Micah, was choosing which one of the five we would keep. I said the words all parents have said.

'You'll have to help look after them'.

Micah replied in the expected way.

'I will,' she agreed, nodding vigorous in her agreement.

Cut to a montage of me cleaning out the kitty litter, purchasing cat food and more kitty litter, feeding the cats, changing their water, and waking up most mornings with a kitten on my face. We called the kitten designated 'ours', Jaff. She was orange and brown, like a Jaffa chocolate. Before long, the kittens were weaned and Liquorice could have her post-poned operation. Micah cried over her enforced barrenness. The kittens all went to other homes, except Jaff. Micah cried when each one left. I remained stoic but missed them. They'd brought extra joy into our house, and you can't have enough of that stuff.

'Mumma, where's my daddy?'

My feet may have lifted off the ground with the fright triggered by this sudden question. If I'd managed to stay in the air, I might have flown off like a startled bird. Unprepared for the question, I gave no thought to an answer for Micah. I blurted.

'I don't know.'

'What's his name?'

'I don't know.'

Confusion furrowed Micah's face.

At what age, should this question be answered with the truth? Or is this truth harmful to my daughter?

'Mikey, I'm not sure how old you should be to know about your father. I think you're a little bit young still, to understand. I promise I'll tell you when you're old enough.'

'You always say stuff like that.'

'I know.'

'So, what am I *spost* (supposed in Micah speak) to tell the kids at school?'

Tell them to fuck off.

'I don't know. Maybe, make something up?'

'Lie, you mean?'

'Just a little bit.'

'Maybe, I'll tell them he's dead.'

Micah enjoyed dramatics.

I hope he fucking is.

Wow, my thoughts are pretty sweary.

'Tell the kids you don't want to talk about it. It might shut them up for a while'.

'They've been asking me stuff since Fathers' Day.'

'Wow. Nosey bunch of...'

Jaff skittered past in a floor scratching hurry to get somewhere at speed. Micah, quite distracted, went off after the kitten, laughing. Thank you, Jaff. In the meantime, I had a bit of a lie down.

My frequent need for a lie down was developing into a matter for investigation. I couldn't figure out what was the matter with my matter. Tiring wasn't the usual MO. It was typical of me to weary in the mind, while physical stamina kept me chugging along, not well but upright. Now; it was time to see a doctor. A 400,000-kilometre overhaul was required, stat. Trying to undress at night, I had the energy and physical abilities of an unappealing rotting banana.

Help, I'm trapped in my bra, I called out to the universe, weakly, weekly.

An appointment was made.

CHAPTER 38

There Be Dragons

Astreak of sad pale draped in a smothering manner over day-to-day life about then. One night we drove home to find Liquorice lying in a furry unmoving mess in the drive-way. She'd been hit by a vehicle or something very, very solid. The cat was her usual purring self, she just couldn't move.

Everything happened in a blur at the vets. Our beautiful black cat was euthanized before we had understood the gravity of her injuries or had been given sufficient time to say goodbye. Nothing was explained well, and our cat was handed to us in a box to dispose of in our own way. When Liquorice's kitten, Jaff, grew to an age to be de-sexed, we did not return to that vet's practice. They needed far more 'practice' at tactful treatment of bereaved pet owners.

Not long after this loss, we reached our house after a day out, driving in unprepared for awful, I found the house had been robbed. The zoom lens for my old SLR camera lay on the living room rug, which struck me as odd, until I realised there was a lengthy list of electrical products I could now mark as 'missing.' Without admitting to Micah that we had been raided, I put the six panes of rectangular glass from the louvre windows back into their positions and closed them up. At least the glass hadn't been broken; what thoughtful burglars.

As soon as Mikey had left for school the next morning, I rang the Police. My zoom lens was still sitting on the rug, I'd wanted to preserve the crime scene. Hours later one policeman turned up.

'Looks like you caught them in the act. They've made a sudden exit. Obviously piling things onto rugs to pull up like a sack.'

'Yes. The duvet is also missing from my bed. Probably gone off, filled with my diamonds and tiaras.'

'What else is missing?' continued the officer without looking up from his notebook. I'm not sure whether he wrote down my tongue-in-cheek 'diamonds and tiaras' but he continued scribbling in his little black note pad.

I reeled off the list.

Microwave. DVD player. CD player and CDs. Camera. Jewellery box. Hair dryer... Blah, blah, blah.

'Insurance?'

'No.'

'Shame. They were evidently professionals.'

And then he left! No searching for fingerprints. No checking for footprints. Nothing CSI-like at all. I cannot tell you how disappointed I felt. Okay, I can. I have. I shall continue to do so. To amplify my feeling of inferiority, down my street there is a woman whose mansion I clean; her burglar alarm went off while she was at work. Police were called, and arrived within minutes, including plain clothed detectives. My fingerprints were later taken to rule me out of the investigation. Nothing had been taken, nor had any thieves accessed the interior of the house. But there they were, dusting the exterior window sills for fingerprints and interviewing neighbours. After my break-in, I never heard from the police again. When I telephoned them about the next robbery, they didn't even bother to come out to see me.

Yes, it became a thing, robbing the house next to the reserve. I put a sign on the window.

Burglars, please note
WE HAVE NOTHING LEFT!

Conversations with Micah were sometimes strange after we'd been robbed.

'Mumma, where's the DVD player?'

Not wanting to lie, I answered, 'I gave it to the poor people.'

Another time, 'Mum, where's the microwave?'

'I donated it to the poor buggers.'

'Where's the computer, Mum?'

'I gave it to the bloody poor buggers.'

Much later, 'Mum, why come the poor people have more than we do?'

It's, 'how come'.

'How come?'

'Because we are very generous', said I, through gritted teeth.

'I want to play my new DVD.'

'I know. Tell you what, I'll take my telephoto lens to the pawn shop and see if I can get enough money from it to buy a DVD player.'

'Why? Don't you want to zoom anymore?'

'No. Anyway, it's pointless now, since I gave my camera to the bloody poor buggers.'

'You should stop doing that.'

After the first losses, I tried to get household contents insurance, having replaced a few of the more indispensable items.

'Have you been robbed at that address before?' asked the insurance sales department. I could hear the sound of a keyboard clicking as my address was typed in.

'Yes'.

'Does it have louvre windows'? (It was like they knew).

'Yes.'

'Can they be locked with a key?'

'No.'

'Then, I'm sorry, we can't insure the contents of that premises.'

'Of course, you can't'.

I sighed the sigh of the luckless.

As a considerate tenant, I looked after the yard well. Micah and I were outside gardening one weekend morning when we were approached at the front gate by a woman.

'Have you seen my cat? It ran off in this direction.' The lady seemed distraught.

'No. What does it look like?'

The cat was described with exceptional thoroughness, right down to brown markings on its belly in the shape of a lizard.

'I'll keep an eye out,' I told the woman. She left, and I restarted the lawn mower and finished the lawns.

If I had been keeping 'an eye out' while the woman was speaking, I might have seen her children entering our house and coming out with the contents from our refrigerator. Micah had noticed them move on to our veranda but assumed they were staying out of the sun while their mother was talking to me. This thievery was not noticed until I went to make sandwiches for lunch. The margarine was missing.

'What the?' I said.

'What's wrong, Mumma?'

'I can't find the margarine. And my last beer's gone! And the milk. And cheese. For crying out loud, the ice cream's gone from the freezer, too! Are you kidding me?!'

'Where'd it all go, Mum? Have you given more stuff to the buggery poor people?'

'It seems I have.'

Living next to a bush reserve and also by a river makes one's house a prime target for pilferers. They've been supplied with two extra getaway points at the side and the rear. Or three, if they owned or had stolen a boat. Now, I had to lock the doors if I were gardening and have a padlock fitted to the chest freezer. A sticker alerting unwanted visitors to an alarm system, was stuck to every window, although we didn't have alarms.

The frequent space invasions by petty thieves shook extra mayhem into my already disordered trust ability. At night, I slept with a softball bat under the bed. I'd almost never slug anybody else, but if we were robbed again, I might smack myself upside the head with the bat in frustration. If people came to the door, I suspected ill will; even from bicycle riding Mormons.

But I never felt unsafe in the house. I'd be more alarmed by Dooley and the Shadow Man's unexpected appearance, rather than the arrival of mortal intruders. The plan for now, was to brandish the softball bat if I felt Micah were in danger. I would kill for her. I would die for her. I would fight. For Micah, I would always do what I couldn't do for myself. It may have been misguided but I believed adrenalin would jerk me out of my all-encompassing tiredness, which made lethargic and heavy both body and mind, if I were confronted by a serial killing burglar, and I'd come out swinging. Adrenalin, enough to allow me to whirl that softball bat like a madwoman.

Regarding that tiredness, the GP decided, because my period was often heavy, to schedule blood tests and a Pap smear. Being a woman who had never had consensual intercourse, the idea of a smearing grew formidable as test day approached. To be lying there vulnerable and then have the mediaeval torture device known as a speculum crank open your bits, is horrible. The instrument has the cruel capacity to both stretch and pinch at the same time, while also leaving your dignity in tatters. The tests came back abnormal. I was to take iron for my blood and have a colposcopy plus biopsy to investigate non-standard cells in my cervix. It takes courage to be a woman.

It takes courage to face the speculum again. To have a gynaecologist peering inside with some sort of mining lamp on his head, while aiming a magnifying camera inside your uterus, to film interior walls in high definition. To hear him say with amusement,

Your abnormal cells are massed into the shape of a dragon!

It takes courage.

CHAPTER 39

Then I Was Falling

There was a familiar sound to overhear when I awoke. It was the buzz of an electric door opening, closing, locking shut. Locking. Locking shut. Next, there approached a recognisable smell. Industrial cleaner.

Then

I was

falling. Deep, way deep down inside myself. Falling. Not to sleep. To despair. Toward madness; with its adjoining crescendo jags of unhappy sound and muddy despondency. Too much of everything. Not enough of anything. Landing near the precarious edge; the closest a mind can move, without tumbling forever unreachable into the dark long endless nothing. It pitches you near into death but stops before the body fails and leaves you ready to let go but still very much afraid.

Micah!

I dream again of tsunamis dragging my child from my inadequate clutching hands, drowning all hope and leaving me forever searching. It was lonely at the bottom.

Micah! The desperation in my voice scared me more.

'She's at your Mum's', said somebody.

'What?'

The plains of my nightmare shifted, rumbled, water poured away and as the fault line dropped on one side, I saw a nurse.

'Dianne?'

'Yes?'

'Where am I?' I asked, looking at the jagged, wounded landscape.

'You're in the hospital.'

The noise was right. The smell was right, but I was in a different visual landscape. Dianne kept disappearing and floating back when she spoke.

'How do I get there?' I asked.

'Where?'

'The hospital'.

'You're here already..

'I'm not', I said, stepping away from the gaping, broken fault line. It was rupturing open further and I didn't want to fall anymore. The noise hurt.

I'm lost.

I disappeared.

They say I was 'lost' for five days.

'What happened?' I asked Vivian, when I was close to found.

I could now see my body was in the psych ward, although I was surrounded by an impenetrable yet invisible box. My hand kept reaching out to touch the ghostly sides. Over the next days, it moved in closer and closer to my skin before it suddenly pierced my side and settled within. I felt solid again, but heavy. There, but not.

'Don't you remember what happened?' asked Vivian, after I inquired again.

'No. I wasn't in hospital and then I was. There's nothing in between.' Vivian seem to be a little uncomfortable or hesitant.' Do you not want to answer? Has it something to do with this? I held up my bandaged left arm.'

'Not really and yes. I don't think you're strong enough yet to process what happened without being retriggered.'

'Jesus. Did I kill someone?'

'No. No. Nothing like that. You only ever hurt yourself. No, I'm worried that a reminder from me, will just flash you back into a horrible moment with your uncle and stress you even further. An incident at your gynaecologist's rooms triggered an appalling memory for you. Just know, you didn't kill or hurt anybody. Far from it. Also, I have your knife back in my possession again. We seriously need to work on that before you damage yourself irrevocably.'

That information was a great deal to process. I drooped quiet under the weight of its heaviness.

I asked the question I'd asked a hundred times, 'Is Micah okay?' I knew she was, I craved reassurance.

'She's fine. I even spoke to her yesterday. She loves you very much and wanted me to pass on her love to you'.

The need to cry filled me; nevertheless, umpteen assorted medications had rendered my capacity for tears parched and inadequate. How did this happen without me glimpsing its dark advance? Dooley, who, although frightening, had not turned up as the harbinger, to at least signal disruption ahead. Wherever my blindside was, there must lay a portal to tumble me through to land unwell. How can a person prepare for the thief, the dragon, that is psychosis if it can hit without warning? Medication to resolve the madness robs you of the facility to come to terms with the collateral damage of each episode; to cry and grieve.

'I don't want to be that person who keeps fucking up,' I said to Vivian when self-pity had taken hold.' I don't want people to think, 'Poor Micah, having a mother like that'.

'Hmm.'

'This is shit,' I mumbled.

My neediness wanted Vivian to say, 'No, Maddie, nobody will say that,' but she stayed at 'hmm.' This for me, meant Vivian was also thinking, 'Poor Micah.'

Was I reading too much into her silence? The pitfall of falling, is the quicksand pit of self-pity you're sucked into on what you assumed was solid ground at your landing site. Falling is easy. Touchdowns are hard. It's difficult to avoid the self-pity pit when you are made groggy by medication and heart-damaged by the brutality of a rapid unforeseen psychosis slam; the treachery of a mind turning on itself. It leaves you stumbling for quite some time after reaching a safe place. The problem of clinginess, the neediness, makes sense; it's clutching for stability. But Vivian was having none of it.

'You've been here before. You'll get past the insecurities. You'll start fresh.'

As much as I liked and admired my doctor, I had an urge to smack Vivian then. Or empty threaten her with a wooden spoon, the way I did Micah. There is such a physical exhaustion on resurfacing from the quicksand, that starting over seems a Sisyphean waste of precious energy. I tried to force myself to death by lying very still. It didn't work. Dying of natural causes looked an honourable way to go, but it became apparent it wasn't going to happen overnight. It still hasn't happened. So far, I appear to be immortal, although prone to allergies.

When Micah came to visit me, along with my mother, I felt ashamed of myself. My self. My happiness at seeing my daughter was tainted by the damage I thought it might be doing to her, to see her Mum in such a place. We sat out in the courtyard and tried to pretend we were somewhere else. Somewhere nice. Was I planting a third generation of pretence to graft onto our family tree, by fake smiling for Micah?

'Sorry, I'm here,' I said to her. 'I'm not going to pretend it isn't awful. It is. But I'll be out and back with you soon.'

My mother looked horrified at my truth telling. Micah didn't say anything but climbed into my lap the way she used to when she was small. It was nice and bolstering us both.

'Doctor Brooker is helping me to find ways to stop this happening,' I added.

'I was frightened. Nobody picked me up from school.'

My heart tore into small spikey pieces.

'I'm so sorry,' I whispered into Micah's right ear. 'I don't know what happened.'

'You went nuts!' Micah said very loud, astonished I didn't know.

'Oh. Is that what happened?' I laughed. That explains a lot.

My mum remained horrified.

At the sliding door, I was surprised to see Helen come outside. Micah saw too and rushed over to hug her.

'Are you doing an afternoon shift or just here to see me?' I asked.

'Both,' she answered.' I'd been trying your phone number for days. It wasn't a huge surprise to see your name up on the board when I arrived just now.'

I wished it had been. That it didn't surprise anybody my being locked up, saddened me further. Waking up in Room 13 had come as a complete gigantic shock to me. Micah was back on my knee and I nestled my head upon her little shoulder and shrunk into my self and self-pity yet more.

'Hey, come on you,' Helen said to me. 'You know things get better from here. Don't they, Micah?'

'Yes. Nan will buy me McDonalds® drive-thru on the way home.'

I smiled and wanted to cry at the same time. Mikey had called my mother's place 'home.' My need to self-harm grew large and in my weakened self-esteem-less condition, it was a battle not to surrender. To my horror, I ached to be in the bathroom with something sharp, to release pain. Un-screamed screams tore at my insides, looking for a place to exit. Helen noticed my agitation.

'Do you need something?' she whispered.

I nodded. Helen left us.

'When are you coming home, Mumma?' Micah asked me, earnest.

'Soon, my baby. Very soon. I just have to sort a few things first.'

Helen was back with some syrup in a cup and she handed it to me. I didn't care what it was, I just drank it like a shot. Like a shot of vodka. It worked better than alcohol. I mellowed some over the next few minutes and the need to cut, distanced itself, but was not gone.

'Are you allowed to come out for a chino?' (Micah's word for coffee from a machine, combined with cappuccino).

'I think mum, could actually do with a sleep', my mother said, observing my medication induced dullard-ness. 'Let's you and I go shopping and perhaps buy mummy a pair of jeans and come back this afternoon'?

I was wearing old trackie dackies or sweat pants for non-Australians. My attire did not suit my mother's sensibilities on dressing for sanity.

'Okay'! Micah jumped off my lap and was keen to go. That girl loved to shop.

Within minutes they were gone, and I was sleeping the weird dreaming sleep of the pharmaceutically altered. In the dream, I was begging Vivian to give me back my pocketknife while a boa constrictor wrapped itself about me. Not a restful sleep. When I awoke, sweating and buffeted, the need to cut into myself was still tapping a constant insistence at my brain.

Tap.

Tap.

Tap.

It was a torture of a persistent kind. The tapping brainwashed all other thoughts out from my mind until my autonomy was shattered, and I was beaten. But, time soaked, my wounds healed to thick red scars. The faulty mind restored to basic function and I was allowed to leave the hospital, as long as Helen and Doctor Brooker kept a close eye on me for a week or two. I still had to see the gynaecologist again because Human Papillomavirus had caused pre-cancerous changes, mutating my cells into a CIN 3 grade. If nothing was done, it would lead to cervical cancer. I was so loaded with Valium for the laser treatments, I may have slept through part of each process, but nothing triggered me off into the unknown deep. The feeling of invasion after the procedures was expected; and strict self-control stopped overwhelm from smashing into me full-fledged and gruelling. This required positive self-talk, hugs from my baby and beer.

CHAPTER 40

Dark Border Control

I became seriously ill around the time of Micah's 19th birthday. So very hard for her to stand by and watch her mother wither, approach death, back off, approach again and back off. Love was the only thing, I think, that kept her in that hospital room with me, as breakable as she was with anxiety.

'Make sure people know I died of natural causes,' I asked of her, lying small in that hospital bed. 'I don't want them assuming I offed myself. I DIDN'T GIVE UP.'

There was a strong possibility that I would die, I even called for death on the nights that crowded me with too much pain and dark. Not by my own hand, I wanted God, or whoever was in charge, to show some fairness. But it wasn't death I craved, just an end to pain, ffs. That's right, I said, 'for fuck's sake' to God. That could be why I was not smited on the spot. I wanted it too much. For this, I have forgiven fate, but not God; or whoever the fuck is in charge. It was cruel. Merciless too, the amount of pain to bear before everything eased again.

'I should have been a dog', I whimpered. They would have killed me by now. Please, take me to a vet. Far more humane.

But, as the end of the year approached, I held on. Death was not going to be allowed around Christmas or New Years'. There came a reprieve. Some might say a miracle, but it was a cumulative effect of treatments kicking in and winning a round.

'Over my dead body,' I objected in the rasping whisper of what was left of my voice. I'm not about to die and ruin holidays for you for the rest of time. Not going to die until I am old. I did look pretty darn old right then. But I began to grow younger as each day passed and we all felt a little better.

I could see Micah wasn't sure what to do. Parents die. It happens. Nonetheless, you expect them to be all shrivelled and maybe smelling like pee, before death wins. You know, when the candles on their birthday cakes set off smoke alarms, or they get tottery at store check-outs. Although, I've always been a bit dithery when it comes to sorting out money exchange. 'Tap and go' was a happy technology innovation for my kind, and even that I can botch, tapping too quickly or hitting the wrong part of the machine.

Yes, parents are supposed to grow old first before they go. I saw Micah become quite angry with me for being ill. It was an anger illogical, but understandable. There was and is, a truck load of friends watching out over her. Sometimes the driver of that truck is a bit reckless and friends fall out, but they climb back in, or take a dip in the shallow pool that is social media to check on how Micah is. Drag her to the pub or some sporting activity. Most of them would come running if she called.

Mothers push your buttons, don't they? Its unavoidable. Mum pushed my buttons and I push Micah's. She, in turn, will push the buttons of the next generation. If there is one. For the world's in a pretty violent mood, which leaves her unsure about bringing a new-born onto this planet. As a remedy for the miserable global atmosphere, I suggested she pursue optimism, as if life depended on it. Because, it did. I blamed the brutal assassination of my own blithe optimism during infancy and the subsequent trauma, as one trigger for mental illness and ensuing physical illnesses. By the time I'd slid halfway down the bumpy theoretical mood stairs, I was unable to turn things around and climb up. Momentum had been cartwheeling me toward the base, leaving no alternative except a painful halt at the end.

'The trick is to stay, at the very least, above the halfway mark', I told Micah. 'It lessens the uphill battles. You have to re-scaffold your optimism, so it doesn't drop away.'

But she wasn't listening at the time. Or perhaps was listening on some sort of delay system and heard what I'd said, well after the words had been spoken. I wanted to tell her the fight is not over and to be happy and not give up. I'm not sure if she'll ever say, 'I hear you, my Mumma.' But I might have missed these words because I slept a lot. Sleeping is a major part of recovery, even though it seems a small death each time. The world was not right when I slept in the daytime. There was a constant confusion. A frantic search for anything to hold on to; like a clock. A clock at least, could hold me firm in time, once I'd worked out if it was am or pm.

They'd put me in hospice care for a while, not in the dying wing. In the respite wing. It was surreal and made me uncomfortable to be so near to death, at first. Kind of weird how soon we adapt to being around the dead and dying. The nights were a bit Hellish. Death loved the nights. Brought people to their knees. Nan and John would come down from the coast every other week. They somehow made me miss my place more. The desolate house, echoing my absence at Micah. It was no longer a nest. Just rooms full of empty, which Micah tried to fill with noise.

I cried sometimes. Alone. Pieces of my hard fought for autonomy dwindled fragment by fragment by the long-term care I needed, until all that was left was a wilting outer casing and a small spark of humour. Micah was tough. A fighter. A fighter that did not deserve this fight. Sometimes the strain on her weighed burdensome. I couldn't help carry any of it. I could barely carry myself.

'At least I can take it out on other people', Micah said, after a dust up in the car park.

In the hospital carpark, a driver wanted her parking space.

'Fuck off! You, you, impatient prick!' she'd yelled through her sliding down window. 'I just got here.'

His car had moved away, and a modest amount of anger had been released in the hiss at the man, like a pressure cooker valve activated.

'Micah!'

'It's okay, Mum. You know I win all my fights by at least five hundred
metres', said Micah retelling the story.

'I don't want you ending up in the next bed.'

Micah told me my mother and John were coming during evening visiting hours.

'Nan asked if you had anything special you wanted from her?' said
Micah. 'I said, 'no, but Mum said not to let you choose her funeral outfit, if the worst happens.' Pop laughed out loud. It made me giggle and
then Nan smiled, too.'

I grinned.

'What did Maddie think I was going to do? Lay her to rest in a beige
cardigan?' Micah mimicked.

'It's a strong possibility. That's why I want you to choose my
clothes,' I said.

Nan also asked me who my father was, Micah told me, and I could
see her need to know, too. I felt weak, too weak for truth. Was it the lies
killing me? Not that I'd lied, it was just a tiny omission. Okay, an un-
truth. A big one. Fortunately, a nurse had come in with a wheelchair and
I'd had to roll off for some tests. Leaving Micah to sit with the question.
I needed to talk to Vivian about my daughter. Would the truth be too
damaging for her? What if I died and left her with only the knowledge
of such a horrible heritage? A fruit loop and a rapist. Shit.

Fuck the questions, they'd been ripping my insides. I did not, then,
have the strength.

Nights were hard. It's never dark in a hospital ward and that's a com-
forting thing in times of Cimmerian thinking; when you stand at the
edge of the land of the dead. The glowing lights from machines and the
outside world helped the night thoughts stay away from the shadows.
But they slipped easily into the inky overwhelm. Many times, I turned
on the overhead lights to breathe in brightness.

CHAPTER 41

Ignore me, I Might Go Away

Sleep long, sleep hard. Nightmares await in the morning. Reality is not always the place to be. The sand had barely left my eyes after the long sleep which was the daze I called the 'serious' part of my illness, when I realised, I'd not heard from Dooley and the Shadow man for a long time.

'It can't be the meds working,' I told Helen, when she came for a visit. 'Because I've been throwing up most everything I've been swallowing. If anything, my mental health should be worse.'

If it's possible to look sceptical, Helen did. You can sound sceptical by calling 'BS', but Helen remained silent.

'I've been cured of my delusions,' I said, and Helen could be quiet no longer.

'You've been here before,' she said. 'Don't grow complacent about your mental health. Remember that time you went off your medication, because you were cured? Vivian found you bleeding in your bathroom and nobody knows who gave you the black eye.'

I hated reminders of the bad days.

'Way to knock me down with the truth.'

'Sorry. But, you know, I care. Just enjoy their absence, but keep an eye on your mental health. Eh, Maddie?'

'I will. It's not like I've got anything better to do,' I punctuated the words with a sigh.

'That's the spirit', Helen said, when it clearly wasn't.

'Is it, though?'

Helen smiled. 'It's the Unsinkable Maddie Kitchener.'

'I sink plenty. I sink, therefore I am.'

'Well, salvage is my business. What time's Micah coming?'

'Now,' said Mikey, walking through the door.

She looked tired, my child. I wondered if my illness was harder for her than me. I'd hate for this situation to be the other way around. If Micah had such an illness, I think my heart would break. Rip open and my reason for being would fall out.

'I was wondering if you could nip down to my car and grab some chokies I brought for your Mum, but forgot to bring up.'

'Sure,' Micah said. 'Where's your car?'

'Staff carpark green level. You can see it from the lift. Straight ahead.'

'No problem.'

Helen pulled her keys from a pocket and tossed them to Micah, who fumbled, tried valiantly to keep them in her hands but dropped them.

'And that's why I don't play cricket for Australia,' she said bending to retrieve the keys.

'And that's why there's no U in team,' I added.

Helen laughed.

After Micah had left, Helen resumed our talk.

'You need to remain vigilant about your mental health. I mean it.'

'No, I want to enjoy this. I've very little to be happy about. If you don't mind, I'll replace my old delusions with this new one that I'm cured of my mental illnesses. I promise, if there's any sign, I'll let people know. The staff here, are on me all of the time, anyway, about what I'm hearing or seeing. It pisses me off that I can't be treated like any other dying person. I want the things I say to be taken on face value and not have people dissecting every word to check for signs of mental disorder, or asking how my 'nerves' are. If I die, I want to die like a cancer patient not a weirdo. Two thirds of my life's been hard or been eaten away by psychosis, it's not taking my death... Isn't that right, Dooley?' I asked an empty space to the left of Helen, croaking some, with tiredness, but smiling.

Talking so long was exhausting and I flopped back onto the pillows behind me.

'Great monologue. You're an arse,' Helen said, just as Micah returned, chocolates in hand. She threw Helen's keys to her and was disappointed to see Helen catch them cleanly and slide them into her pocket.

'Why is Mum an arse?' she asked, while placing the chocolates on the bedside table.

'She was teasing me.'

Micah smiled. It was a good sign.

When Micah and Helen had left, I felt lost. Empty. I realised that Dooley and the Shadowman had stolen my interior life. Filled my mind with their mess, quashed dreams and filled the holes they'd dug with things I didn't need. Like self-doubt. Fear filled spaces.

Even though, I'd craved death at times, now I panicked, not for me, but my child. I had fought hard all my life to keep Micah. Until she was eighteen, I feared the authorities would swoop in like angry birds and take her from me for 'her own good.' Now, she was deemed an adult, that fear lived no longer, but I was scared I would abandon her through death. It was so fucked. Couldn't we have some fear-free time together? Just a week. A weak little week with no anxiety. Micah's whole being was shrivelling with the fear of losing me. I could see it. Part of me considering end it all, right then, so that it could be over and Micah might not be as severely undone by a protracted illness. But hope, fucking hope, kept me there and I battled on.

Battled on, not without an anxiety attack; that pilfered enough oxygen to push me unconscious and concerned the nursing staff. I quite enjoyed the lapse of consciousness. Coming to, not so much. The woman in the next bed, told them I looked fine but had just passed out. Good to know I had such a professional poker face. My interior had felt not even close to fine. I didn't want to tell them I'd had an anxiety attack.

It would probably have me labelled neurotic on top of everything else. A schizo-affected, complex post-traumatically stressed, depressed, neurotic cancer patient.

Obviously not neurotic enough. My mother and John came visiting often; to give me neurosis top ups. That's not true. Okay, maybe a little bit true. In my early forties, I still couldn't reconcile the mother I had now, with the one with which I shared a house during my childhood. This one seemed to care about me. This one attempted nurturing. This one sometimes laughed at my jokes and never called me stupid. When, or how she changed, I couldn't say, but I couldn't take it for granted that she wouldn't turn back into the person that hadn't liked me. I remained wary and vulnerable when my mother visited. And prone to masking up into a happy parody of myself.

'You look good,' my mother said. That's how well I wore my mask.

'Cancer must agree with me,' I said. Glibness fell from me like sweat.

'I brought you some new pyjamas,' my mother said, choosing to ignore my words, or me.

'I think that's best for everybody.'

CHAPTER 42

Garden of the Green Jesus

The doctor's dropped a bombshell. Shrapnel flew everywhere in my brain and I wasn't quite sure how to react.

'We're going to say the 'R' word.'

'You what now!?'

'Your cancer is not actively killing you. Each test result has shown a drop in cancer cell percentage. Your numbers across the board are good. This might be a temporary diminution of the severity of your disease, but we're calling it a partial remission, and are now very hopeful for a complete one.'

'Well, fuck me,' I said, shocked into swearing. 'Sorry. Well, good gracious. What a turn around.'

My oncologist looked both smug and happy.

'We did it,' he said. 'Against the odds.'

'Does this mean I can go home?'

'Not quite. Because of your troubling peripheral neuropathy, from the chemo, we think rehab is the next best step. Pardon the pun. Just a couple of weeks to get you on your feet properly and get some strength back in your legs. You'll still be seeing me and taking synthetic maintenance medications, potentially for the rest of your life. Monitoring is very important. But you'll be home by next month. All going well.'

I ignored the caveat at the end and allowed some light into the gloom of the last few months.

But I do now have the rest of my life?

All indications...

That's enough for me.

'When do I leave?'

When Miss Havisham died the day before I was moved to rehab, I went to pieces. Just a cat. Just a bad tempered, underfoot in the kitchen, food stealing, tail flicking, cat. When she flipped that tail, it was an obvious middle finger up gesture. Miss Havisham, a bitch of the highest order could turn into a smoochy, purring ball of love. Gone. I think she died without pain. Micah said there'd been no sign of illness. Havie was an old moggy and quietly went off to sleep and didn't wake up. This is the way I want to go. I'd like to be mentally away from my body when it happens. Crikey, I'd like to be mentally away from my body right now.

After a search, Micah had found poor Havie on a pile of clothes, in a sunny spot, on the laundry floor. Surrounded by a little nest of knickers and things, she'd fallen into the big sleep. I howled, locked in a small ensuite bathroom, with the shower running. Howled in a way I hadn't known was in me.

Or maybe it was for more than a dead cat?

Whatever was going on, it sunk me. So hard, I hit the floor. At a certain age, you stop bouncing. You rise, fighting the gravitational pull of trepidation, uncertain of footing and go forward with a new hesitance, expecting it might happen again. That is the damage of sorrow, and as one of my friends said, it's also the sorrow of damage.

PTSD seeped in. There was that old flinching to my demeanour, that comes from the expectation of another blow. That almost 24/7 vigilance that was there, the second I woke from anything. I expected the doctors to come and tell me my cancer had recurred. My interior was hunched over in expectation of bad news. I worried about self-fulfilling prophecy. Worried about worrying.

I guess I was genetically predisposed towards gloom, whether traumatised or not. I couldn't say I'd been newly traumatised. Not by Miss Havisham's death. But again, I couldn't say I hadn't. Maybe I learnt the lessons of pessimism on my mother's knee but, it didn't matter. I was filled with glumness and it added a layer of anger to everything, because I didn't want to be sullen. I'd turned into a grumpy old man in the body of a forty-year-old woman. It wouldn't surprise me if I rushed outside to yell at the neighbours' children, get off my grass! This would necessitate a big old stick to wave windmill style, to show I mean business. Show that I'm in the mean business. In the meantime, I could wave my new walking stick, if I had the energy.

Maybe I needed a break. A breakdown? I needed something.

Later, I went to pieces about the cat when Vivian came for a visit.

'Poor old Miss Havisham,' she said, sympathising while I tried to stop tears. 'That cat bit me on the foot once,' she told me. 'An unprovoked attack'. The doctor laughed, and I couldn't help but smile.

'Havie would have had her reasons, they'd just be a bit... cat.'

'What did Micah do with her?'

'Had her cremated, then scattered her ashes in the garden down near Kitchener's Bench.'

'That's nice. Aside from all of that, you still look quite weary. Everything okay?'

I was near tears again, and I didn't know why.

'I think this PTSD thing has become a malaise again, rather than an emotional reaction to everything. I'm worn out. I should be happy. Partial remission, you know? I am happy. But not. What's wrong with me?'

'You need time to take it all in. Good news can still be unsettling.'

'Yeah, for people like me.'

'For everyone. Just ask any first-time pregnant woman.'

'I don't want to be unsettled by good news.'

I heard myself sound like a whiney child and clamped my mouth shut to a determined line. Remembering how I'd asked the higher power for a week without fear and here, now I had one and was throwing a man-made fear into the mix; a self-inflicted injection of anxiety. How I hated my fucked unit brain.

'You'll be fine,' Vivian reassured. 'As you know, if I could, I'd shake the pessimism out of you.'

I laughed, 'It's always nice to know you'd consider physical violence as a therapy tool... I just need a break from myself, is all.'

'Why don't you go and sit in the garden for a bit and I'll see you when you get back from rehab?'

'Okay.'

I asked a nurse to wheel me into the garden of the Green Jesus after Vivian left. I'm not sure if garden had an actual name, but a statue of the son of God lived there and it had turned green as it aged.

'I know how you feel,' I told Green Jesus.

Coming from the building, had been like leaving a cinema. The brightness of the day was surprising and intense. It seemed in opposition to my mood and I was glad of it. There was trouble with my assorted temperaments. I'd just settle into one mood and boom, it would change. While I was in the garden, I asked Green Jesus to take care of Miss Havisham.

Boom, I felt quite light. Perhaps, even cheerful. I grabbed at the mood, so wanting to keep it. In order to maintain the buoyancy, I carried that mood within me, as if it were a fragile egg. How bizarre to go from thinking I was dying to thinking I was living. In less than two weeks. It lifted me dangerously high. High enough that any sudden drop might kill me. But I grabbed the new happiness with both wobbling hands and held tight. Throttled it.

The in-patient rehab facility my doctors managed to get me in to, was too far for anyone to drive up for a visit. That was nice for both Micah and I. She didn't worry so much having had my feebality (okay, feebleness) moved well out of eye witness range, and this eased my mind. I planned to be a new woman when Micah saw me again.

Did it amuse you, 'eased my mind'? Like I had an easable mind? Erasable mind, sure. The damage the cancer drugs wreaked on my brain left me with an even faultier short-term memory, if that was possible. I spent most of my new life looking for my phone.

'I can't find my phone', I said.

'The one you're holding?'

'That's the one. For the love of Green Jesus, do I ever get any brain cells back?'

CHAPTER 43

We Three Queens of Disorient Are

I left rehab after a gruelling month. Walked from the building on my own legs. That's right, my legs. They were skinny; looked fragile but now held my weight, which was increasing. The maintenance oral dose of chemo was gentle on my insides and I could almost say I felt well. Happy, even. Happy; is a happy word. I'm superstitious about saying the word 'happy.' It's an obvious invitation to disaster. I'm up, bring me down universe. Let's not tell anybody I'm happy.

Micah, brought the car to the door so that I didn't have to take the walk to the car park. My mother was in the back seat, seat belt on and ready to assume the crash position. She had driven to the rehab centre, so that Micah could drive back to our house. If there is an award for the world's worst back seat driver, my mother would surely be on the short list by selection time. She appeared apprehensive, but that's how she always looked in a car.

Micah jumped out to help me into the front passenger's seat.

'Belt up', my mother said before I'd hit the seat.

'Yes, mum.'

I tried to remain happy but within an hour my body was aching. With stealth, I slipped a diazepam from my purse and put half into my mouth, to help my muscles ease and relieve the pain.

'You okay?' asked Micah.

'Sure am.'

'We can stop if you need to stretch your legs.'

'I can make it to the mountains. We can stop for a stack and a wretch there.'

Micah laughed.

'I haven't had pancakes at Katoomba for years. It'll be great,' she said.

Once upon a time, I used to take Micah for drives on every other Sunday, the traditional day of driving. A few of her school friends wouldn't be about because they'd 'have to' go to their father's houses for the weekend; leaving Micah at a loose end. Quite often we'd end up in the Blue Mountains. It became a thing to say 'a stack and a wretch' instead of 'a snack and a stretch because we'd go to the little pancake place and inevitably eat too much.

'Remember that time Rachel's dad couldn't have her, so we took her with us?' asked Micah.

'Ah, yes. The day of misadventures.'

'You had a flat tyre and were trying so hard not to swear undoing the wheel nuts.'

'And Rachel was watching me and said, 'Well, this is a bit shit'.'

'And then we all ate too much and were green all of the way home. Good times,' Micah said. She gave a sigh filled with nostalgia and fell quiet.

We were climbing higher into the mountains and the scenery was mesmerising. Giant mountains, harsh and jagged where the weather had bitten great slices from their sides. Beautiful and dangerous. At least once a year a hiker had to be plucked all broken from a ledge by a helicopter. These mountains fought back trying to rid their surface from the cancer that is humans.

'Speaking of father's', my mother said from the back seat.

'Who was?' I asked, confused.

'You were. Rachel's father couldn't have her, you said.'

'Did I?'

I allowed my thoughts to slip back into the scenery. I could see smoke. These mountains could be Hell in the summertime.

'Hope that's just a back-burn,' Micah said, glancing at the puff.

'Speaking of father's,' my mother said again. She obviously wanted to talk about something. Fathers.

We weren't, really.

'While it's just us women, are you going to ever tell me who Micah's father is?'

'No,' I said.

Does Micah know?

'No,' Micah said.

'Don't you think she should know? You nearly died and...'

'It's not that important, nan,' Micah interrupted. I could tell by mumma's continued reticence to talk, that the whole thing must have been distressing. The fact that my father is not in my life is a clue that he's a jerk. That's enough for me. I don't need to meet him. Or even know anything about him.

'But,' said my mother, not ready to give up.

'Honestly, Nan, I don't care and neither should you.'

I've never been prouder of my daughter. It pushed me to look for something in my handbag, so that nobody could see my tears of over-welm. The love I felt for Micah quivered my whole being. She had now given me permission to not tell. Anyone. There was a weight shift; a lightness new.

'I was just...' began my mother, but fell silent. 'He should be made to take some responsibility,' she said, trying again.

'I don't want a father who is made to do anything.'

My mother gave up then. It was beautiful. I pulled my phone from my hand bag, like it was the reason the search had begun and tapped a few keys.

'That pancake shop is still there and open,' I said, my voice tight with leftover emotion.

'Yay! I'm going for the royal stack.'

'Wretch,' I said.

Micah took my hand and squeezed. We sat there happy in the small contact. I saw, in the rear-view mirror, my mother was also smiling. The smile looked real. We three might be okay. Although, I could feel my mother tapping her imaginary brake on the floor behind me.

She, my mother, was a puzzle. The woman of now, I could not match to the woman I knew as my mother growing up. As an adult, I was vaguely aware that I feared her still, but it was a fear left over from childhood. My mother had done or said nothing to warrant such feelings toward her in well over a decade, but I couldn't quite put the apprehensions away. I still remembered the times I'd needed a mother, to be only pushed away by her anger. A piece of me couldn't quiet forgive. The me I'd been after the rape was still inside wanting to be held and loved by a mother. Ancient resentments die hard. But holding hurt this long was my problem. Mea culpa. Forgetting might be hard but I needed to forgive.

'We won't be able to stay long at the pancake place,' my mother said. 'I don't want John driving us back home in the dark.'

The child in me wanted mumble, 'then why did you even come?'

I needed to forgive.

'No problem,' I said. 'Thanks for coming today, Mum.'

I swallowed the small resentment at being placed on my mother's timetable with the other half of the diazepam tablet and closed my eyes. We three might be okay.

CHAPTER 44

Visits

Old bones were glad to reach home. Fell into my own bed for the first time since... Well, a long while. Brain fog impeded my math skills and I didn't care enough to delve into dates. Micah did all the good-bying to my mother and John and they would have been well home before the sun dipped. Still slightly green from pancake eating, I considered skipping dinner, but Micah said no. That's where I was now. In the land of upside down. Micah was mothering me, and I was har-rumphing like a teenager.

It is peculiar sitting in a place you've lived a long time still feeling like a visitor. It's a talent I have. Maybe I am a visitor to the planet and would never feel 'at home.' Having Micah near me was my closest 'home.'

The next morning, life slipped into a better groove. Not a rut; a rhythmic groove with a soundtrack care of Spotify™. Micah was in the kitchen feeding Lady Hyphen-Hyphen and preparing for her work day, singing along to the acoustic covers playlist.

'Would you like a boiled egg?' she asked me.

'Okay,' I said, not feeling hungry but not about to argue.

Today was the first day my autonomy would be fully returned. I was excited. Not even sure what I would do with such freedom. How do people fill in their days when they're not dying?

'Have you taken your meds?' Micah asked.

'Yes.'

'Well done.'

'That's all I had planned for today.'

'There you go. You've nailed it all ready. But, really, what are you going to do all day?'

Hmmm. Have you ever forgotten how to live? What it is you actually 'do' to be a functional human? I was at a bit of a loss after Micah went to work. Breathing, I could do. Anything after that took thought and planning. I managed to throw my dirty laundry into the washing machine and planned the walk out to the clothes line when it was ready for drying. There is more to life than this, but I guess that was an accomplishment for Day One of my restart.

As time ticked the days away, the mixed feelings I had about being alive again, and the fear that always lived with me, moved to a different part of my brain. Still there, but at the back somewhere. Micah decided to move from the house after I had settled back in and was feeling well. She was moving out of the first home she'd ever known. This was not a bad thing, but it wasn't a good thing, either. Micah felt she couldn't be an adult in the same place where she only knew how to be a child. I fully understood, but felt slightly redundant. This was my issue; my low self-esteem sulking and I chose to push the thoughts away, remembering instead the feelings when I visited my own mother these days. It kicked the adult right out of me. I understood Micah completely. After some hunting, she moved to a tiny studio flat in the inner city. The rent was stupid, but Micah had a strong bank balance, a good job and after graduation, the world would be her bivalve mollusc.

The move, written in a few sentences, sounds easy. But it wasn't. I had to part with a big piece of my heart, although I was also a rejuvenated powerhouse; burbling with excitement. Proud of my daughter for embracing the future; her future. I've always liked a beginning. Much better than ends. Here was a fresh start, a resurrection. You wouldn't know I'd been tapping on death's door, for eighteen months or more. I helped Micah pack, clean, unpack, clean, showing a circumstantial weariness and not the bone deep tiredness of my illness. For her, there was a month of regrets and enthusiasm before the actual move. It took so long to organise and pack; transforming Micah into a sighing, worn out, carbon copy of my mother. I teased her about this and she sighed at me. The move was no quick stripping of the Band-Aid; more, a slow painful peeling. I was relieved when it was done; my heart all filled with pride at the woman my daughter was becoming. To think, I nearly missed it.

The first night in her new flat Micah found overwhelming, but she said it, 'felt right.' Next, she sold her car and bought a second-hand Vespa Primavera 50. Inner city parking is a fright and 'Tilly,' the scooter, was easier to slot into small spots. On my first visit to her flat as a visitor not removalist, I bought and brought a bright yellow helmet, for Micah because I was frightened people wouldn't see her. The helmet was such a high vis yellow; I was sure individuals flying over in aeroplanes could spot her. For the benefit of eyes, I secured a sticker of a pink daisy to one side, to break up the yellow a little.

'I hate to say it,' I said to Vivian. 'But I think I'm happy. Like almost fearless. It's kind of quiet in here, I tapped the side of my head. No shadows. Yes, happiness.'

Her smile was as bright as the yellow helmet.

'That's good, isn't it?' she asked.

'I don't know. Once you have something, it can be taken from you. If you never have happiness, it can't be stolen.'

'You may be right, but it would be sad to ban happiness in case its temporary. Cake is temporary, but I wouldn't want to miss some. You've been happy before.'

There's an old saying, *expect the best, prepare for the worst.* I've been prepared for the worst my entire life. Preparing for the best is hard. Unnatural. Not a position I revert to automatically. I have to say I was unprepared for happiness. It was bordering on a discomfort; because of the rarity. How sad to be made apprehensive by the first approach of happiness.

'I know, I've been happy. And it was seized, ripped away, by illness or trauma. Maybe both. But, this new happiness, it's all mine, right? If

I lose it, it'll be sheer carelessness on my part. You know? I've labelled it with my name, but I can still misplace it, like a favourite jumper or the car keys.'

'You're one up on some. At least you know when one happiness is lost you can find a new one. If this latest bout of happiness is stolen, there'll be another strain. Perhaps an even stronger one.'

'I guess.'

'Enjoy this time. If you overthink it, you might wear it out'.

'How can a person shut the sabotaging part of their brain up?'

'If I knew that...'

My happiness remained in a stable condition.

Micah would come back often, to sit with me at Kitchener's Bench and be by the river. The ease of our togetherness would allow my brain to switch to a kind of neutral whir, not off, but not advancing. Eyes closed; I would feel the flow of the river rather than see movement. Much like life. For all of the enterprise and blur going on around me, I'd missed my own progress.

'I'm doing it, Mumma,' she said. 'I'm doing life.'

'You are kiddo. You are.'

When a river is flowing, life is undeniable. When life is undeniable, growth is guaranteed. I felt grown. Not strong, but strong enough. Not breakable, but flexible. What a thing resilience is. You don't realise you have it, until its almost nonessential, when you've already made it through to the other side. If you swim across a river and then swim back again, it will land you in a different place. Why exhaust yourself trying to get back to the exact same spot? Why fight the flow? You wait until you've reached dry land and go in your chosen direction from there, right? I might still find my direction.

It doesn't matter which direction you're going, just look ahead a little, in case you're going to tread in something. I told Micah on one visit, but I think I was telling myself, too. Look ahead a little. You're lost if you stop, so keep moving. I had, it seems, a strong navigational bent in in my motherly advice.

242 - ROO STOVE

The day edges were showing in the sky and we rose from the bench for goodbyes.

'You're lost if you stop,' I said aloud and stepped into a blob of dog poop.

Look ahead a little, you dick! I told myself. Shit.

Micah was just laughing. There's nothing like a visual illustration to help push advice home. After scrapping and dipping my boot in the water, it was clean enough to bring back dignity. Micah kissed me and said; I'd better get home. And I marvelled at her ability to call her place 'home' already. I waved until Micah was out of view then settled back onto the bench for some contemplation.

The river was flowing a gentle rhythm. There was war and pieces of me lost in the mild burble; and taken downstream somewhere, to be diluted into nothingness; washed and tumbled out of the system.

'I've come for Micah', said Dooley, settling beside me.

As if he'd never been away.

THE END.

1.   Yes, I did make up that word. Carry on. ↑
2.   An explanation of the acronym isn't necessary; such is the state of the world. ↑

Jen Hutchison, you are remembered with love. Thank you.

www.ingramcontent.com/pod-product-compliance
Lightning Source LLC
Chambersburg PA
CBHW070558120726

47909CB00007B/2382